CONJURING THE FLESH

CONJURING THE FLESH

Brandon Fox

Leyland Publications
San Francisco

Library of Congress Cataloging-in-Publication Data

Fox, Brandon.
    Conjuring the flesh / Brandon Fox.—1st ed.
    191 p. 22 cm.
    ISBN 0-943595-79-7 (pbk. : alk. paper)
    I. Title.
  PS3556.08772C66   1998
  813'.54—dc21   98-36714
                                                                      CIP

Leyland Publications
P.O. Box 410690
San Francisco, CA 94141
Complete illustrated catalogue available for $1 ppd.

1

"REMEMBER, ANDER. Pleasure alone isn't enough. Skill is required. A moment's carelessness could be fatal, if we find blood magic in the kei."

Thane leaned over the book they were examining, his boyish features intent. Nineteen forever, or at least so long as he practiced the art, he looked like Ander's contemporary instead of an experienced mage. But Ander was no longer deceived by appearances. He had seen the fierce intellect and determination that burned behind his lover's gray eyes.

They leaned comfortably against each other, their soft white robes falling open, on a round leather cushion that appeared to float among the stars. Oil lamps flickered atop tripods, their flames reflecting infinitely in mirrors covering the subterranean chamber's walls, floor and ceiling. A ring of double-sided mirrors in freestanding frames formed a broken circle around the black cushion. Ander glanced up and saw his reflection: widely spaced brown eyes beneath a thick sheaf of raven hair, high cheekbones, a straight nose, lips that always seemed on the verge of a smile. It was a face he had always taken for granted, although customers at Lady Tayanita's House of Companionship had swooned and professed amazement at his beauty.

A large book lay open before them. Thane turned the page to reveal a painting of an athletic young blond in the arms of an exotically beautiful russet-haired boy. They pressed against each other, hard cocks aligned between their flat bellies. Complex patterns painted on their bodies emphasized hard curves of muscle, almost tricking the eye into believing the figures moved. Neat handwriting filled the opposite page. Ander had already read the text, studied the concepts behind the art's physical aspects. "Nicolai and Sorel again," he said. "Why do you paint them more than anybody else?"

Sorel returned from the chamber's far corner carrying a brazier heaped with red-hot coals. His lithe body, clad only in a black silk loincloth, seemed to approach from every direction as he entered the inner circle of mirrors. He knelt and put the brazier on the floor near the cushion. "Thane paints fast, but it still takes time. Nobody can stay hard longer than Nicolai."

A thump echoed around the chamber as Nicolai entered the room and swung shut the heavy door. He carried an amphora made of blue glass, and wore nothing but a silk loincloth and a grin. "Don't believe it," he said. "Sorel can keep *any* lover hard for as long as he wants. He's merciless." He crossed the chamber, dodging mirrors with the grace he had learned as a professional acrobat, and placed his amphora beside the brazier.

Thane closed the book. "I paint them because they're beautiful," he told Ander. "And because they're always ready for love. Like you."

Ander blushed as he felt the throb of Thane's desire in his core. The bond pulsing between them at the moment was only a shadow of what they shared when fully joined in mind and flesh, but it still linked them. His heart quickened as his body responded to Thane's eagerness.

Thane met his gaze and smiled gently. Ruggedly sensual, with short brown hair and a muscular body, the mage could easily be mistaken for an unusually handsome hunter or farmer. Ander had mistaken him for a servant when they first met, and been seduced by his playful flirting, before learning he was the master of the estate.

"Your flesh calls to me," Thane said, his voice low. "It's time to continue your training."

Ander shivered despite the underground chamber's warmth. Morning sun sparkled outside Thane's castle, bathing the winter landscape with clear light, but the mirrored chamber beneath the castle's great tower was a different world. Or at least a gateway to a different world, a new reality he was eager to explore. "I'm ready. Will this be like last time?"

Thane handed the book to Nicolai, then turned back to Ander. "This time we'll do more than touch the kei. We'll shape it, create a manifestation."

Ander licked his lips nervously, then nodded. "I read about it in the Gramarye Curiosa. I understand the principles. But I still don't know *how* it's done."

"It's something you have to feel. You can't learn it by reading." He grinned, irrepressible with enthusiasm for the art, and lowered his voice to a husky whisper. "Your body will show you the way. Yield to pleasure, and you'll see." He put an arm around Ander's shoulders and drew him into a kiss. His other hand slipped beneath Ander's robe and grazed over taut flesh.

Ander's body arched under the light caress. His robe slipped off to reveal a tightly muscled body and a thick erection that extended to his navel. Thane's fingers moved lower and slid along the shaft's underside.

"I've done enough reading," Ander said, his breath fast. "I'm ready to learn. And I want *you* to teach me."

Thane smiled and shrugged out of his robe. Tawny skin glistened over hard muscle. He rolled on top of Ander and moved his narrow hips in small circles, rubbing their cocks together, as his tongue sought entrance to Ander's mouth.

Nicolai chuckled softly. "Help me pry them apart, Sorel. Poor Ander is never going to learn the art if we don't keep Thane off him. Maybe we should have washed him in the cold pool instead of the warm."

"Wouldn't have worked," Sorel replied. "It takes *hot* water to get the grime off a rowdy beast like Thane. Too bad we can't let him grow up a few more years."

Thane rolled off Ander and looked at his friends in mock alarm. "What, and get stuck a tired twenty-two like you and Nicolai? Ander's only twenty and won't get any older, once he learns the art. I'd never be able to keep him satisfied!"

Nicolai crouched by Thane's side with clear oil cupped in his right hand. He let it dribble across the mage's broad chest and rippling abdomen while Sorel did the same with Ander. The northerner began spreading the slippery fluid over Thane's skin. "We'd help you tend to Ander," he offered. "As long as he doesn't mind. But I know better. We could never keep you away from the art long enough to start aging again."

Ander gazed at the mirrored ceiling and watched Nicolai apply oil to the mage's body. Thane's phallus stretched across his lower belly, twitching slightly as the blond's fingers grazed it. The sight made Ander gulp. He settled into the soft cushion and tried to relax under Sorel's massage. He still couldn't believe his luck at finding Thane and his band of mages, and suspected that more than luck might have been involved. Ghostly remnants of Lucian, Thane's first love, still lingered in the kei. The shade was determined to conceal his existence from Thane, wanting to shield him from doomed dreams of reunion, but he had helped Ander in times of crisis. The ghost hoped Ander might heal the grief and loneliness that still haunted the mage ten years after Lucian's death.

Whether fate or simple good fortune, the event had transformed him. He was no longer a simple musician, an ornament to entertain customers in a brothel. Thane had sworn to bring down the zamindar, and Ander had pledged himself to the cause. The task would have seemed impossible had he not seen the art's power with his own eyes, felt it with his own flesh. He squirmed as he thought about the magic Thane fashioned out of pleasure.

"What's on your mind?" Sorel asked. The curly-haired youth looked searchingly into Ander's eyes, perceptive as always. "You're not worried, are you? You've already proven you can contain pleasure long enough to touch the kei."

Ander reached to the side and slipped his fingers around Thane's hand. "I'm just thinking how fortunate I am."

Thane rolled to his side and traced the hard ridges of Ander's abdomen. Then he wrapped his fingers around the thick shaft of Ander's cock and gave it a leisurely stroke. "No luckier than us," he said. "I know how you feel. And you know how I feel. Or you *will*, when we renew our bond."

Ander shivered as Thane fondled his cock. The hardest part of the art was keeping lust at bay long enough to weave the spells that warped reality and conjured magic. But at least the struggle was with pleasure, the opposite of the blood magic used by the zamindar's sorcerers. He sat up and turned to Thane, spreading his legs wide.

Thane grinned and sat up. He put his legs around Ander's slender hips and pulled their bodies close. They sat crotch to crotch, their erections touching, while Nicolai and Sorel applied sandalwood scented oil to their backs.

"We'll use trance smoke this time," Thane said, running his hands along Ander's sides. "A mild form, just enough to help you slip into the kei easily. But you'll have to concentrate to maintain control of your body."

"That's the main purpose of the mirrors," Sorel added. "It can be confusing when you're deep in a bond. The mirrors help you see what you're doing."

Ander nodded, his eyes half shut as he returned the mage's caresses. "Will this be the same as last time, then? We'll share everything we feel?"

"It'll be harder," Thane said. "This time you'll have to be more active. But don't worry. I'll let you know what to do."

"You don't have time to worry, anyway," Nicolai said. He picked up a robe and wiped his hands while examining their glistening bodies. He looked satisfied. "Too bad I can't paint. You'd make a fine illustration in the Gramarye Curiosa."

Sorel knelt beside the brazier and sprinkled dried leaves over the coals. Aromatic smoke filled the air, sweet and pungent at the same time. Ander felt lightheaded. Thane leaned forward and gently pushed him onto his back.

"As always, the art starts with love. Kiss me, Ander."

Their lips came together, brushing lightly, as their bodies flowed together along their full lengths. Ander's hands slid over Thane's broad back, then down to his firm buttocks. The muscles bunched beneath his fingers as the mage ground his cock against the slippery ridges of Ander's abdomen.

Ander looked up and saw Thane's muscular back reflected in the mirror above them. His tanned body moved with powerful deliberation. The smoke was thicker now, wispy purple strands floating through the air.

Ander slid his hand up to Thane's shoulders and pushed him up slightly. Their cocks stayed in contact, twitching, smearing each other with sensitizing oil. "Roll over," he urged, giving Thane a sultry smile. "Let me show you what I've learned."

Thane cooperated quickly, rolling onto his back and waiting breathlessly. Ander crouched next to him, then slid his hand from the mage's neck down to the navel. Hard flesh tensed beneath his fingers and a pearl of precum drooled from Thane's penis. Supporting himself with a hand on each side of the youth's waist, he lowered his head and licked the clear fluid. The dreamsmoke beguiled his senses, making the precum taste like honeysuckle nectar. Then he took a deep breath and let the glans slide between his lips. He held himself motionless, gently pulling the cockhead, while Thane's body tensed.

"Take me, Ander! Show me your skill!"

Obligingly, Ander let the smooth shaft slip into his throat. Although it was a good nine inches long, he accommodated it easily. The virile power of the rigid organ made his heart race.

Thane put a hand on Ander's hip and urged him into a straddle. Without letting his partner's cock leave his mouth, Ander swung around. Then he lowered his pelvis until his cock brushed Thane's lips. Sorel gripped the shaft lightly and angled it down. It slid into the wet heat of Thane's mouth in a single smooth glide.

Ander began to undulate, sliding his cock between Thane's lips as he sucked. He fell into an easy rhythm and forgot about the kei, forgot about the fragrant smoke swirling around them, forgot about the two youths who crouched beside the cushion and watched intently. He closed his eyes and ignored everything except the warm glide of lips over his cock and the satisfying hardness of Thane's penis in his throat. His balls pulled tight against the base of his cock and his legs began to tremble.

A hand caressed the back of his neck. "Patience," Nicolai said. "It's the smoke, making you forget your goal. Open your eyes and see what you've done."

Ander opened his eyes. Red haze colored his vision. Startled, he realized that the glow came from Thane's body and his own; they were already touching the kei. He stopped his movements and let Thane's cock slip from between his lips. It slapped back against the mage's flat belly. Then he withdrew his penis from Thane's mouth and lowered himself to the cushion, bemused by the effects of the trance smoke.

Thane didn't give him time to get distracted. He sat up and moved to a crouch between Ander's legs. Nicolai and Sorel eased Ander onto his back, then each grasped a leg and pushed it toward his chest.

"Clear your mind," Thane said as he poured scented oil into his palm. "Learn from your flesh. It will lead you."

Ander squirmed, his ass clenching and unclenching as Thane spread sensitizing oil into the crack between his buttocks. "It's working," he gasped. "I feel *everything*! I think my skin can even taste the smoke."

Thane slid a finger through Ander's well-oiled ring of muscle. Ander gasped with pleasure, his body trembling.

"You'll learn to feel smoke," Thane said. "To hear light, smell sound. In the kei anything is possible." He rotated his finger gently, loosening the tight muscle, then slipped a second finger inside Ander's ass. "Don't worry about learning, for now. Experience it fully. Understanding will follow."

His heart pounding, Ander glanced at the overhead mirror as Thane withdrew his fingers and positioned his cockhead against the lubricated opening. "Go ahead," he gasped. "Put it in." He lowered his gaze from the mirror and locked eyes with the handsome youth preparing to enter him. "I love you, Thane. Let me show you."

The mage leaned forward. The lust in his young face mingled with tenderness. "I love you, too. Now I can say it. And it would be useless to deny it anyway." He pushed his hips forward. His cockhead slipped into the waiting ass with only the slightest resistance.

Ander threw his head back, his expression ecstatic, as Thane's long phallus eased into him. The slippery oil, blended from herbal extracts developed by Thane and the other mages, increased his control over his body at the same time it magnified his sensitivity. He relaxed his ass muscles until his lover's cock was fully encased in the warm glove of flesh. Thane waited, motionless, his pubic hairs grazing the creamy flesh of his partner's buttocks.

"You feel so good inside me," Ander said softly. "Like we were made for each other."

Thane made a slow withdrawal, no faster than his leisurely penetration had been. "Perhaps we *are* meant for each other. You make me so hard. Do you feel it?"

"Every inch!"

Smiling, Thane set up a slow movement in and out of his partner's clenching ass. Ander milked the cock, loosening as the shaft penetrated and tightening as it withdrew. Wonderment blossomed on their faces as their pleasure spiraled.

They rocked against each other, mesmerized by the silky glide of flesh against flesh. Ander's cock drooled profusely. A pool of precum formed beneath the dusky glans. He heard something like distant music, and felt a faint caress of slippery warmth stroking the length of his penis. His eyes opened wide.

"It's happening! I'm starting to feel what you're feeling!"

Thane nodded and slowed his movements even further. "You renewed our bond quickly." His voice lowered to a throaty whisper. "I feel your sensations, too. *All* of them."

He began to move faster, barely pausing at each end of the stroke, keeping the steady slide of his penis in and out of Ander's ass perfectly controlled. Ander's muscles stood out in clean lines as his body soared on waves of pleasure. Nicolai and Sorel gently pulled his legs higher, opening his ass even further to Thane's delving cock. The red halo outlining their bodies began to sparkle with bright points of white light.

Ander moaned softly as he fought to keep sensation from overwhelming him. His back flexed powerfully, in time with Thane's movements. "Don't push me too fast," he pleaded. "It feels like I'm fucking and being fucked too. It's so real!"

"It *is* real," Sorel said. "Your bond with Thane is strong. Look up, into the mirror. Seeing your body helps anchor you."

Gasping, Ander looked at the mirrored ceiling. His body, and Thane's, shimmered with red light. The mage's cock was brightest of all. It shone like burnished copper every time it emerged from the slippery sheath of ass. Sorel and Nicolai crouched by the side of the leather cushion, each holding one of his legs in a powerful grip. They looked like muscular acolytes, immovable witnesses to the straining bodies between them. Points of light receded to infinity all around them as lamp flames echoed between mirrored surfaces.

Ander relaxed slightly as he regained his orientation. He still felt the slippery grasp of a clenching ass stroking the length of his penis, the bunching of strong muscles in his buttocks and back, as well as the glide of Thane's thick phallus deep inside him. He basked in the intense stimulation. Then he started to lift his hips in time with Thane's thrusts. The welter of sensations made coordination difficult, but he soon sensed how to tell his own body's perceptions from the sensations flowing through the bond. He shifted and squirmed, squeezing Thane's cock from different angles, feeding their mutual pleasure through the bond.

Thane groaned with appreciation as Ander milked him. Precum oozed from his cock in a steady stream, further lubricating the slippery sheath. Ander's flesh grew more sensitive as his senses soared. He could feel Thane's shaft pulsing in time with the youth's heartbeat.

Thane's body trembled as he fucked, straining between lust and efforts to prolong their lovemaking. Sweat streaked his torso. "You're as skillful as Sorel," he gasped.

Ander grinned and gave Thane's cock a slippery squeeze just as the glans reached his ring of muscle. "He's been giving me suggestions. And I'm a good student."

"I'll vouch for that," Nicolai said. "When Sorel and I tested him, he took us both by surprise. A randy boy if ever we've met one."

Thane slid his hands behind Ander's knees and shifted the boy's legs to his shoulders. Nicolai and Sorel sank back on their haunches as the mage leaned forward and supported himself on outstretched arms. Ander's hips rose clear of the cushion, pulled up by the press of broad shoulders beneath his knees. Thane's fucking slowed. As the leisurely strokes sent waves of ecstasy through their bodies, a swirling ball of energy materialized above them. Gold with green streaks, it pulsed in time with their heartbeats.

"We're one flesh, now," Thane whispered, his lips nearly touching Ander's. "Our bond is complete. What do you feel, beyond the pleasure?"

"It's . . .like we're floating in darkness, but there's a light inside us. What is it?"

"Touch it with me. Then you'll understand." His lips touched Ander's and they kissed. At the same time he pulled his cock partway out, so the tip rested against Ander's most sensitive flesh. Their tongues wrestled, adding to the whirlwind of shared sensations. Ander closed his eyes and moaned as Thane began a series of short jabs. His shuddering pleasure coursed back to the mage through their bond.

Lips together, their bodies pressed tight, Thane tensed into a solid slab of muscle. Then he lifted his head, a throaty cry escaping deep from his chest as the first jet of his ejaculation flooded Ander's clenching ass.

Ander groaned as the shock of Thane's orgasm triggered his

12

own shattering climax. His penis jerked strongly and a fountain of semen gushed between their hard bellies. Again and again, in perfect synchronization, their cocks emptied their seed.

The sphere above them sizzled with an influx of anima. It changed from gold to blue and expanded to the size of a large melon. Rainbows of light caromed around the mirrored chamber as the manifestation of the kei stabilized.

Ander was limp with reaction to the wrenching dual orgasm. Thane's sweaty body pressed down on him, heavy and hot, as the last spurts of cum oozed from their cocks. When both of them were completely drained, Thane gently withdrew his penis and lowered Ander's legs.

Sorel and Nicolai stood, their bodies shining in the magical sphere's coruscating light. "Roll over, Thane," Nicolai said as he slipped his thumbs under the top of his loincloth. "Finish the ritual. We're aching!"

Thane rolled off Ander while Nicolai and Sorel slipped out of their meager silk garments. Their cocks were rampant, upthrust and drooling precum.

Ander propped himself on an elbow as Sorel knelt by his side. The handsome youth's cock speared up from his groin, curving so the glans touched his navel. Ander caught the strong scent of his excitement. He leaned forward and captured the slippery glans in his mouth.

Sorel's back arched and his muscles went rigid as Ander's tongue tickled the sensitive skin where the cockhead joined the shaft. A jet of semen splattered against the roof of Ander's mouth, bathing his tongue with earthy flavor, as the cock slid deeper into the accommodating mouth. Ander gently caressed Sorel's tight scrotum as the rest of the ejaculation emptied itself deep in his throat. Nicolai was equally primed, gasping as his cock flooded Thane's mouth with milky cum.

Sorel ran his fingers through Ander's hair, tousling it affectionately, then pulled back. His cock slid from between Ander's lips, leaving a residue of sweet-tasting cum. The four collapsed together in a tangle. Wispy blue smoke drifted around them, playing games with the glowing sphere. Ander pondered the ball of energy while they caught their breath.

It's a part of me, and Thane. Maybe I can learn the art after all. Finally, here was evidence he had the skill needed to become an initiate. His head rested on Thane's shoulder, and the mage's arm circled him protectively.

They rested while the last of the specially prepared leaves burned to ash. As their senses returned to normal they began to stir. Ander wasn't surprised when Thane was the first to wriggle free and roll to his feet. The mage was a relentless worker.

Thane stood beside the cushion, hands resting on his hips. "Maybe I should paint a picture of *this*. I'd call it *When Mages Turn Twenty*. I'd use it as a caution to initiates, warn what happens if they let themselves start aging."

Nicolai gestured with a rigid middle finger, then curled up with fluid grace. He put his hands on the floor beside the cushion and smoothly pushed himself into a handstand. After a few seconds he launched into a series of back flips, narrowly missing several mirrors and lamps as he crossed the chamber. He came to a stop next to the door and gave Thane a sunny smile.

"You're welcome to paint me if you can keep up with me. Last one into the bath has to wash Thane behind the ears!" He tugged the door open and darted out of the room.

Sorel got to his feet. "That sounds like a job for you, Ander." He patted Thane on the buttocks, then followed Nicolai.

Ander could tell from Thane's smirk that his barb had achieved exactly the desired result. He got to his feet and put an arm around Thane's waist. They strolled across the mirrored floor, content. When they reached the door Ander turned and nodded toward the sphere of energy that still hovered above the leather pad. "How long will it stay?" he asked. "Do we need to do anything with it before leaving?"

"It'll be stable for an hour or so," Thane assured him. "After we've washed, we'll store it in a hearth crystal. I have plans for it." They entered a passage leading to the bathing chamber. Fine tapestries lined the walls, interspersed with oil lamps in niches, and a soft rug warmed their bare feet.

"What kind of plans?" Ander asked. "I thought you used the spheres for things like light globes and fire starters."

Thane nodded. "We do. But this is a new blending. Your anima and mine, together for the first time. It will have properties different from any other blend."

"It will?" Ander found the idea appealing. "How come? I thought you worked different spells by how you *use* anima, not how you make it."

"You're partly right. But every mage is different, so the anima from each is different. And the blend created by any different grouping of mages will vary. The blending is part of the art, part of what makes it a great challenge." He gave Ander a strong squeeze. "And it's why we keep looking for new initiates, like you.

New initiates mean new magic."

"And new lovers," Ander said as he returned the hug. "That's what *I* like about the art. Sex for love, not for money."

"We were lucky to have found you," Thane said.

Ander nodded, though he suspected more than luck might have been involved. They entered the washroom. The chamber was lined with rose-colored marble and was dominated by three large terraced pools. Water from a hotspring flowed from a spout into the top pool. A sluice on the pool's opposite end created a waterfall into the middle terrace, and another waterfall splashed into the lowest pool. Stairs along the front of the pools provided access.

Nicolai and Sorel were already in the central pool standing under the sluice and washing each other with eucalyptus scented soap. Water splashed off their powerful bodies as they scrubbed each other. Ander and Thane joined them beneath the downpour.

"I thought you two had gotten lost," Sorel said. "Or more likely, gotten lost in each other's slippery fingers." He began to wash Thane's genitals with a soapy hand. "What a sight you two were! It's a good thing Erik and Skorri weren't there. We wouldn't have been able to keep them off you."

Ander scooped soap from a niche and lathered Thane's back with it. "Sounds like fun. I've heard of their prowess."

Thane sighed. "A few short weeks, and his modesty has vanished. Sorel, you and Nicolai have a remarkable way of bringing out the debauchery in boys."

"I was horny when I *met* them," Ander corrected. "I think that's why they liked me."

Nicolai grabbed him from behind. He squirmed strongly but couldn't wiggle out of the northerner's grip. Nicolai took a few steps to the deep end of the pool and dropped him in. "We liked you because you were such a shy beauty. Or so we thought. Maybe you just knew the best way to seduce us, yes?"

Ander grinned, finding a submerged ledge and settling onto it. He leaned back, arms propped behind him on the pool's marble rim, and gave Nicolai an innocent gaze.

Sorel laughed and slapped Nicolai on the shoulder. "I wager he could seduce anyone he wants. He even ensnared Thane!" Settling into the water beside Ander, he beckoned for the others to join them. "Take a rest, Thane. At least for a few minutes. We've been too busy repairing damage done by the damned cuirassiers. We need to talk about what the zamindar will do next. We won the battle, but not the war."

Thane's expression turned serious. "Good counsel, as always."

He and Nicolai took seats on the pool's opposite side. "We destroyed the zamindar's device, at least. I think it must have been one of a kind. They were using everything at their disposal just to get it working."

"I think you're right," Sorel agreed. "But they'll surely build another. Especially if you're right, that it can preserve the zamindar's life. He'll do anything to gain that power."

Thane's scowl showed his agreement. "We have to stop him. But how? A direct attack could never work. No force we can gather could match his guards. And our magical attack worked last time only because they weren't expecting it. They won't make that mistake again."

"Perhaps we could deprive them of the materials they need," Sorel suggested. "Those crystals they were using, they must be rare. If we could find out where—"

"Did you feel that?" Ander surged to his feet, his eyes wide. The others looked at him mutely. His surprised expression changed to confusion.

Thane crossed the pool and put a hand on his shoulder. "What's wrong? What happened?"

A shiver ran down Ander's back. He took a deep breath before answering. "You didn't feel it? It was like . . . a warning? But there were no words. Only alarm."

Thane glanced at Nicolai and Sorel. "I didn't feel anything, did you?" They both shook their heads.

He turned back to Ander. "Maybe it was some kind of reaction. You're new to the art. Your body might be sorting out the experiences you've just had. It's confusing, at first."

"Maybe," Ander said doubtfully. "It certainly felt real, though. It was almost—" He stopped in mid-sentence, his breath catching in his throat. A feathery voice whispered in the back of his mind. *Ander. Danger . . . Pella, here. The kei!*

"The kei," Ander muttered, realization dawning. *Lucian! He's warning me!* He grabbed Thane's wrist. "Come on! I . . . I don't know how, but I think something's wrong with the magic we worked." He released Thane and splashed out of the pool. Before he reached the bottom of the steps the others were following him. They sprinted down the corridor, water flying from their bodies, and rushed into the mirrored chamber.

The energy manifestation still hovered above the leather cushion, but its color had changed to red streaked with black. As they approached it a sense of evil imminence blossomed. Nicolai warily raised a hand toward the spinning globe.

Thane lunged against him and pushed him back. "No! Don't touch it!" Spinning around, he grabbed a large framed mirror and pulled it loose from its supporting stand. It crashed to the floor and shattered, scattering sharp fragments. Thane grabbed a long piece, heedless of the sharp edges, and thrust it like a sword into the sphere.

A banshee shriek made them step back, all except Thane. The mage closed his eyes to a squint. Ignoring the painful screech, he twisted the shard of mirror inside the mass of energy. It began to expand and contract, then to deform. The screech became deafening. Beams of light lanced from the sphere, like spears, streaking their bodies with ocher and cerulean light. Thane's jaw was clenched tight and blood trickled down his arm from a cut on his palm, but he didn't waver.

Suddenly the sphere flew apart in a burst of blinding red light. The banshee screech vanished, and a stench like burned meat filled the air. Thane staggered back, dropping the bloody shard of mirror. Ander caught him as he started to topple. He lowered the mage onto the cushion, peering anxiously into his lover's dazed eyes.

Thane was already recovering. He sat up and blinked, then rubbed his eyes. Sorel and Nicolai crouched next to them and touched Thane reassuringly.

As soon as his vision returned Thane turned to Ander and grabbed him by the shoulders. "How did you know? How could you feel what was happening, when the rest of us didn't?"

Ander stared back, speechless. "I . . . I don't know." He felt miserable, but was bound by his oath to Lucian. "Maybe because my anima was in the sphere? Here, let me look at your hand." He held Thane's hand and gently pressed the fingers back. A long gash across the palm oozed blood, but the cut wasn't deep.

Thane sighed, his shoulders slumping. "I'm sorry. I didn't mean to grab you. I'm just worried."

"It's all right," Ander assured him. "Has anything like this happened before?"

"No. But the zamindar didn't know there are mages opposing him, until last week. He's discovered a new threat. He didn't waste any time coming after us."

Sorel nodded. "We should warn the Lyceum. This attack came right after you and Ander used the art. Maybe the zamindar's sorcerers are searching for disturbances in the kei."

Thane scrambled to his feet. "You're right, we can't let anyone enter the kei! Hurry!"

2

THEY RAN BACK to the bathing chamber, threw on their clothes, and raced up the stairs. Crisp winter air and bright sun greeted them when they emerged into the courtyard. The buildings of the old fortress, long since modified to emphasize comfort over defense, spread around them. Thane led them across the courtyard at a trot. "Sorel, spread the word around the dormitory and greenhouse. Nicolai, you check the yurts. Round up Katy or somebody to cover the women's side of the ravine. Ander and I will check the workrooms. Tell them to stop *everything*, at least until—"

The clatter of hooves on cobblestones made them turn. A stallion charged through the gateway at full gallop, carrying a lithe youth with tightly curled blond hair. He reigned the horse in hard and leapt off its back, nearly running into Thane. His brown leathers were soaked with sweat.

"A patrol is coming! We don't have much time! It's not as big as the last one, but—"

Thane grabbed him by the shoulders. "Slow down, Skorri. Where are they now?"

"They were just crossing Battle of the Roses Bridge when I saw them. About ten, I think."

"Were they moving fast?"

The youth took a deep breath, starting to calm. "No, just a canter. But they'll be here soon!"

Thane nodded grimly. "Nicolai, Sorel, get going. Tell everyone to conceal what they can. And don't forget to tell them to stop using the art. Skorri, you can help Ander and me in the manor house, after you get your horse to the stable." They split in three directions, Ander staying close to Thane.

"How long before they're here?" Ander asked as they ran into the manor house's entry hall.

"Under an hour. And that's if they're not in a hurry. Go to the tower workroom and tell Anna. She'll know what to do. I'll find some initiates and start to work in the library."

Ander turned and started up the tower's spiraling staircase. The Lyceum's largest workroom was on the tower's uppermost floor, near Thane's private rooms. He glanced out slit windows as he climbed, but it was impossible to see far into the thick forest. They wouldn't have further warning before the patrol appeared at the gate. He burst out of the stairwell, startling two female initiates who were cuddling in a window well.

"I have to see Anna! Can I go into the workroom?" The art worked differently for men and women, and each gender was scrupulous about not prying into the other gender's secrets.

"You shouldn't be here," one of the women objected. She left her seat and started toward Ander. "She'll be done after lunch, if you'll—"

"A patrol's coming! Thane said to tell her *now*."

The woman blinked, then turned and pounded on the main workroom's iron-banded door. It was always barred from the inside when delicate magic was in progress; the forces in play could be deadly if the mages working the spell lost control at a crucial moment.

Ander fidgeted a few seconds, then joined in pounding. A few seconds later the door opened a crack and a middle-aged woman peered out. Her irate expression changed to surprise when she saw Ander.

"You know better than to interrupt—"

"There's a patrol coming, Anna! It'll be here in a few minutes. Thane wants you to start getting ready."

Her mouth snapped shut and she nodded. "I understand. Beth, you and Maris spread the word." She turned back to Ander. "Thane's in the library?"

"Yes. He said that's where he's going. And that you'd know what to do. You have a plan for visitors?"

"Thane looks too young, so he plays a servant and I play the lady of the manor when we get visitors." She gave Ander a quick appraisal. "You could pass for a kitchen boy yourself. You can help. That'll make it easier for Thane to eavesdrop. But first we'd better clean up in here." She opened the door the rest of the way and let Ander in.

The workroom was littered with the paraphernalia of the art: jars of dried herbs, bottles of extracts and oils, assorted crystals, and soft leather cushions the mages favored for sex. A huge block of black granite, a pool carved into its center, dominated the middle of the room. Light poured through prisms set in leaded glass windows and bathed the walls with rainbows.

"Pile the cushions in the storeroom over there," Anna said, pointing to a door on the chamber's far side. "I'll pull out the perfume bottles."

"Perfume bottles?"

"We're mages, but we still have expenses. The Lyceum *does* sell wine and perfumes. And it helps us explain all the equipment and ingredients around here, when we need to."

Ander heaved cushions into the storeroom while Anna removed magical apparatus from work tables. The room soon looked like a perfumer's laboratory, or at least it did to Ander.

Anna surveyed their work and gave him a pat on the back. "This should do, if there's a search. Now let's get down to the library. Books and talismans have to be concealed."

They left the workroom and descended the tower. Voices and the sound of frantic activity came from the library.

As they entered the room, Thane was just emerging from a door that had been concealed behind a tapestry depicting a boar hunt. "Good," he said. "We need more help." He pointed to a bookcase that was still filled with treatises on magic, and Ander joined the toiling initiates. When the last of the gramarye were hidden, Thane released the hooks holding the tapestry back and let it fall into place over the door.

"Anna thought I might be able to help with the visitors," Ander said. "She said you pretend to be a servant."

Thane looked doubtful. "Anna and I have a sign language we've worked out. But you don't know the signs, and you're not experienced with our business dealings."

"I could still help," Ander persisted. "I served guests at Lady Tay's, I'm good at it. You'll be more free to listen."

Thane thought a moment, then nodded. "With your charms, you could walk on a customer's toes and spill wine on him, and he'd still be happy. But maybe you're right. If they're distracted maybe they won't look as closely at the Lyceum."

Ander grinned happily. "It's decided, then. Let's get out of these leathers. We look a bit too rough for house servants."

They went to Thane's rooms and changed quickly, coming back downstairs wearing brown cotton pants and loose white shirts. Anna was already in the library, standing anxiously by a large window that faced the central courtyard.

"They'll be here soon," she said. "Do you think they know what happened to the last patrol?"

"They know it was destroyed by sorcery," Thane said. "But not that we did it. If they did, they wouldn't be approaching the way they are. It'd be a full-out attack."

"I hope you're right." She shuddered at the recollection of their recent encounter with cuirassiers, which nearly ended in disaster for the Lyceum. "They did more than enough damage the last time. It was too close."

"No warning last time. We're better prepared—"

"They're here!" Ander interrupted. A patrol rode into the court-yard, led by a dour officer who looked around impatiently.

Anna nodded to Ander. "Go invite their captain in. Remember to act like a servant."

Ander ducked his head, then trotted outside. The column had already come to a halt. The captain glared at Ander, his battle-scarred face scowling beneath a closely trimmed black beard. "We're here on the zamindar's business, boy. Where's the master of the estate?"

Ander bowed smoothly, his expression calm. "That would be Lady Anna, sir. I'll show you to her study." He glanced at the rest of the column, twelve men on armored horses. "I could have the kitchen prepare a meal for your men, if that would suit you."

The captain swung down from his saddle. "You'd best not let their minds wander from their duties. We've been in this damned province a week, and they're restless."

Ready to rape and plunder, he means. Ander nodded politely, then stepped back and gestured toward the manor house's door. "This way, captain."

The officer beckoned his second in command to accompany him, then followed Ander to the manor house. His stench made it plain he had told the truth about their time in the field.

Ander ushered them into the library. Thane was sitting at a writ-ing desk, bent forward and holding a quill as if taking a letter. Anna stood by his side. She turned and tilted her head slightly as they entered.

"Pour our guests some wine," she told Ander. "Then you and Thane may attend us while I see what we can do for our visitors."

The captain scowled. "There's no need for escorts, Lady. We're here on the zamindar's business. You've nothing to fear as long as you cooperate."

Anna smiled demurely. "The zamindar's household holds us in high regard, captain. His concubines are fond of our perfumes. I merely want servants on hand should we require refreshment."

The man snorted, then accepted a pewter goblet from Ander. He downed the wine in a gulp. "Suit yourself. I've no time to waste. We've had reports of evil doings, and I'm looking for the source. Has anything unusual happened here in the last week or two?"

Anna blinked slowly, a puzzled expression on her face. "Un-usual? I suppose it's been colder than usual this winter. Is that what you mean?"

The captain thrust his goblet toward Ander. "I'm not searching this damned backwater to talk about the weather." Ander refilled the goblet and the captain took another drink before continuing. "Has there been anything *strange*? Sounds in the night? Lights in the sky?" He drained the wine, then slammed the goblet down on a table. "We've been searching for a week, and I want to get this job done. Don't try my patience."

Anna held up a placating hand. "I assure you, captain, we'll do nothing to delay you."

"No. You won't." His suspicious gaze swept the library. "This is a strange little estate. You're secluded, out here in the forest. You have comforts that bandits might covet. I'll have my men look around, for your protection."

Anna was looking past the captain. Glancing sidelong at Thane, Ander saw the mage make a series of subtle gestures. Anna's eyes flicked back to the captain.

"Thank you for the offer, captain. But that won't be necessary. Our hunters keep a close watch on the forest. We'd know if there were bandits around."

"I insist." The flat tone of the officer's voice left no room for argument. He turned to his aide. "Split the patrol into four squads and get them started. Tell them to be quick about it. We have another hamlet to search before nightfall." The aide raised a clenched fist in the zamindar's salute and left.

"I'll look around in here myself," the captain said as he walked over to a bookcase. He pulled out a volume and flipped it open, squinting at the handwritten manuscript, then dropped the book on the floor and reached for another volume. Thane's jaw clenched and his eyes narrowed to slits, but he remained motionless near the door. The captain moved past the bookcase and opened a chest beneath a window.

"I assure you there aren't any brigands hiding in the library," Anna said sharply. "I appreciate your concern for our safety. But this is hardly necessary."

The officer ignored her as he rummaged through the blankets and footwarmers that filled the chest. He let the lid fall with a bang and turned to Anna with an irritated scowl.

"You might sell perfume to the zamindar's concubines, but he won't be interested in your complaints. Neither am I. Something evil is loose in the land and we've got orders to find it. You'd best stay out of my way."

Anna wavered, realizing the officer couldn't be deterred. She glanced at Thane, who looked alarmed.

The captain returned to his search, flinging books aside and jerking drawers open as his irritation increased. Ander could see how tired he was, how the days of fruitless search had worn him thin. After the officer had gone through all the drawers in the desks and cabinets, he glared at them belligerently.

Anna glared back. "Are you satisfied? I hope you realize I'm going to send a letter to the prefect about this."

The officer's mouth twisted in a snarl. He strode over to Anna and towered above her. "Send letters any damned place you want! If I don't find what the zamindar seeks, he's likely to have my head." He paused, breathing hard. "And I'm *not* satisfied."

He spun around and encompassed the library in a sweeping gesture. "Half these bookshelves are empty. What happened to the books, Lady?"

Anna paled, but stood firm. "Books, captain? We have little need for them. I thought you were looking for bandits. Perhaps if you'd tell us what you're really after, we could help you find it."

He ground his teeth together. "I'm looking for sorcerers. For their tools and their secrets." His fist slammed down on a table, making a heavy pewter candlestick wobble dangerously. "I was told to look for anything unusual. So I'll damned well look!" He strode to the nearest wall and yanked a tapestry down, ripping the delicate stitching along the top of the panel.

He turned and started toward another tapestry, the one concealing the chamber where the gramarye were hidden. Thane moved forward, silent as a cat, toward the table holding the pewter candlestick.

Events were racing out of control. Ander caught Anna's eye, looking for inspiration, but she stood frozen in horror as the captain stalked across the room. As Thane reached for the candlestick, Ander saw the captain's aide in the foyer outside the library. Even if Thane managed to subdue the captain, the aide would see everything. Ander's heart pounded. It would be disastrous if Thane attacked the officer.

"Uh, captain? You're looking for anything unusual?" Ander shuffled from foot to foot, his mind racing.

The captain wheeled around, his gaze fixing intently on Ander. At the same moment Thane saw the aide entering the library. The mage diverted his reach and picked up a goblet instead of the candlestick.

The officer regarded Ander impatiently. "What is it?"

Ander cleared his throat, then coughed nervously. "Well, I wasn't feeling too good last night, and decided to take a walk in the forest. The fresh air helps. It was, um, unusual."

The captain grimaced. "Unusual how? What did you see?"

Ander spread his hands, extemporizing wildly. "Well, it's hard to say. I mean, it was so strange. There were these lights in the sky. Colors . . . I don't know, it's hard to explain. Um, . . . they were *moving*."

Although the officer stood as if frozen, his eyes burned with excitement. "What colors? Was it dark outside, the sun had already set?"

What should I say? He caught Thane's eye. The mage had already guessed what he was doing, and nodded slightly. Ander's mind began to work again. *Treat the captain like a customer at Lady Tay's. Keep him distracted.* He squinted as if remembering, then nodded vigorously.

"Yes, the sun was down. It was well past dinner. And the lights, they moved like serpents! Writhing and twisting. But with colors like flaming brands! At first I feared there was a fire in the forest."

The captain moved closer, intent on Ander's words. "Did you see anybody else in the forest?"

After pausing thoughtfully, Ander slowly shook his head. "No, there was nobody else. No *people*, anyway. But I heard something really strange. Like a moan, only . . . kind of strangled. Or maybe like it was coming from deep underwater, faint and low." Ander shivered, beginning to get into the spirit of his story. He lowered his voice to a whisper. "But then, after that sound, was when it really got strange."

The officer and his aide were within arm's reach, reeking of sweat and horse. Ander could see the captain thought their long chase was nearing its end. "Go on," the man urged. "What happened next?"

"Everything began to spin around. Like a whirlwind! And my throat got as dry as a man lost in the desert." Licking his lips, his eyes flicked to the goblet Thane was holding.

"It makes me thirsty just thinking about it. Could I have a sip of that wine, Thane? Just a little one?" He began to sway slightly, and Thane picked up on the cue.

Thane placed the goblet on the table, then crossed his arms and looked at Ander sternly. "You know better than to ask. And in front of Lady Anna, even!" Thane turned to Anna and held his arms out in a gesture of exasperation. "He promised to stay in his room after we finished the dishes last night. I can't watch him *all* the time, Lady. Even servants have to sleep."

A low growl came from the captain's throat. "What're you talking about, boy? Why would you be watching him?"

Anna stepped forward, coming between the captain and Ander. She grabbed Ander's left ear and twisted it sharply.

"Ander! Did you sneak down to the wine cellar last night? Answer, or you'll be doing dishes the rest of your life!"

Groaning, Ander turned his head to relieve the pain she was inflicting on his ear. "Please, Lady. I didn't have anything to drink. You know I've been good."

Anna twisted his ear again, playing her part to the hilt.

"Nothing at all, Ander? You're sure? If you're lying, I'll punish Thane along with you."

Ander moaned, then glanced sideways at Thane and sighed. "Well, maybe I had one glass of wine. Just to settle my stomach. So I could sleep, and get a lot of work done in the morning."

Thane shook his head mournfully. "Just one, Ander? You're sure?"

"Well, maybe two. Or three. I . . . don't remember very clearly. Perhaps I lost count."

The captain let his breath out in an odorous snort. He pushed Lady Anna aside and cuffed Ander on the side of his face. Blood flowed from a split lip as Ander rocked back with the impact from the blow.

"You drunkard! What are you doing, wasting my time like this? I ought to have you drawn and quartered."

Ander fell to his knees and groveled at the officer's feet. "Please, sir, I was only wanting to help. I meant no harm."

Thane crouched beside him and put an arm around his shoulders. He looked up at the officer imploringly, his handsome features stricken.

"Have mercy, sir. He can't help himself. I failed him. It's my job to keep him out of the wine, but he got by me."

The captain stepped back, his mouth twisting with disgust. "Another backwater awash with drunks and simpletons! By Yataghan's sword, I swear I'll puke if I have to stay out in the provinces much longer." He turned to his aide. "Have the rest of the buildings been searched?"

The man nodded. "There's not much to see, except for a lot of plants. They said it's for perfume, they make it—"

"I know about the damned perfume," the captain snarled. "I already heard more about it than I wanted to hear. Get the men back to the courtyard. We're leaving."

The aide raised a clenched fist, then hurried from the room.

The captain stalked to the door, then turned and pointed a finger at Anna. "You're to send word to the prefect at Fochelis if you hear of anything unusual. And you'll be held personally responsible if you waste the prefect's time. Be thankful I don't have time to discipline your household."

Anna nodded meekly, not giving the officer any excuse to linger. He spun on his heel and left the room. The crash of the door as he went into the courtyard was oddly comforting.

Thane and Ander got to their feet, then joined Anna at the window overlooking the courtyard. The patrol was already starting to mount, hastened by the captain's curses.

Thane used the back of his hand to gently wipe blood from Ander's chin. The split lip was slightly swollen, but the injury was minor. "I was right about you," he said. "Beauty is only the beginning. You've brought us wisdom as well."

Anna snorted. "Luck's more like it. I half expected the captain to lop off his head, then continue the search."

Ander shrugged. "It was worth a try. But you're right, we were lucky. We'd best not rely on luck the next time."

Sorel entered the library just as the cuirassier column rode out the gateway. "They made a mess," he reported. "But they didn't discover anything."

Thane nodded wearily, and Ander's heart went out to him. Despite his immense native intelligence, and wisdom accumulated during the thirty years of his life, the mage still had the body and spirit of a youth just entering manhood. Responsibilities weighed heavily on him.

Thane rubbed his eyes, then squared his shoulders with characteristic determination. "All right. Anna, would you check on the initiates and make sure everyone's all right?"

After she left, Thane took a seat on the sofa facing the fire. Ander sat at his side, and Sorel took a chair.

"Let's start with what we know," Thane said tiredly. "Cuirassiers are scouring the countryside looking for us. Sorcerers are doing the same thing in the kei. Anything else?"

"I'd say they're doing more than *searching* in the kei," Sorel ventured. "They seemed to be waiting to attack. If it hadn't been for Ander's premonition, who knows what would have happened? I think they were in the process of manifesting something physical, when we interrupted them."

Thane put an arm around Ander's shoulder and squeezed gently. "It's a good thing we were the ones using the art when it happened. I don't know why, but you felt more than anybody else around here would have."

The warmth in his voice made Ander glow, but the words were

troubling. *Should I tell him I had help?* It was tempting, but his pledge to keep Lucian's ghost a secret was solemn. Thane had nearly died from grief when Lucian was killed. Knowledge that a fragment of his first love still lived in the kei would throw the mage into turmoil. Lucian wanted to free Thane from the past, not ensnare him in it.

Ander decided to trust the shade's judgment. He leaned against Thane, putting an arm around his waist and hugged back. "Maybe it's just because I'm so new to it," he said. "I might notice things you ignore."

"Perhaps. We'll find out soon." Thane released Ander and sprang to his feet. When he got involved with a problem he was tenacious as a hungry lion. "I'm going to the workroom. Maybe I can find a way to enter the kei without being detected. You two, think about the zamindar's tactics. We can't afford to be taken by surprise again."

"We'll do what we can," Ander answered. He watched Thane leave the room, wishing he could stay with him, but knew the mage was right. There was work to be done. He turned to Sorel.

While Sorel was a loyal friend, he was uncannily perceptive. As the son of a wealthy merchant, he had learned how to detect evasion. Ander blushed under his friend's scrutiny.

A corner of Sorel's mouth lifted in a sly grin. "You have a charming lack of guile. I'll regret the day you learn how to control that blush."

Should I tell him? He already suspects something. Caution overcame his desire to speak. He shook his head slightly, which Sorel correctly interpreted as a wish not to be pressed.

"Let me know if you ever want to talk about it, Ander. You know you can trust me. I'm willing to trust you, too. If you have reason to hold something back, you must think it's important."

"I'm grateful for the offer," Ander admitted. "I'm not as sure about it as I'd like. But I think that speaking might harm Thane. He's suffered so much already. I don't want to risk it."

Sorel put a hand on his shoulder. "We all share your concern for him. I'm grateful you're trying to protect him. But remember, we live in dangerous times. Pain is sometimes the price for survival."

"I'll remember. And . . . thank you for trusting me. It means a lot to me."

Sorel gave his shoulder a quick squeeze. "It's more than trust, Ander. We've already begun to form a bond. I know your heart. Now, let's get to work."

27

3

A NDER MARVELED at the change a few weeks could bring. Snow still covered the ground, but the journey was completely unlike the last time he had ridden the trail between Thane's estate and Pella. This time he wore warm clothes, and no cuirassiers pursued them. Best of all, he had spent the night in a warm tent and warmer embraces.

Thinking back to their campsite brought a smile. Thane and Nicolai were excellent traveling companions. Their high spirits and lurid stories had kept him laughing as they huddled around the campfire, and their tender passion when they finally took refuge in the tent had left him exhausted. He had slept nestled between them, filled with the contentment.

Thane rode at his side while Nicolai took a turn breaking the trail. "You look like a cat who found a warm hearth," the mage said. "I thought you didn't like snow."

"I was thinking about last night. The only way it could have been better was if we had used the art."

"True," Thane agreed. "But you'll need skill at sex without the art, too. Your partners won't always be initiates."

"Like when Sorel and Nicolai were going to test me at Lady Tayanita's house?" Ander's smile widened. "I remember. They had me so excited, I almost couldn't talk."

The reminder of their destination changed the direction of Thane's thoughts. "I'm still nervous about this plan," he said. "We know Lady Tayanita escaped from the citadel in Fochelis, but are you sure she'll go back to her brothel?"

"I'm certain. She built her house into Pella's finest. And her companions are her family. She'll go back."

Thane nodded thoughtfully. "And you say she has customers high in the empire. You're right, she's in a good position to hear gossip. I just hope she's willing to help us."

"She will," Ander said confidently. "Customers like to impress their companions. Especially when they're with someone as smart as Lady Tay. You'll be surprised at what she hears." He hoped he was right. Lucian's brief warning had mentioned Pella, and Ander was convinced the clue was vital. Persuading Thane to go to Pella, without revealing the ghostly warning, had been a challenge.

"We'll soon find out," Nicolai said, dropping back to join them. He pointed a short distance ahead. "A real road. We're getting close."

They left the forest trail and found themselves on a dirt road along a riverbank. The road soon widened, and they were able to ride abreast as they passed through the fields on Pella's outskirts. The city's stone walls loomed before them as stars began to glimmer in the indigo sky.

They soon arrived at Lady Tayanita's House of Companionship. They left their horses in the attached stable and entered the brothel through the kitchen door. The portly cook's eyes went wide when she saw Ander. She dropped her ladle and grinned widely, showing several missing teeth.

Ander put his arms around Thane's and Nicolai's shoulders. "These are my friends, Annie. I'll introduce you later. But first I want to surprise Lady Tay. Is she here?"

She nodded vigorously. "Aye, she hasn't gone out tonight. Welcome back, Ander!"

A knot of tension dissolved in the back of Ander's neck. While he knew Lady Tay had escaped the dungeons in Fochelis by contacting one of her many loyal customers, he hadn't known for certain that she'd made it back home. He opened the kitchen door and peeked into the main room.

A huge fieldstone fireplace filled the cavernous room with warmth. Customers and their companions occupied cushions and sofas, sharing drink and conversing in hushed voices. Above, hidden in shadow, a balcony ran along three walls and provided access to private rooms on the second floor. Like many older buildings in Pella, no attempt had been made to cover the log walls or the huge wooden beams supporting the roof.

Ander felt a pang of homesickness as he watched the companions mingle with their customers. While he had rarely bedded customers, he had sat near the fireplace and played the guitar nearly every night. Lady Tay and her companions were the closest thing he'd had to a family while growing up. He saw Lady Tayanita near the brothel's entrance and broke into a wide grin. She was as beautiful as ever: an elegant woman of indeterminate age, with deep red hair and high cheekbones. She wore a green velvet gown and a necklace of finely made glass beads.

"Wait here," Ander said. He crossed the room quickly, coming up behind Lady Tayanita, and touched her lightly on the shoulder. "Lady Tay. I've missed you."

She whirled around and wrapped him in a fierce hug. After a few seconds she pushed him back and held him firmly. "You rascal! Where have you been? I feared the cuirassiers had caught you!"

"It's a long story. One you need to hear in private." He glanced over his shoulder. Several people were looking their way, mostly companions who had noticed Ander. "Can we use your parlor? Two of my friends are here, they can explain."

Her eyes narrowed. "I can always tell when you're up to something. And I've got that feeling now." She glanced across the room. "Those are your friends? I recognize the blond beauty. Nicolai, isn't it? He helped you escape the seraskier."

Ander nodded. "Nicolai, yes. The other is Thane."

Lady Tay nodded knowingly. "I might have guessed you'd find the handsomest boys in the kingdom to disappear with. I think I know what you've been up to."

Ander shook his head, blushing. "No. Well, yes. But there's more than you're thinking. I can't say much about it. Thane will tell you, if he thinks it's wise."

Lady Tay lifted an eyebrow. "The brown-haired buck? Why, he's no older than you! Why do you think *he's* so wise?"

"Please, Lady. It's important. It's his decision."

Releasing Ander, she raised a hand to beckon Thane and Nicolai. They crossed the room, and she showed them into her private parlor. Ander made introductions and they settled into chairs around a small table.

Lady Tay served brandy from a crystal decanter, then settled back and fixed her gaze on Ander. "Now, tell me what's going on."

"Well, you know that Nicolai and Sorel helped me get away after Seraskier Reincken fell and broke his arm. I've been with them ever since. They're both friends of Thane's."

"I'm not likely to forget Seraskier Reincken," Lady Tay agreed. "He hasn't darkened our door since that night, but he still made trouble for us. He even had me arrested for treason. A difficult charge to dispose of."

"I know. We heard about it. Nicolai and I even went to Fochelis to try to rescue you, but you'd already gotten away."

Lady Tay bowed slightly toward Nicolai. "Thank you, both of you. But what did you think you were doing, trying to rescue people from the zamindar's dungeons? No offense, but it would take more than two youths to do the job. Far more."

Ander squirmed, pledged to silence but understanding Lady Tay's skepticism. He looked at Thane for guidance.

The mage had been sitting quietly. When he leaned forward his gray eyes gleamed like silver in the soft light. "Ander has told me a lot about you, Lady Tayanita. I'm honored to meet you. I think we share some common goals."

Lady Tay sipped her brandy, regarding Thane with open curiosity. "What goals might those be?"

Thane paused before answering, his expression serious. When he continued he spoke in a soft but determined voice. "We feel the same way about the zamindar's tyranny. It must end."

Lady Tayanita sighed. "Spoken with the brashness of youth. But brave words can't defeat the zamindar's army." She turned to Ander. "Do you know what you're doing? You've worked here. You know that judgment is passion's first victim."

Ander blushed again, but didn't look away. "You're right, Lady. I love him. I'd never deny it. But it's not just talk. Thane and his friends are the kingdom's best hope against the zamindar."

Lady Tay shook her head. "I'm sorry. I believe you mean well, but I don't see how you can challenge the zamindar. You're all so young. You probably don't even know what you're up against."

Thane sat motionless, his jaw clenched. Ander could tell the mage was beginning to doubt the wisdom of coming to Pella.

Nicolai shifted uncomfortably. Despite his physical prowess, the northerner disliked confrontations. "Perhaps we should leave," he suggested. "We all need time to think."

Ander surged from his seat, aching with frustration. "Wait, not yet." He knelt beside Lady Tay's chair and took one of her hands between his. "You're right to be cautious. So is Thane. You both understand the danger. But you don't have to trust each other, not yet. Trust *me*, for a first step."

Lady Tayanita's stare was unwavering, but she finally turned to Thane. "Tell me why you're here. I'll listen."

Thane gave Ander a grateful nod, then met her gaze. "Ander says you hear gossip from customers. That you've got friends everywhere, like that officer who helped you escape from the dungeons in Fochelis. We need to learn what the zamindar is doing."

Lady Tayanita frowned. "You don't need friends in high places to know he's ripping the kingdom apart, looking for something. I've never seen it so bad. So many people being seized for questioning, so many searches. I'd almost think they were expecting an invasion."

Ander tilted his head. "Invasion? Why do you think that?"

Lady Tay took a sip of brandy before answering. "Well, the city guard *has* been busy. Escorting convoys, mostly. More than any time since we had that border dispute with Eeloia twenty years ago."

Thane leaned forward eagerly. "That's exactly the kind of information we need. Do you know what the convoys are carrying?"

"Hans would know, but I don't. The wagons are covered.

Despite what you might think, I don't pry into my customers' business. I listen if they talk, but no more."

"Who's Hans?" Thane asked.

"Hans Stecher. Commander of Pella's garrison. He's been a customer for years, and he's a good man. Far more cultivated than most soldiers. He's a soldier out of family tradition, not loyalty to the zamindar."

Nicolai looked bewildered. "Why would we be interested in convoys? What could they have to do with what the zamindar is looking for?"

"If two unusual things happen at the same time, there's a chance they're connected," Thane said. He turned back to Lady Tay. "I'd like to learn more about these convoys. How can I meet this garrison commander?"

"If you're thinking about bedding him and getting him talking, think again. Hans is only interested in women."

"I don't have a plan yet. Maybe I can trick him into revealing more if we talk. Is there any way I could meet him?"

Lady Tay looked exasperated. "You're barely a man! I certainly couldn't introduce you as a merchant. You're old enough to enlist in the guard, I suppose, but that wouldn't necessarily get you close to Hans."

Ander watched with quiet amusement. Lady Tay was stubborn, but Thane was relentless. He took a sip of brandy, letting the fiery liquid roll over his tongue, and settled back.

Thane surged out of his chair and began to pace. "You're right about enlisting in the guard," he said. "It'd probably be useless. I have to get closer. Into the commander's household." He came to an abrupt halt. "That's it! If I can get me a job in his household, I'll have a chance to look around. There's bound to be information about the convoys in his records."

Lady Tay snorted in disbelief. "You *are* a dreamer. Maybe you could sneak around his house guard, but he's got a sorcerer too. There's no sneaking past *that*."

Thane frowned and stood silent. Ander began to fidget as the silence stretched painfully. Finally he cleared his throat. "Listen, Thane. Lady Tay was willing to trust me. You know me even better than she does. Better than anyone else ever could. I'm telling you, Lady Tay can be trusted."

Their eyes met, and Ander felt a pulse through the link that joined them. He knew Thane loved him, but that wasn't the same as having faith in his judgment. Time seemed to stop, and then Thane's warm presence blossomed in his heart. The mage's anxiety faded as Ander's calm certainty flowed through the bond.

"All right," Thane said at last. He returned to his seat and faced Lady Tayanita. "I trust Ander too. Give me your word that what you learn won't go further than this room."

Lady Tay's eyes narrowed, but she nodded slowly. "You have my word."

Extending a hand, palm up, Thane narrowed his eyes in concentration. A light the size of a robin's egg materialized above his hand. It glowed with a golden light that seemed to shine through his hand's flesh.

Lady Tay gasped and jerked back. "Bloody sorcery!"

"No, Lady Tay," Ander protested. "It's not sorcery like the zamindar uses. It's completely different. There's no blood, no torture. I . . . I can't say more. I'm sworn to silence. But you know I'd never harm people like the zamindar's sorcerers do. I can't believe you'd think I would!"

Lady Tay's breathing gradually slowed. "No. No, you wouldn't. But I still know sorcery when I see it."

Thane curled his fingers into his palm and the light vanished. "Sorcery is merely knowledge. But knowledge is power. That's what the zamindar is so worried about. As Ander said, my friends and I are the only real threat to his stranglehold on the kingdom."

"Ander vouches for you. And I remember how Nicolai and his friend fought the seraskier when they first came here. Perhaps I don't need to understand anything beyond that."

"You'll help us, then?" Thane asked.

Sitting back, Lady Tay tapped her fingers on the arm of her chair. "There might be a way. I remember Hans mentioning that some of his servants were beset with fever. His wife has been complaining about it. He might take you on until they recover." She grinned wickedly. "I could tell him you're a companion recovering from crotch itch. You're easily handsome enough to work here, so he'd believe it."

"I'll go too," Ander said. "It'll be safer if he's not alone."

"Impossible. Seraskier Reincken meets with Hans regularly, and Reincken still wants your blood. No, the only safe place for you in Pella is here at the house."

Ander's jaw clenched, but he couldn't refute her. If the seraskier saw him, neither he nor Thane would escape alive.

"You're both right," Nicolai said. "Somebody should go with Thane, but it's too dangerous for Ander. I'll go instead."

It wasn't the outcome Ander had wanted, and the thought of being separated from Thane made him ache, but he couldn't fault

Nicolai's logic. Lady Tay was already nodding.

"I'll pay Hans a social visit in the morning," she said. "If his servants are still sick, he'll probably want you to start right away." She looked at Thane sternly. "Are you sure you know what you're doing? You might know a few tricks, but it'll take more than that to do what you seek."

Thane shrugged. "Do any of us know what lies ahead? All we can do is try."

Lady Tay stood. "I've still got one empty room. The three of you can sleep there."

"Where's Leif?" Ander asked as he stood. "I ought to see him."

"He's with a customer. You'll have to wait for morning." A smile returned to her lips. "And be ready to answer some questions. He's been driving everybody crazy, asking what they think happened to you."

Ander groaned. "He's not going to learn much. My oath, remember. Maybe I can try to keep him distracted."

Thane thumped him on the back. "If you can't, you haven't been studying hard enough."

Lady Tayanita gave them a quizzical look, then opened the door and escorted them to a room on the second floor before returning to her business.

Ander sat on the bed's edge. Like all beds in the brothel, it was large enough for any gathering a customer might care to pay for; the three of them would be cozy but comfortable. The other furnishings were spare. Notched logs made the walls, and a window with small glass panes overlooked a dark street. A small fire in the hearth kept the room warm.

Ander looked at Thane mournfully. "I don't know what to say. I'll miss you. How long do you think you'll be away?"

Thane sat beside him. "Hard to say. It depends on how good his defenses are, how carefully we're watched. So let's make the most of tonight." He put a hand on Ander's crotch and gently squeezed the bulge.

Ander's cock quickly expanded, making a long mound beneath his soft leathers. He leaned into Thane and returned the caress. He shuddered as Thane slid a hand beneath his shirt and caressed his torso. Then the mage slid his other hand under the shirt and lifted it off.

They kissed, then Ander took Thane's hand and tugged him to his feet. "Let's get Nicolai undressed. We don't want him to get lonesome." The young northerner had been standing at the door, watching quietly.

"A fine idea," Thane agreed.

Ander moved next to Nicolai and touched his smooth cheek. "Would you share with us, Nicolai?"

Nicolai smiled and caressed Ander's bare side. "I'm *always* ready to share pleasure with you and Thane." He tilted his head and kissed Ander, his thick blond hair obscuring their faces as their tongues began to quest.

Thane stepped behind Nicolai, pressing against him as he unfastened the blond's belt and unbuttoned his pants. The leathers slid down Nicolai's strong legs. He cupped the youth's balls in one hand and his cock with the other. In seconds the penis was throbbing, thick and hot.

Nicolai unfastened Ander's belt without breaking their kiss. The pants soon joined Nicolai's on the floor. The blond pulled him closer and rubbed their cocks together.

"Thane's turn," Ander murmured. He crouched briefly to remove his boots. When he stood again he was completely naked. His perfectly proportioned body shone in the hearth's soft light, like a golden statue dedicated to youthful virility. Disheveled black hair concealed his eyes, and a mischievous smile played about his lips. He approached Thane with outstretched arms while Nicolai slipped out of his shirt and boots. "You're in *my* lair now," he said. "There's no escape."

Taking it as a challenge, Thane attempted to dodge. Ander yelped and tackled him. They tumbled onto the bed, grappling for holds.

Nicolai whooped and joined the wrestling match. His years as an acrobat had honed his body to lean slabs of muscle. With Ander's help he pinned Thane and held him fast while Ander removed the squirming youth's clothes. Soon all three were entwined, laughing, in a tangle of limbs. Their hard bodies strained against each other, and by unspoken agreement Ander and Thane joined forces to subdue Nicolai. The blond athlete struggled valiantly, but was finally pinned. Once victory was achieved, they released him.

The wrestling had only increased their arousal. Ander turned head to toe with Thane and rested his head on the youth's thigh. His fingers grazed the length of Thane's cock in feathery strokes. The thick shaft quivered in response.

"Go ahead," Nicolai said as he caressed one of Ander's long legs. "Take him down your throat. He's ready for you."

Ander didn't need more urging. His lips brushed the rosy glans of Thane's cock. A thin film of precum stretched between his lips and the turgid penis. His lips parted and slid over the crown at the same moment he felt his own cock being engulfed in Thane's mouth.

Pleasure surged through his body. Nearly mindless with delight, he let Thane's penis slide its full length down his throat. It filled him fully, but there was no difficulty. The long shaft, curving upward from its base to its flared head, seemed made to exactly fit his throat. They began to move in unison, slow and undulating, their strong bodies tense with barely contained passion.

Nicolai leaned close and held the base of Thane's cock as Ander sucked it. The shaft was covered with slippery spit and gleamed wetly in the dim light. "There's nothing more beautiful than pleasuring your lover," he said. "Your lips look so fine wrapped around his cock. You make him so hard! Let me stroke him with you."

Ander put his hands on Thane's waist and rolled him onto his back. He swung over the mage's body and held himself on outstretched arms. They continued feeding their cocks in and out of each other's hot mouths, not missing a stroke.

Nicolai moved to the foot of the bed and crouched between Thane's spread legs. He wrapped his fingers around Thane's cock and masturbated it as Ander avidly massaged the phallus with his lips and throat. Spit and precum drooled from his lips, coating Nicolai's fingers. They continued at a leisurely pace, until Ander's arms quaked at the strain of holding himself above his partner.

Nicolai released Thane's cock, then used his well-lubricated fingers to stroke his own shaft. "His balls are pulled up tight," he said as he watched the lovers. "Give him a rest, Ander. I have an idea."

Ander took one more slide to the base of Thane's cock, squeezing it with his throat muscles, then pulled up and let the penis escape from his lips. It slapped against the mage's flat belly, shiny and rock hard. Ander eased onto his side and pulled his cock from Thane's mouth, then looked to Nicolai.

The handsome blond held his drooling phallus in a light grip. The gleam in his eye revealed his intense arousal from watching their lovemaking.

"Let us suck you," Ander offered. "We don't want to leave you out."

"Maybe later," Nicolai replied. "First I'd like to see you fuck Thane. I know you'd both like to do it."

Flipping around on the bed, Thane gave Nicolai a wolfish grin. "Who *wouldn't* want Ander to fuck him? You just like to watch!"

"True," Nicolai agreed. "What could be more beautiful?"

Thane put an arm around Ander's shoulders. "Would that please you? Or we could take turns fucking Nicolai. He'd like that, though he's too polite to ask."

Ander smiled shyly. "Let's take Nicolai's suggestion."

The blond slid off the bed and retrieved his cloak. He opened one of its inside pockets and took out a thin leather case, then returned to the bed. His upthrust cock swayed provocatively as he walked. He laid the case on the bed and flipped it open. An assortment of small vials, filled with colored liquids, crammed both halves of the case. He selected a vial of clear liquid and removed its stopper. A mild fragrance reminiscent of fresh-cut heather filled the air. He leaned against the wall at the head of the bed and spread his legs wide.

Nicolai made an appealing image: shaggy blond hair framing the face of a strikingly handsome northern boy with sky-blue eyes; broad shoulders and chest tapering to a narrow waist; and powerfully muscled legs spread in an inviting vee. His long cock stretched across ridged abdominals and his balls, lightly coated with fine blond hairs, made a solid mound at his base. He poured oil into the palm of his left hand, then gave the vial to Ander.

Thane shifted around so his shoulders rested against Nicolai's chest. He lifted and spread his legs, his muscular buttocks gleaming like ivory in the soft light. Ander's cock throbbed at the gift being offered.

Nicolai reached forward and wrapped his lubricated fingers around Thane's rampant cock. He held it gently, motionless, as he nuzzled Thane's ear. "Open for him," he urged. "Let me see his cock sliding inside you."

Thane took a slow breath, calming his eager body, and the opening of his ass widened before Ander's eyes.

His heart pounding, Ander crouched before them and poured part of the remaining oil into his hand. He used his fingers to funnel a trickle into Thane's open ass, following it with first one finger and then two. Incredibly slippery oil coated the smooth skin and made it glisten wetly. He poured the remaining oil into his hand and spread it over his aching cock.

Thane looked up at him, his eyes shining like burnished silver. Despite his vast experience, he exuded an irresistible innocent sensuality. Nicolai began to gently stroke Thane's cock.

Ander took another moment to admire his lover's perfect body, then shifted forward on his knees. He put his cockhead against the boy's winking ass, then pressed gently. A smile blossomed on Thane's lips as the glans slipped through his ring of muscle.

Ander gasped and closed his eyes, afraid to move, afraid the warm grip of Thane's body would propel him to a climax before they even started. Before he knew it, half his cock was ensheathed in Thane's ass. He opened his eyes and saw Thane watching him with a wide smile.

"So smooth and hard!" Thane said. "Put it the rest of the way in. Go slow, you'll be fine." He pulled back on his knees, lifting his legs higher and opening his ass for even deeper penetration.

Shuddering, Ander let his cock creep forward until his balls pressed against Thane's upturned ass. He held himself motionless, his lean body arched backwards, waiting for the waves of pleasure to subside.

Nicolai reached around Thane with his free hand and fondled Ander's balls. "You can do it. I can tell you're almost ready to cum, but you can control it. Try to forget what you're feeling. Think about pleasuring Thane."

Your partner's pleasure is more important than your own, Ander remembered. He nodded, and forced himself to examine his lover's body. Thane was pressed against Nicolai's broad chest, feeling the thrust of Nicolai's hard cock against his back. His stiff phallus glistened in Nicolai's hand, and his youthful features seemed lost in wonder.

Locking eyes with Thane, Ander began a slow withdrawal. The ring of muscle stroked his cock like a lover's lips, squeezing precum out of the shaft and further lubricating the hot channel. He paused when all but the head of his cock was withdrawn, then slid forward again.

Nicolai moaned, entranced by the spectacle of Ander's cock sinking into Thane's ass. He held Thane's penis upright, away from the youth's flat belly. Then Ander's glans hit the sensitive spot inside Thane's ass and the mage gasped. A spurt of clear fluid flowed from his cock and down the shaft, coating Nicolai's fingers anew.

"You feel so big," Thane whispered. "As big as Nicolai. Go ahead. Fuck me faster."

Ander started moving in slow strokes, marveling at his cock's hardness. At each inward stroke he felt his cockhead glide over the spot that gave Thane greatest pleasure. The mage began to lift his slender hips in time with the thrusts. Nicolai kept his left hand around Thane's cock, and reached down with his right hand to feel the bottom of Ander's cock as it slid in and out of Thane's ass.

Beads of sweat snaked down Ander's torso as he struggled to control his thrusts. His hips moved back and forth as if gripped by an irresistible force. "I can't last much longer!" he gasped.

Thane smiled blissfully. "Kiss me."

Ander lowered his head. Their lips pressed together at the same time Ander's penis sank deeply into the hot, slippery ass. Thane lowered his legs and hooked his ankles around the small of Ander's back, holding him tight. As their tongues jousted, he milked Ander's cock with a rapid series of squeezes.

Ander's cock geysered deep in his partner's ass. His body shook, but Thane refused to release him or break the kiss. Nicolai pressed Thane's cock upward, rubbing the underside of the glans against Ander's hard abdomen. Ander felt the spray of hot semen against his skin, felt the clenching of Thane's ass in time with volley after volley of thick cum. Faint with reaction to the wrenching orgasm, he collapsed on top of Thane.

Nicolai pulled his right hand from between their bodies. Thane's semen coated his fingers. He licked a thick strand that dangled from his fingertips, then held his hand in front of Ander's face.

Ander took a deep breath, savoring the musky fragrance, then licked Nicolai's palm. Earthy flavor filled his senses and his cock began to stiffen again. The press of Nicolai's hand against his tongue reminded him the blond youth still hadn't cum.

He pressed himself up and moved back, carefully pulling his cock out of Thane's ass. The shaft was slick with semen and clear oil, glistening wetly as it emerged into the light.

Thane stretched languorously, then sat upright and wrapped Ander in a brief embrace. "Now for Nicolai," he said. He released Ander and turned to their athletic friend.

Nicolai was breathing quickly, powerfully aroused from watching their lovemaking. His heavy cock throbbed against his belly, its glans slimy with precum. The organ twitched in slow pulses.

Thane pulled the penis away from Nicolai's abdomen. "Go ahead," he told Ander. "Give him release."

Kneeling between Nicolai's outstretched legs, Ander lowered his head and put his lips to the dusky glans. Thane squeezed the cock and stroked upward, and a surge of fluid flowed from the slit in its end. As it began to ooze down over the cockhead Ander opened his mouth and slid his lips over the crown. He swept his tongue over the taut skin, tantalizing the sensitive areas around the ridge and just below the slit.

Ander's lips followed Thane's fingers up and down the shaft, his spit mixing with Nicolai's juices to coat the phallus. The blond arched his back, his buttocks lifting off the bed, as Thane jacked his cock in slow strokes. His muscles stood out in hard slabs as his friends coaxed ever more pleasure from his body. Overwhelming sensations consumed him. "I'm coming!" he gasped.

Ander backed off until just the cockhead remained in his mouth. He rubbed his tongue lightly against the bottom of the glans while Thane stroked the rigid shaft.

The first jet of Nicolai's semen fountained from his rock-hard penis. Ropy streamers of semen, thick and hot, coated Ander's mouth. He wrapped his lips around the cockhead and tried to capture the copious ejaculation. He laved the glans with his cum-drenched tongue as the young blond continued to shoot. A thin stream of semen leaked from each side of his mouth.

When Nicolai's cock finally stopped jerking and spewing, Ander slipped off the cock. The blond stretched on his back and Ander lay on top of him. As their bodies ground together Ander pressed his lips to Nicolai's. The handsome blond opened his mouth. Ander's tongue immediately entered, carrying with it a slippery load of cum. Their tongues wrestled as Nicolai's ejaculation passed back and forth between them, until the last of it had been swallowed.

When Ander looked up he saw Thane watching him fondly. The mage reached forward and caressed Ander's lustrous hair.

"You've given us something to remember while we're apart. Not that we were likely to forget you."

Ander grinned. "Maybe the memory will speed your return." He slid off Nicolai and made a space for Thane between them. Thoughts of impending separation were forgotten as they drifted into sleep, wrapped in each others' arms.

4

Sᴏғᴛ ᴋɴᴏᴄᴋɪɴɢ roused Thane from peaceful slumber. He stretched, feeling Ander's sleeping form pressing against one side and Nicolai on the other. Their blanket had slid off during the night, leaving them naked to the golden light pouring through the window.

The door swung open and a blond boy Ander's age peered through. His eyes were wide with curiosity, but they lit with joy when his gaze fell on Ander. *Leif, I wager. I see why Ander's so fond of him.* While Ander and Leif had shared the pleasures of the flesh for years, jealousy wasn't in Thane's nature. And he knew beyond doubt that the love he shared with Ander was unshakable.

The boy stepped into the room, his trim form clad only in a robe. He nodded slightly to Thane and signaled for silence. Dark blond hair fell loose over his forehead and in back was braided in a heavy ponytail. Despite the blond hair, his looks were different from Nicolai's classical northern features. A broader nose and slanted eyes spoke of mixed bloodlines, as did chocolate brown eyes. He was slender but beautifully proportioned and sleekly muscled, as the hairless chest exposed by his open robe revealed to good advantage.

He padded over to the bed and knelt next to Ander. He brushed back a lock of raven hair, then let his hand slide to Ander's shoulder and squeezed gently. As Ander opened his eyes, Leif kissed him. Ander responded warmly, lifting his upper body and wrapping his arms around the boy.

Thane couldn't guess how long the kiss would have continued if Nicolai hadn't wakened. The northerner lifted himself on an elbow and smiled. "Aren't you going to introduce us?" he asked, reaching over Thane and prodding Ander's shoulder.

Ander broke the kiss and turned to his friends, grinning widely. "Sorry, Nicolai. This is Leif." He turned back to Leif. "And these two are Nicolai and Thane. You've seen Nicolai before, remember? The night I had to run away?"

Leif nodded solemnly. "How could I forget? We were all worried about you." His gaze lingered on Thane's and Nicolai's nude bodies. "But now you're back. I can see why you took your time."

Thane chuckled. "Ander told us about you. We'd be honored to make your acquaintance. Would you like to join us? Or would you like to be alone with Ander?"

Leif sighed, looking at Thane wistfully. "I'd give a month's pay to spend the morning with you. But Lady Tay sent me to wake you up. She wants you to have breakfast in her rooms. She said she has news."

Thane slipped out of bed and started to pull on his leather pants. Nicolai followed. Leif's eyes widened in stunned admiration as he watched them dress. Even in Lady Tayanita's House of Companionship and Refreshment, the finest brothel in Pella, youths of such beauty were rare.

Ander cuffed Leif's shoulder. "I see your fevered imagination hasn't cooled," he said. "That's good. You'll need it, to keep up with these two."

Leif blinked and turned back to Ander. "I'm willing to try! Are you going to be staying?"

Ander got out of bed and started dressing. "For a while. I don't know how long." He glanced at Leif, who sat cross-legged on the bed watching them dress. "We'll talk later. Are you having breakfast with us?"

"No. Lady Tay said your business is confidential." Leif radiated curiosity, but nobody volunteered any information. He sighed and slid off the bed. "I'll be napping in my room this morning, if you have a chance to visit. I was with those randy Lukaan twins last night. I didn't get much sleep."

Ander stopped dressing long enough to give him a hug. "I'll be there as soon as I can, I promise." He gave the braided ponytail a playful tug. They exchanged another kiss, then Leif slid off the bed and left.

"Too bad Sorel and I didn't have a chance to linger last time we were here," Nicolai said. "It would have been interesting to test Leif."

"What do you look for when you pick somebody to test?"

Thane pulled a boot on, then looked up. "It's mostly intuition. But you and Leif are both good examples. Strong bodies, an aura that sizzles with sex. And the capacity for transcendent pleasure. What do *you* think, Ander? Could Leif reach the kei?"

Ander pulled his shirt over his head, then nodded. "I'd bet on it. He loves sex, and he's a considerate lover. He can prolong pleasure for hours."

"Perhaps we should test him, then. But we also need to know if he'd join our cause. Do you want to feel him out?"

"I'll do it," Ander promised as he opened the door and led them into the hallway. "Provided he gives me time to talk."

Thane looked around Lady Tayanita's private dining room with growing respect for their hostess. Furnished with understated elegance, the room would make even the most discriminating customer comfortable. Lady Tayanita was a courtesan of the old school. Her establishment, as well as its stable of companions, reflected the finest the kingdom had to offer.

Lady Tay rose from her chair as they entered. Thane and Nicolai bowed graciously, while Ander went straight to the sideboard where a breakfast buffet had been laid out.

"I really missed the meals here!" Ander declared as he picked up a plate. He glanced at Thane sheepishly. "I like oatmeal, too. But Lady Tay's cooks are especially talented."

Lady Tayanita gave Thane a puzzled look, then joined Ander at the sideboard. "Why are you apologizing to Thane? I got the impression he was your lover, not your cook."

"Um, it's a long story, Lady Tay." Ander heaped his plate with hotcakes and sausages. "He just likes oatmeal a lot."

Lady Tayanita didn't look convinced, but she dropped it. They filled their plates and settled into chairs surrounding a linen-covered table. The perfect hostess, Lady Tay let them enjoy the excellent food in peace before bringing up business.

"I sent a message to Hans Stecher last night," she said. "He always works late, at least when he isn't sneaking over here for a visit." She shook her head sympathetically. "Considering his wife's disposition, it's surprising he ever goes home at all. Not that I'm complaining. Shrill wives and boorish husbands are good for business."

"Did he send a reply?" Thane asked.

Lady Tayanita sipped tea from a porcelain cup before answering. Her expression was serious. "Yes. He said he'd take you on, and was grateful I'd thought of him. The sickness among their servants gave his wife something new to complain about, and the poor man's desperate. You can start this morning."

Thane grinned excitedly, but Ander looked glum. "I hope you'll be careful," he said.

"I hope so too," Lady Tay agreed. "There are two things to remember. First, if Hans finds out you're spying, you're dead. And I assure you it won't be an easy death. Second, don't let his household know you've come from my house. Especially his wife. She doesn't know about his diversions. The steward knows where you're coming from, but he's completely loyal to Hans."

"We'll remember," Thane promised.

"Very well. It's best that you go right away. You'll attract attention if you stay around here for long." She looked at them wistfully. "Are you sure I can't interest you in becoming companions? You'd both make a fortune."

"A gracious offer," Thane replied. "But impossible. We're pledged to our task."

"So serious, for one so young." She sighed, then nodded in acquiescence. "But I'm glad Ander has found such worthy friends. I always felt he was destined for something great."

Ander blushed crimson, embarrassment at Lady Tay's praise mixing with pride in his friends. "Meeting them has been my great fortune, Lady."

"Well then, let's hope you get them back alive." She stood. "May luck be with you. But even more, be damned careful." She held Thane's gaze a few seconds, then turned and left the room.

"A formidable woman," Thane said. "You were wise to suggest coming here, Ander."

"I hope so. I'll know when you return safely."

Thane and Nicolai explored the awakening streets, heading for the garrison commander's house. Servants trudged through the narrow streets with buckets of water and vendors crowded the plazas. The smell of sewage being emptied into gutters mingled with the dust and aroma of farm animals tethered to stalls.

Nicolai surveyed the scene curiously. "It's hard to believe Ander grew up here. It's a wonder he's not an ignorant bumpkin. He's innocent, in that sexy way of his, but more sophisticated than you'd expect coming from a backwater like this."

"Probably Lady Tayanita's influence," Thane replied. "I'd like to know more about her. I'll wager she had a good education before opening her house of companionship. She takes pride in her staff, and treats Ander like a son. He was probably encouraged to learn."

Nicolai snorted. "That wouldn't be hard. He's as curious as a cat."

"Speaking of big cats, how's Sorel doing? I've been working so hard lately, I haven't bedded him since before the two of you left on your last journey."

"You've been busy teaching Ander everything you know about fucking," Nicolai corrected. "I'd hardly call that work. I'm not complaining, since I've had Sorel all to myself. Fun, but we're still eager to get you and Ander into the same bed with us."

Thane grinned eagerly. "First thing, when we get back!"

His grin faded as they rounded a corner and saw the garrison commander's home. The house was timber and stucco, like most of the buildings in Pella. Three stories high and dark, its white-washed stucco suffering from years of neglect, it presented an ominous facade. A stone wall twenty feet high extended from each side to enclose a large courtyard in back. The garrison barracks were directly across the street, along with stables for the cuirassiers' steeds.

"Why is everything the zamindar builds so ugly?" Thane asked, bitterness tinging his voice. Every encounter with the zamindar's minions reminded him of Lucian's death.

Nicolai put a hand on his shoulder. "We won't be here long. Remember, we need to act like companions recovering from crotch itch. Don't let anger show."

Thane nodded, then squared his shoulders. "Let's go. There's a job to be done."

They went to the servant's gate, a cave-like arch built into the wall a short distance from the house. A door made of iron grating blocked the passage. They rang a bell hanging from a rod set into the wall. Soon a door swung open on the side of the house and a man emerged, bent with age but obviously a giant in his prime. From the look of his dour battle-scarred face, his military career had been long and bloody. He stalked across the courtyard and then peered at them through the gate.

"What's your business?" he asked gruffly.

"We were told the household is in need of servants, and we're looking for work," Thane answered. He gave the old man a winsome smile. "We were told to see the steward."

The old man scowled fiercely. "I'm the steward. Name's Ivan. You're the boys from Lady Tayanita's place?"

Nicolai nodded. "Yes, sir. She said we could find work here for a couple of weeks, while your staff is sick. We have an ailment ourselves, and need some time off from Lady Tay's house."

"I don't want to hear about it," Ivan muttered. "And don't you be yammering about whoring while you're in this house. The commander's got problems enough, without having to explain you to his wife."

"Lady Tayanita told us to be discreet," Thane assured him. "We won't be any trouble."

Ivan reached into a pocket and produced a large key. He unlocked the gate and allowed them into the courtyard, then carefully locked the gate again.

"You're sturdy boys," he observed, looking them over. "More than I expected, considering your line of work. You'll do fine for heavy labor."

Thane grinned roguishly. "You've never seen us at work. It can be very demanding."

Ivan snorted. "You'll have more demands than you can deal with if you don't watch yourself. You'd do well not to let the men in the garrison think your services are available." He led them to a woodpile at the rear of the house, then showed them where the axes were stored. "Come to the kitchen at noon," he said. "You'll eat with the other servants. And don't be lax with your chopping."

Thane and Nicolai began to split logs into firewood. The labor was strenuous, but at least it kept them warm. Soon both were sweating heavily. They took off their shirts and continued working, sun glistening on sweat that ran down their torsos. Nicolai wielded his ax with ease, swinging the tool with relentless strokes and never seeming to tire. Small bits of wood flecked his hair, and the healthy smell of his sweat mingled with the fragrance of freshly cut wood. Thane kept pace, his young body responding strongly to the challenge.

By late morning they had chopped a formidable pile, and had attracted a small audience. Four soldiers, assigned as guards to the commander's household, had come around to the courtyard to watch the new servants at work. They lounged against a wall where they were concealed from the house. Their muttering and laughing got louder as the sun climbed higher in the sky.

One of them began to rub his crotch as he watched. "Ain't they ever going to take a break?" he asked one of his companions. "They're working too damned hard." He waved at Thane. "Hey, brown fox. Come over here and rest. I'll give you something to put your head on." He rubbed his crotch again, leering as Thane glanced in his direction. Thane turned back to his work, keeping his eyes turned down, and swung the ax furiously. Wood chips flew. The soldiers laughed raucously.

"I like the blond one," another soldier declared. "I had a girl from the north once, but she weren't half as pretty. Those blue eyes look cold, but northerners are hot enough once you get inside!"

"I still favor the brown fox," the first soldier replied loudly. "I can tell he wants it, too."

Thane's knuckles were white, his jaw clenched.

Nicolai moved closer, turning his back on the soldiers. "Ignore them," he whispered. "We're not likely to win a fight. And we'd lose our chance to learn what's happening here."

Thane's eyes narrowed to slits. After a few seconds he took a deep breath, then exhaled slowly and glanced at the soldiers. They whistled and hooted, but he turned away like Nicolai had suggested. "I'd like to kill them," he muttered. "For what their kind did to Lucian, and so many others." He took another deep breath, then wiped sweat off his forehead. "Don't let me lose my temper," he said grimly. "You're right, we can't afford it."

The soldiers jeered and tried to coax him to turn around, but Thane ignored them and they finally tired of the game.

After lunch Ivan gave them respite from splitting wood and put them to work in the stables. Cleaning stalls all afternoon, they ended the day starving and exhausted. They had to wash in a horse trough, in nearly freezing water, before Ivan would let them into the kitchen for dinner.

"You'll sleep in the attic," Ivan said as he served them bowls of beef stew and scraps of hard bread. The rest of the servants watched from the other end of the huge kitchen, their eyes wide and their heads bent together in whispered gossip. Ivan glared at them, then turned back to Thane and Nicolai.

"Remember, you're to mind your own business. I don't want you spreading crotch itch around this house, or doing anything else that might embarrass the commander." The reference to Lady Tayanita's House of Companionship was veiled, but clearly understood. Nicolai and Thane nodded mutely. They also heard the implied threat of retribution if the commander's wife heard rumors of brothels. Ivan brought them mugs of ale, then stalked off. His hostility only made the household staff more curious.

"The attic," Thane said, picking up his spoon. "The other servants probably have quarters in the basement. Is he really afraid of rumors about us, or is there more?"

"Like what?" Nicolai asked between bites. He was concentrating on his food like a famished wolf.

"Maybe he's afraid of *us* hearing rumors," Thane said thoughtfully. He took a bite of stew, then blinked in surprise at the surge of hunger that swept through him. He joined Nicolai in devouring the simple but well-prepared meal. No sooner had they put down their mugs than Ivan returned to their table carrying two threadbare blankets.

"They're not much," he said gruffly. "I'll burn them when you leave. Don't want your damned diseases around the house." He handed them the blankets, then gestured for them to follow. "You'll have everything you need in the attic."

They followed Ivan up a flight of servant's stairs, narrow and steep. Doors at each landing were shut; the only light came from a candle the steward carried. The stairs emerged directly into the manor's warm attic. A faint breeze blew through slit windows at each end, whispering past in dusty zephyrs. One corner was empty save for a thin straw mattress and a chamber pot. The rest of the attic was filled with chests and crates, piles of rusting armor and cracked pottery.

Ivan pointed to the mattress. "You'll have to share it. I only want to burn one, and you'll stay warmer sharing a bed anyway." He looked at them contemptuously. "You'd probably be in the same bed by the time I got to the kitchen anyway. Whoever heard of whores sleeping alone?"

Thane glared, but Nicolai gave the steward a cool gaze. "Your jealousy is showing, Ivan. But don't even think about it. You couldn't afford us."

Ivan spat, almost hitting Thane's boots, then went back to the stairs. "You'll start back to work at dawn." He slammed the door behind him. They heard the loud thunk of a lock being turned before he stomped down the stairs.

Nicolai sat on the straw mattress. Thane joined him and they sat quietly, tired from their labors, watching the light fade. "Spying isn't going to be easy," Thane said at last. "I think Ivan plans to keep us too exhausted to get into trouble."

Nicolai grunted. "What I don't understand is what he's got against companions. Even back home in Norvaal I never saw anyone get so nasty about it."

"Maybe it's just because you northerners are so polite. A lot of northerners don't like companions, but just don't say so."

"Perhaps. Sometimes we're *too* reticent."

Thane grinned. "Is that a hint? You don't need to be shy around me. I know how your mind works."

Nicolai returned the smile. "If anyone knows how randy minds work, it *should* be you. But you look so tired."

Thane scooted behind Nicolai. He spread his legs and pulled the handsome acrobat against his front, then rested his hands over the full mound of Nicolai's genitals. The leather was warm and soft. In seconds he felt his friend's cock start to grow. He kneaded softly, enjoying the feel of Nicolai arching against him as the thick penis expanded to its full nine inches. "I'll never be too tired to share pleasure with you," he whispered in the blond's ear. "Besides, this is probably the best way to start our quest. Maybe we can use the art to explore."

Nicolai twisted his head and looked sidelong at Thane. "Is that wise? What if we're discovered?"

"We won't enter the kei. I'll just look around the edges, stopping at the first sign of danger."

Nicolai shrugged. "I trust your judgment. And as you say, we can make love even if we can't use the art."

Thane rubbed the mound of Nicolai's cock again, then stood and began slipping out of his clothes. Nicolai did the same and in seconds they were nude. They faced each other in the nearly dark room, erect cocks pressed between their hard bodies.

"Stay alert for danger," Thane said as he cupped the hard mounds of Nicolai's buttocks. "We'd best keep it simple. Perhaps just kisses and caresses. Would that suit you?"

The athletic youth answered with action. He put his arms around Thane's back and pulled them together tightly. Their stiff cocks jousted and their lips met in a kiss as they rubbed sensuously. Fatigue disappeared as each reveled in the muscular response of the other's body.

They sank to their knees without breaking the embrace. Nicolai eased onto his haunches and then his buttocks. He spread his legs and let Thane settle into the space between them.

Still kissing, Thane wrapped his legs around the blond's waist and pulled their crotches close. Nicolai reached between them and held their cocks together.

Their kiss intensified as Thane's tongue explored beyond his partner's lips. Nicolai squirmed against him, enjoying the penetration and inviting more. Thane ran his hands along the young acrobat's torso. The blond's flawless skin was warm beneath his fingers, hard muscle moving beneath it.

Nicolai leaned back and smiled. "It's good to feel you against me. But I know, we have a task. What's your plan?"

"I'll enter the fringe of the kei," Thane said, his lips an inch from Nicolai's. "If I'm in a waking trance, I should be able to sense danger in time to avoid it."

"You brought echinde leaves? I thought we were going to leave all implements of the art behind."

"I can enter a trance without the smoke. You and Sorel probably could, too. You're skilled enough. It's just harder."

"You can lie back while I pleasure you, if you'd like. It might make it easier to maintain the trance."

"No," Thane answered softly. "I'd rather stay in your arms. Pleasure both of us. Sharing with you is far better than making the journey alone."

Nicolai squeezed his heels behind Thane's buttocks and drew them more closely together, then put one hand behind the mage's back to help hold him upright. "I can hold you like this a long time," he said. "You'll feel my pleasure, never fear."

"Let's begin, then." Thane closed his eyes and rested his left hand on Nicolai's shoulder, then slid his right hand between their lean bodies. He wrapped his fingers around Nicolai's phallus, while the blond shifted his grip entirely to the mage's cock.

Thane paused to feel the throb of Nicolai's pulse in the straining shaft of flesh. With his eyes closed, the penis felt even more massive than usual. Thane explored it with leisurely familiarity. He knew it intimately, knew the depths of Nicolai's pleasure and the movements that made him feel best. Moving his lightly clenched fingers only an inch up and down, he worked the foreskin back and forth over the crown of Nicolai's glans. He was rewarded with a fresh outpouring of precum that coated the glans and trickled down the shaft's underside.

Nicolai matched his movements, stroke for stroke.

They used their long-established rapport to bring each other to the brink of climax and then stop at the precipice; a steady ascent based in equal parts on physical perfection and control over pleasure that only an adept of the art could fathom. They strained against each other, panting, as flesh screamed for release. The movement of their hands on each other's slippery cocks slowed to nearly imperceptible movements as they trembled on the brink of orgasm.

As his body's demands swelled, Thane channeled the torrent of sensation in a new direction. It flowed through him, echoing and rebounding between his inflamed body and his mind, amplifying in intensity. He felt the pleasure throbbing in Nicolai's phallus, felt it in the flood of precum that coated his fingers as Nicolai ascended the peak beside him. Even though his eyes were closed, he could sense the red halo surrounding their bodies. Pleasure engulfed him. Suddenly his mind burst into a different reality, a realm woven integrally throughout his body and extending to infinity.

Thane let his consciousness drift. He was aware of his body, focused on the stimulation of Nicolai's stroking hand, and was dimly aware of the blond's thick phallus in his own grip. But he also seemed to float above the crude mattress. In his mind's eye he could see their bodies: two lean males, entwined and vibrantly aroused, outlined by a red glow that beat in time with their hearts.

He turned his vision back to the kei's swirling colors, and sensed something stirring. Using the detachment inherent in his trance state, he split his attention between maintaining the bond with

Nicolai and extending his awareness toward the disturbance in the kei. His mind expanded, quivering with tension that was driven only in part by the clamoring of his masterfully stimulated body. The disturbance took on a more distinct feel, like the slithering of scales over rock. The smell of blood suddenly blossomed.

Swirling colors coalesced into a shape, a colossal red serpent with the head of an obese man. Bloody fangs stabbed below his lower lip, and his eyes were flat like a snake's. A large crystal, sparkling brightly, pierced the scales just below the point where the head joined the body. The coiled body rested on an ornately carved ebony chest, and rotting corpses lay around it in twisted and torn heaps. The creature's head swayed wth slow deliberation.

The serpent's gaze turned in Thane's direction. He froze, blanking his mind, becoming a passive observer and nothing more. Unblinking serpentine eyes, unreadable, seemed to peer into his own. But instead of the attack he feared, Thane sensed only a guarded watchfulness. Unbidden, a new image flashed through his mind: a large desk with a locked center drawer. A key protruded from the keyhole, with beams of violet light streaming out around it.

The snake creature hissed and lifted its fanged head as if to strike. Thane stopped thinking, his consciousness merging with lines of force flowing through the kei's unseen dimensions, becoming part of the flux. After a few moments the serpent resumed its regular swaying, its head raised as if sniffing the air for the scent of prey.

Thane waited before allowing thoughts to form. Then he eased away from the foul apparition. It faded from his awareness like a bad dream. He retreated along his bond with Nicolai, letting awareness of their bodies grow as the kei faded.

The trance broke and his double vision faded. He found himself nestled between Nicolai's legs, held tight by the young athlete. Nicolai was using a finger to gently stimulate the underside of his cockhead, moving his fingertip in small circles through a thick coating of precum.

Thane's cock was hard and aching, his balls pulled up tight. Full perception of his body brought a shocking jolt of pleasure. He cried out and wrapped his arms around Nicolai as a geyser of semen fountained between their bodies.

Nicolai squeezed their cocks together, belly to belly, using both hands. He grunted softly as his phallus spat ropy streamers to mingle with Thane's ejaculation. Hot cum smeared their chests and ran down smooth skin in long streaks.

As their orgasms subsided, Thane fell against Nicolai and

pushed him onto his back. They lay together, chests heaving, as their slippery cocks rubbed and spewed cum in weakening surges.

Nicolai caressed Thane's back, letting his hands linger against the firm mounds of buttocks. The mage sighed contentedly and let his weight press his friend into the mattress. They rested quietly for several minutes, savoring the pleasure they had shared. Thane finally rolled onto his side.

"Did you learn anything?" Nicolai asked. "For a moment you stopped breathing. I feared you might have been snared by whatever's loose in the kei."

"Almost. I found *something*, and it nearly found me." He frowned as he thought about the apparition. "I don't know." His voice was soft and hesitant. "The mind struggles to make sense of what it encounters in the kei. I don't understand what I saw, the meaning behind the visions."

Nicolai brushed his fingers through Thane's short brown hair. "Just describe the visions. Maybe I can help."

Thane sighed, then rolled onto his back and nestled against Nicolai's side. Slowly at first, then more rapidly as the words began to flow, he told Nicolai about the serpent, the ravaged bodies and the ebony chest, the perplexing image of a locked desk. The different elements of the vision had to be clues, metaphors for some reality encountered in the kei, but he couldn't see how they were connected.

"The serpent must be a sorcerer guarding the kei," Thane said. "That much seems obvious." He shook his head in frustration. "But it didn't really seem to be looking for me. When its eyes met mine all I got was an impression of that desk, and light coming from the keyhole. Did the vision come from the serpent, or somewhere else?"

"Maybe the sorcerer isn't guarding the kei at all," Nicolai suggested. "He might be guarding something *from* the kei."

Thane paused, then nodded. "Maybe. And that reminds me of something else, a feeling of *closeness*." He shivered. "Whatever's going on, Nicolai, I think we've come to the right place. But we're going to have to get around Ivan somehow. We won't discover anything if we're stuck in the courtyard and attic all the time."

Nicolai rolled on his side and pulled Thane into a hug, nestling together front to back. "Don't worry, you'll think of something. You always do."

Despite his friend's confidence, Thane wasn't so sure. They were in enemy territory, under the supervision of suspicious eyes, and dared not use any strategy that might implicate Lady Tayanita.

Was I foolish to think we could learn anything without using the art? But what else could we have done? He lay awake a long time, listening to the faint city sounds filtering through the attic's windows and feeling the slow rise and fall of Nicolai's chest at his back. Finally, his mind still troubled, he fell into exhausted slumber.

5

A NDER LOOKED at the swirling crowd of spice vendors on the street beneath his window, but he didn't hear their haggling voices or notice the pungent aroma of their wares. The scene, which had greeted him every morning for years, seemed irrelevant. Thane and Nicolai would be at the commander's house by now, and there was no telling how well Lady Tay's story would protect them. He rubbed his eyes, wishing fervently that he knew what was happening.

A soft knock on the door made him jump. He blinked and turned from the window. "Come in," he answered.

The door swung open and Leif entered. He had just bathed, and dark blond hair flowed over his shoulders. He still wore his robe. He smiled widely, his almond eyes squinting nearly shut. "I was worried you'd disappear again," he said. "I heard about your friends leaving before I even got out of the wash house. I've never heard companions talk so much about visitors."

Ander grinned. "Are you surprised? Thane and Nicolai are enough to make even a companion swoon."

Leif looked at the floor. "No, I'm not surprised," he said softly. "I'd probably have gone with them myself, if I'd had the chance." He looked up, his gaze searching. "What happened, Ander? Have you started working for another house? Why didn't you let us know where you went?"

Ander went to Leif's side and wrapped him in a tight hug. "No house of companionship," he whispered. "I didn't tell you where I was because I couldn't." Brushing aside the long hair, he gently kissed Leif's neck. The tawny skin smelled faintly of mint. "I'm sorry," Ander said as he stroked his friend's back. "I came back as soon as I could." Leif returned the embrace, his tense body slowly relaxing.

Leif turned his face to Ander's. Sharing the same age, they had been confidantes since boyhood and frequent lovers since awakening to the pleasures of the body. They kissed, responding hotly to each other's familiar flesh.

Ander parted Leif's robe and slipped a hand beneath the soft garment. He stroked the length of the blond's lithe torso, feeling the ridges of muscles and the nub of a nipple. Drifting lower, his fingers grazed over Leif's lean belly and through soft pubic hair. Finally, as his tongue slipped between Leif's parted lips, his fingers slid around the upthrust shaft of Leif's cock. He held it loosely, stroking the satiny skin with exquisite lightness, until Leif quivered in his grasp.

As Ander drew back, Leif opened his eyes and gave him a sultry smile. "You're more skillful than ever. Been learning from your new friends?"

Ander grinned back, giving Leif's throbbing penis a gentle squeeze. "I've learned a *lot*. They know ways to fuck you've never dreamed of. And Thane . . . well, he's more than a sexy tumble, Leif. Much more."

Reaching down, Leif took Ander's hand between his own. He raised it to his lips and kissed it. "You're in love, aren't you?"

Ander blushed, wondering how his old friend would feel about the depth of his attraction to someone else, but he need not have worried. When Leif looked up, a sunny smile lit his face.

"I'm glad for you. You deserve it." He tugged Ander toward the bed. "Braid my hair and tell me what he's like. Aside from him being the most beautiful boy in the kingdom, next to you. I can see that for myself."

They settled onto the bed and Ander began to braid Leif's thick hair into a ponytail. The familiarity of the task brought a flood of memories. He shoved them aside and turned his mind to his new life at the Lyceum.

"First of all, I didn't leave here to be with anybody else. I had to flee when Seraskier Reincken got hurt. Everything that happened was unexpected."

"I was still downstairs when it happened," Leif said. "I saw it all. Where did you go?"

Ander hesitated, feeling awkward. "It's really complicated, Leif. And . . . I promised not to talk about some of the things I've learned. You understand, don't you? I can't betray their trust."

Leif nodded. "I understand promises. But I've got ears. You're mixed up in politics, aren't you? I heard Lady Tay talking politics this morning, and I doubt it's a coincidence."

There's no reason to deny it. As long as I don't mention the art. He continued braiding the ponytail, giving Leif a chance to dwell on his question, then sighed. "You know how dangerous the zamindar is, Leif. I trust you, but my friends don't know you and I couldn't lie to them. Do you really want me to answer?"

"I knew it!" Leif twisted around and looked at Ander anxiously. "Do you know the risk you're taking? Do you want to end up gutted at a public torture?"

Ander put a hand on Leif's shoulder and squeezed it reassuringly. "I can't deny the risk. I've already looked death in the face.

That's why we have to be careful, Leif. It'd be foolish to do anything that makes the danger even worse."

Leif took a deep breath, his eyes never leaving Ander's, then nodded slowly. "Maybe you're right." He put a hand on top of Ander's, then turned around again. "So don't tell me about politics. Tell me about Thane. What's he like? He seems very serious for somebody his age."

"He *is* serious. He had a lover who died in the zamindar's dungeons. After being tortured." Ander's voice thickened as he thought of Thane's intense pain and grief. "He's amazing, Leif. Brilliant, and dedicated to a noble cause. He has many followers."

"He *must* be exceptional, to gain a following at his age. Or are they all just smitten by his beauty?"

Ander gave the ponytail a playful tug, then finished the braid. "If you really want to be smitten, take a tumble with him. He'll show you pleasures you've never imagined."

Leif flopped onto his back, resting his head on Ander's lap. His robe fell open to reveal smoothly rippling muscles. His cock, still thick and semierect, lay across his lower abdomen. "I'm certainly willing to learn. And what about the northerner? He moves like a dancer."

"He's an acrobat. He's strong as a tiger, but gentle." Ander let his fingers trail over Leif's chest, enjoying the silky feel of his friend's honey-brown skin. In moments Leif's nipples were hard nubbins, and his cock started expanding again in slow surges. "He can do things in bed that even Thane can't. He's very . . . supple."

"Supple?" Leif lifted an eyebrow. "You're always so discreet." He moved his head in lazy circles, rubbing Ander's growing erection. "Go ahead, tell me."

Ander blushed, but couldn't resist Leif's horny curiosity. "Well, he can fuck you and suck you at the same time. It feels wonderful! Sorel says he can suck himself, too. All the way to the balls, while being fucked at the same time."

Leif's eyes got wide, and his rigid penis twitched against his belly. "I'd like to see that! Especially if he'd let me do the fucking!"

"I'll tell him you're interested as soon as he gets back, if you'd like. You have to be direct with him, though. He'd never press you the way most people do. You know how northerners are."

"They're as horny as anybody else," Leif said confidently. "And it feels to me like you're just as horny as your friends." He arched his back, pressing his head more firmly into Ander's lap. His robe fell open the rest of the way. Light streaming through the window bathed his body in a golden haze, like a magical vision. He smiled and reached up to touch Ander's cheek.

"Want to show me what you've learned? Why don't you get out of those clothes? The leather looks good on you, but it must be getting confining." He pressed his cheek against the long mound of soft leather that covered Ander's erection, then reached for Ander's belt and deftly unfastened it.

Ander needed no further encouragement. He pulled his shirt off, mussing his thick black hair as the garment went over his head. Leif rolled off the bed and crouched at his feet, pulling off one boot and then the other. Then he hooked his thumbs in the waistband of Ander's pants and gave a tug. The leathers snaked down Ander's hips. His eight-inch cock sprang free, spearing up from a bush of black pubic hair. Leif started to reach for it, but Ander stepped back.

"The first thing I learned is that your partner's pleasure is more important than your own. Let me show you."

Leif shrugged out of his robe. He stood before Ander naked and aroused, his ponytail hanging over the front of his right shoulder, before sitting on the bed's edge.

"Lean back," Ander said as he crouched between Leif's legs. The boy obliged, supporting himself on strong arms thrust behind his back. He spread his legs to give Ander plenty of room. His long cock lay across his belly, its head straining against the small indentation of his navel.

Ander licked his lips, aching to press against his friend's hard body, but held himself back. Instead he reached forward and brushed his fingertips over the fine golden hairs of Leif's inner thighs. The penis jerked in response. He continued caressing, using both hands and tracing the length of Leif's thighs from the knee to within an inch of his balls. Silky hairs on Leif's scrotum caught the light as the balls moved.

Leif spread his legs wider, pressing the balls of his feet against the floor. Droplets oozed from his cock and glistened in the morning light. "Don't stop!"

Ander's cock ached. He ignored it and continued his feathery exploration. The young blond squirmed as the caresses reached the sensitive spot between his balls and ass. A pool of precum smeared the skin beneath his cockhead.

Leif started moaning, but Ander didn't relent. Instead of allowing release, he extended his light strokes to Leif's scrotum. The sack pulled up tight and hard against the base of Leif's straining cock, and the youth's pelvis began to rock as if he was trying to shove his cock into an invisible partner. Ander continued tickling the wispy hairs covering the scrotum while the other hand trailed over Leif's inner thighs in leisurely swipes.

"Such restraint!" Leif gasped.

Ander grinned but didn't stop. "Thane likes to take you to the edge of release, then make you wait. Again and again. You'll see, Leif. Even a companion can learn from him. See how long you can make it last."

Leif groaned and shook his head, his ponytail lashing against his chest. "I'll try. But you're making it difficult!"

Ander knew how he felt; his own cock was rigid as a sword. It swayed between his legs, thrusting upward like a post, the glans wet with his excitement. Not touching it was torment, but exquisite torment. Steeling himself with the discipline Thane had taught him he maintained his focus on his friend.

Leif's eyes were half closed and his body shivered. Ander licked his lips, then leaned forward and wrapped the fingers of his right hand around Leif's cock. At first he just pulled it away from Leif's belly while he continued stroking his friend's balls. The well-defined muscles in Leif's legs flexed and his cock strained in Ander's hand. He began to slowly work the cock's sheath back and forth, pulling the foreskin up until it covered the flared ridge of the glans and then all the way back down. Precum streamed down the cock and lubricated its foreskin. Ander kept stroking, his fingers slippery with the natural lubricant.

Leif began to pant. He flung his head back, his ponytail lashing between his broad shoulders. Ander slowed his movements, barely touching Leif's quivering body. The blond's cock thrust upward, the muscles of his legs and torso as hard as granite.

At last Ander leaned forward and licked the underside of Leif's penis, starting at the base and not stopping until his tongue pressed against the underside of the glans. Musky fluid, tasting of earth and moss, seeped onto his tongue. He continued gently stroking Leif's penis and balls while sliding his lips around the slippery glans.

Leif cried out, a muted wail, as jolts of pleasure raced through his body. His fists clenched and his body arched back.

Ander held himself motionless, with Leif's cock and balls in his light grasp and the head of Leif's cock in his mouth. The blond's balls felt as hard as a firm peach, ready to release their store of semen. He held his breath, his heart pounding, trying to help Leif make it last.

Slowly, Leif's body began to relax. His cock still throbbed in Ander's hands, but his breathing slowed and his buttocks settled back onto the mattress. Ander eased his mouth off the cock and looked up, a dazzling grin on his face.

"What kind of tricks have your friends been teaching you?" Leif asked. "Your skill has doubled!"

Ander eased Leif's cock back against his belly. "I'll tell you later, if Thane agrees. But for now, let's finish what we've started." He rose to his feet. Sunlight painted his body with burnished gold. Disheveled black hair glinted with bronze highlights above his princely features. Beads of sweat dotted his broad chest and powerful shoulders. His torso, sheathed in muscle yet showing his ribs as he breathed deeply, tapered to narrow hips. Solid buttocks and long, strongly muscled legs made entrancing patterns as he shifted his weight. His cock, nearly as long as the distance between his nipples, curved up from his crotch in virile defiance of gravity.

Leif stroked the underside of the upthrust cock. "You're more beautiful than ever. I've heard Lady Tay say that being in love can do that to people."

"Your turn will come," Ander said as he gently pushed Leif onto his back. Then he climbed into bed and held himself above Leif on knees and elbows, not touching except for their cocks. They kissed, their lips brushing lightly, while Ander used slow prodding movements to mingle their precum. Warm sunlight caressed his back, soon joined by the slide of Leif's hands along his sides.

As the kiss deepened, Ander lowered himself to press full length against Leif's body. He slid his arms around the blond's back and held him in a tight embrace as the kiss became impassioned. Soon they were grinding against each other, their bodies slippery with sweat.

"Let me taste you," Leif said between kisses. "I want to make you ache, the way I did."

"You'll always make me ache," Ander assured him. "Let's suck each other—"

A brisk knock on the door made him freeze. A second later he heard a feminine giggle.

"What's going on in there?" a girl's voice inquired. "Are you awake, Ander?"

"Tannis!" Leif muttered the name like a curse. "She knows damned well you're awake!"

Ander groaned and rolled off his friend. He reached for the blanket at the foot of the bed and pulled it up, covering Leif and himself to their waists, then propped himself on one elbow and let the other arm rest against Leif's chest. Leif stayed on his back, looking at the ceiling like an insulted cat.

"What is it, Tannis?" Ander asked. "Can't it wait?"

The door cracked open and Tannis looked through. Comely even without her makeup, her brunette curls framed a heart-shaped face with large green eyes. At the moment Ander thought she looked like a harpy.

"I hope I didn't interrupt anything," she said insincerely.

"What is it?" Ander repeated. Leif gave her a look that would have been alarming in a dark alley.

Tannis smiled demurely. "Lady Tay wants to know if you'll join her for lunch. She has some questions about those friends of yours, I think." She fairly radiated curiosity. "What have you been up to, anyway? Where have your friends gone?"

"Tell Lady Tay I'll be there at noon," Ander said, restraining himself with an effort.

"The intense boy with brown hair, are his eyes really silver? I couldn't get close enough for a good look. He wasn't here before, was he? I'd have remembered him—"

"Thank you, Tannis."

The girl sniffed, then gave her head a small toss. "You're most welcome. You and Leif can go back to sleep now." She gave Leif a taunting smirk, then quickly closed the door.

"I'll bet she was listening," Leif fumed. He jabbed a rigid middle finger at the door. "Get an earful of this, Tannis!"

"Never mind, Leif. Who cares what she heard? Come on, give me another kiss." He caressed Leif's chest soothingly, but the blond was still too irritated to respond. Ander stroked the underside of a biceps, a spot that always made Leif relax. "What happened while I was gone?"

"You know about Lady Tay's arrest? *That* caused a panic!"

"Yes, I know about that. Anything else, though? What's it been like around Pella?"

Leif thought for a moment. "Well, Tannis and Nestor had a big fight. You get different stories depending on who you talk to, but I think Nestor got tired of her bitching and started sleeping with Karl." He paused and tugged on his ponytail a few seconds. "Too bad he didn't come visit me. I could've told him a few things that'd keep Tannis from gossiping about him." He wiggled eagerly at the thought.

"Remind me never to get on your wrong side. I hate to think of all the tales you could tell about *me*."

Leif gave him a sunny smile. "You don't have to worry. All the scandalous stories about you would have me in them, too."

"True," Ander agreed. "But what else about Pella? How has the city guard been acting?"

"Come to think of it, that's a strange thing in itself. The military trade has almost run dry."

"Since when did you start sleeping with soldiers?"

"I don't, except for Pavol. He's not a soldier by choice, and he hates the guard. But I've heard the other companions talking about it. Aside from a few officers, there hasn't been a soldier in here for a couple of weeks."

"Have you heard where they are?"

Leif sat up, his shoulders tense. "I hear they're stuck in the barracks when they're not on duty. I hope they go crazy in there, cooped up with each other!"

Ander touched his cheek. "I'm sorry," he said softly. "I didn't mean to remind you of what they did to your sister."

Years before, Leif's sister had suffered a brutal rape at the hands of drunken city guardsmen. They had been young boys when it happened, and Ander had comforted him during his rage and grief. They had touched on a deep level and formed an unshakable bond.

"I'm all right," Leif said. "But why are you asking these things?"

"You already know I'm fighting the zamindar. I can't tell you how, I'm sworn to secrecy. But I think you might be able to help us if you wanted to."

Leif closed his eyes and shuddered. "Don't torment me. I'm just a companion. A nobody. The only way I could defeat the zamindar is if you gave me a knife, and then talked his army into my bed one at a time."

"I think you're wrong," Ander said. "If you *could* make a difference, would you fight?"

Leif fell silent, his eyes hooded. Ander could see the struggle between hope and despair in his face. He waited patiently, hoping their long friendship would outweigh the seeming impossibility of what he was suggesting.

Leif took a deep breath, then slipped out of bed and crossed the room. He stood in front of the window and looked down onto the street. "Take a look at this," he said.

Ander got out of bed and stood behind Leif, his arms around the blond's torso. The scene below hadn't changed much, except for the street becoming more crowded. "What? It's just the usual merchants, and servants doing chores."

"Look how they walk, how they huddle together when they talk. Things have gotten worse, Ander."

Looking more closely, Ander could see what he meant. The perfume vendors looked slightly tawdry, their fine clothes frayed around the edges and their faces shuttered. The air of joviality that usually filled the street was absent. "I see," he said. "It *has* changed. Why?"

"Taxes were raised again last week. They're afraid of losing their homes. And did you hear about the new torture?" Leif sounded sick.

"No. Did they find something even worse?" He squeezed gently, trying to soothe his friend's distress.

"I was in the square, coming back from the farmers' market. They'd had the blacksmith make a big tube of metal, two feet thick and six feet high. They filled it with burning coals until it was red hot. A guardsman held each of the prisoner's arms, and they pulled him against the metal." He shuddered with revulsion. "The screams, Ander! They did it again and again until all his skin was seared off. The smell of burning flesh . . . I think I'll never eat meat again."

"What was his offense?"

"Sedition. He had complained openly about the new taxes. And I think they wanted somebody to try their new torture on."

Leif turned away from the window. He held Ander tightly, almost desperately. "If anybody but you had said I could fight the zamindar, I'd think he was crazy or trying to trick me somehow. But you're my best friend, Ander. I'd trust you with my life. So if you think I can help bring down the zamindar, I'll join you."

Ander nodded solemnly, moved by his friend's trust. "It's Thane's decision, but I'll be your advocate. And I don't think you'll have any trouble, um, impressing him."

"Thane again! He has you enchanted, Ander. I can see why, but it's still hard to imagine how he could unseat the zamindar." His expression changed to curiosity. "Still, I feel something different about you now. Maybe it has to do with Thane. Will you be leaving again when he returns?"

"I doubt we'll stay long in Pella," Ander admitted. "Leif . . . how would you feel about going with us, if Thane agrees?"

Leif's smile was eager. "Yes! Do you think they'd teach me some of the secrets you've learned?"

Ander smiled mysteriously. "Remember Sorel, Nicolai's lover? He and Nicolai showed me a new position for fucking, so I could surprise Thane with it. Nicolai's seed must have flown six feet into the air when Sorel finally let him cum."

Leif's eyes went wide, his renewed erection surging between their bodies. "Show me!"

6

THANE COLLAPSED on the thin mattress, exhausted and still hungry after their meager dinner. Nicolai's collapse was more graceful, though he was no less fatigued. The attic was still warm. Dust motes spiraled through slanting rays of light pouring through slit vents on the room's west end.

"At least you weren't stuck on a ladder all day," Nicolai said as he stretched out on his belly. "I had so much whitewash on me, even the dinner tasted like paste. And I haven't even finished the south side of the house. I don't much like this honest work."

"Quit complaining," Thane replied. He scooted next to Nicolai and started rubbing his back. "My hands are scraped raw from rebuilding that damned stone wall. Why do they want a wall between the garden and the potting shed, anyway?"

"Maybe Ivan's just trying to keep us out of the way," Nicolai said. He flexed his shoulders as Thane kneaded the sore muscles. "He might be afraid we'll say something about Lady Tayanita's House of Companionship. Still, it looked like *you* managed to do a little inquiring. I saw you huddled behind the wellhouse with that scullery maid when you got water for your mortar. Did you learn anything?"

"I tried. But information isn't what she wanted to give me. I had to spend half my time keeping her from pulling my pants off." He grinned and knuckled the back of Nicolai's neck. "I finally convinced her we'll have a much better time if we find a room where we can meet at night. It gave me a reason to ask her about the house, and where the guards are posted." He stopped massaging and sprawled beside Nicolai. "But if we don't find what we're looking for soon, I'm in trouble. She's going to steal a key to the attic. Once she does, she'll expect me to spend the night with her. I won't be able to evade her for long."

Nicolai rolled onto his side and kneaded the sore muscles in the small of Thane's back. "But she told you the lay of the house? Did she say anything that might help us?"

"Maybe. She said to stay off the third floor. Anybody caught on there is in serious trouble."

"Did she say why?"

Thane nodded. "Somebody's there. Eating meals, but staying out of sight. She says there've been strange noises and lights at night. And the commander vanishes for hours at a time. I'd wager that's his sorcerer's lair." A grin flashed. "It was hard to get her to talk about it, though. She was trying to make sure I'd know how to find her quarters once she gets me a key. She must think I'm really dumb, I asked so many questions."

"Doesn't matter," Nicolai replied. "It's not your mind she's interested in."

"No. But I think she's already told us enough. My guess is we'll find what we're looking for on the third floor."

"Why do you think so?"

Thane sat up, wrapping his arms around his legs. "The sorcerer in my vision was guarding something. If we find the sorcerer, we'll likely find the zamindar's secret as well."

"There's one thing to our advantage," Nicolai said as he got to his feet. "The sorcerer is watching the kei for magical threats. He isn't expecting a physical attack in the garrison commander's own home." He began to stretch, loosening his tight muscles.

Thane got up and went to the stairwell door. The last rays of sun fell on his back, highlighting dirt and specks of dried mortar on his leathers. He knelt in front of the door and took a long nail out of a shirt pocket. "Not the best pick, but it's the best I could find in the potting shed."

Nicolai crouched at his side. "I always knew you were a thief at heart."

"Don't look so smug," Thane said as he poked the nail into the keyhole and started feeling out the lock's mechanism. "Sorel taught me how to do this. I understand you two had some profitable adventures before I recruited you for the Lyceum."

"I don't remember anything like that," Nicolai said blithely. "But then we were fucking most of the time, so how could I be expected to remember anything else? You know how distracting Sorel can be."

"Spectacularly distracting," Thane agreed. He jiggled the nail, then slid it forward and twisted sharply. The lock snicked open and he rocked back on his heels, a satisfied look on his face. He turned to Nicolai and grinned. "We've got a few hours before it's safe to explore. Why don't we make some distractions of our own? I have an idea for working those kinks out of your muscles."

"Somehow I'm not surprised."

They leaned together and kissed. Not until well past midnight did their attention turn back to exploring the house.

The ancient stairs threatened to creak at every step; they walked on the treads' outside edges and felt their way through darkness. When they reached the third floor landing they pressed ears to the door, and opened their minds to any strangeness that might signal a magical trap.

All was quiet, but Thane's scalp still tingled. "Do you feel it?" he asked. "Like someone lurking behind us?"

"Someone with a taste for blood," Nicolai whispered. "Just a presence, though. I don't feel a cantrip."

"I don't either," Thane agreed. "But we're on the right track. I'll go first."

He pushed the door open a crack. The corridor that lay before him was lit only by moonlight coming from a row of windows. He opened the door the rest of the way and crept out, Nicolai close behind.

The third floor had obviously seen little use for a long time. Dirt and even a few leaves littered the floor, and the windows were crusted with grime. The crescent moon, glimpsed through tattered draperies, looked mottled and corrupt. Thane sniffed the air. Mold and dust made him want to sneeze.

The first stretch of corridor yielded no signs of habitation, only decay. They turned the corner. The next corridor had doors on both sides, and was dark as a moonless forest. Thane paused to let his eyes adjust.

"It's stronger now," Nicolai whispered. "Like a hunger." He touched Thane's shoulder. "Careful. I smell death."

Thane nodded, then started forward. At every step the air seemed to thicken. He stopped at each closed door and brushed his fingers lightly across its surface. Halfway down the corridor, his hackles rose. A ghostly presence floated just beyond his vision, but close enough to cast a shadow on his mind. He put out a hand to signal Nicolai, then knelt in front of the closest door. A faint light emanated from the keyhole. Choking back the loathing that filled him at the taint of blood magic, he put his eye to the keyhole.

Inside the room, a candle flickered in the breeze from a partially open window. The candle rested on a massive casework desk, a formidable piece of furniture fully enclosed on three sides. Dirty dishes and several large books surrounded the candle. Thane shivered slightly as the desk's lines became clear: it matched the one he had seen in his vision.

A fat man in a black robe rested in an armchair next to the desk. The red sword of the zamindar's crest decorated his robe, and a key hung from a cord around his waist. The rest of the room was lost in shadows. He was motionless, and a trickle of spittle dripped from one corner of his mouth. Though he appeared to be sleeping, a shimmering black veil around the candle's flame revealed magic's presence in the room.

After a few seconds Thane pulled back. He drew Nicolai a few feet down the corridor, then leaned close. "He's in there. Probably in a trance, watching the kei for threats. But he'll come out of it fast if we make any noise."

"I felt for cantrips while you were at the keyhole," Nicolai said. "If there's anything there, it's too subtle for me."

Thane nodded. "As we thought, they're only worrying about magical attacks. If we can get to him before he leaves the trance, we can take him. I'll try the latch."

They went back to the door. Thane put his hand an inch from a metal ring that operated the latch, feeling for tingles, chills or other signs of a cantrip. A sense of menace still simmered in the back of his mind, but it seemed to emanate from the sorcerer. Satisfied that the latch didn't hold a trap, he grasped the cold iron and twisted gently. The ring turned a fraction of an inch, then stopped. He turned the ring back, making sure it didn't bang against the door. They retreated down the hallway again.

"I'll try to pick the lock," Thane whispered. "We'll need luck. He might hear me working, and he might hear the lock's bolt when it's thrown." He scowled, not sure whether the chances of success were good enough to warrant the risk.

"Let me take a look before you start," Nicolai said. "I'll need to know where things are as soon as the door opens." He went to the door and peered through the keyhole, returning a few seconds later. He prodded Thane further down the corridor, then whispered in his ear.

"Maybe there's a better way. Did you notice that the window's not latched?"

"The candle flame was shivering, yes. How does that help? We're on the third floor."

Nicolai chuckled softly. "I spend the whole day on the side of this house, remember? There are framing timbers about seven feet below the bottom edge of this floor's windows. The timbers stick out a couple of inches from the stucco."

"A couple of inches? I don't know, Nicolai. A fall from here would be bad. Even for an acrobat."

"So I won't fall." Nicolai squeezed Thane's shoulder reassuringly. "Trust me, this isn't half as dangerous as some of the stunts I do. And it's safer than trying to rush a sorcerer who hears a lock opening in the middle of the night."

"All right." Thane's agreement was reluctant, but it seemed their best option. "Let's look for a way outside."

Nicolai tried the door next to the sorcerer's study, but it was locked. Thane tried the next door. The iron ring turned without resistance and the latch opened quietly. He swung the door open.

His nose told him what they had found before his eyes could make out the details. The air was ripe with the smell of stale urine, and the shadows held a pair of blocky wooden chairs with chamber pots beneath the seats. Thane ignored the odors. The room had a window.

They unlatched the window and swung it open. As Nicolai had said, a framing timber ran parallel to the ground about seven feet beneath the window. It looked impossibly small, nearly invisible in the faint moonlight, but Nicolai climbed out the window without hesitation. He lowered himself over the edge, then felt with his toes for the shallow ledge. Thane kept a grip on his wrists while he found his footing.

"I'll watch the sorcerer while you're coming through the window," Thane whispered. "If it looks like he hears you, I'll try to distract him. Maybe you can surprise him while he's checking the door."

Nicolai nodded without looking up. "Don't do it unless you're sure he hears me, though. He might launch a magical attack and investigate later."

"Agreed. Good luck."

The northerner nodded again, then began inching along the beam a few inches at a time, the front of his body pressed against the wall. Watching made Thane queasy. The slightest misstep or imbalance would send Nicolai plunging thirty feet into the courtyard.

A glimmer of light caught his eye just as he was about to leave. He glanced up and saw the yellow glow of a torch approaching from a side street.

"Nicolai! There's a patrol coming!"

The northerner immediately stopped moving, his arms splayed across white stucco. The tramp of booted feet echoed in the quiet night. In seconds a patrol rounded the corner and entered the cobblestone street fronting the house.

Sweat beaded Thane's forehead as the patrol approached. In a few seconds they reached the front of the commander's house. But the hour was late, and they were looking for trouble on the street. No alarm sounded. Thirty seconds later they turned another corner and the light of their torch disappeared. "Lady Luck smiled on us," Thane whispered. "Let's hope it holds." Nicolai edged forward again, unable to even turn his head.

Thane watched a little longer, a painful realization in his gut. The thread of his friend's life could be cut at any second. Then he took a deep breath and stepped back from the window. *There's work to be done. Nicolai knows what he's doing.*

He returned to the corridor and knelt at the door to the sorcerer's study. Ages seemed to crawl by without the scene through the keyhole changing. Finally he saw one hand, then another, grip the bottom of the window frame behind the sorcerer. Nicolai found the shutters by feel and swung them open. The candle flame wavered as a gust of wind entered the room. Thane's heart pounded, but the sorcerer didn't react. Within moments Nicolai pulled himself into the window. The sorcerer remained slumped in his chair with his eyes closed.

As Nicolai swung his feet to the floor a cat sprang from the shadows. It hissed and then uttered a low yowl, its back arched and fur bristling. The sorcerer's eyes snapped open.

Nicolai sprang forward as the sorcerer lunged from his chair. He clamped one hand over the man's mouth, then slipped behind the sorcerer and wrapped an arm around his neck. He lifted, bringing the man's feet off the ground.

The sorcerer struggled, thick arms flailing and slippered feet kicking in the air. Nicolai held him fast and tightened the arm around his neck. His struggling soon ceased and the body went slack. Nicolai eased him to the floor. The man was still breathing, though his face was mottled and puffy. The cat hissed from a dark corner while Nicolai removed the key from the sorcerer's belt and unlocked the door.

Thane entered warily. When he got within arm's reach of the desk he felt the air begin to tingle. He extended a hand, then snatched it back. "A cantrip, strong. Made with blood magic. There's no way around it without using the art."

Nicolai prodded the unconscious sorcerer with the toe of his boot. "Who's going to notice? I doubt the zamindar sent *two* sorcerers to Pella. You didn't feel more than one presence in the kei, did you?"

"No, just the one," Thane said thoughtfully. "I suppose we might as well chance it."

"Then let's get started. Delay worsens our odds." Nicolai pulled off his shirt and sat on the floor near the desk.

Thane removed his shirt and knelt in front of his friend. They kissed briefly, a ritual reminder of their bond, then Nicolai spread his legs. Thane sat cross-legged with his back pressed against the northerner's chest. Nicolai embraced him, one arm circling his chest and the other hand cupping his crotch.

Thane leaned against his friend's powerful body. The northerner's familiar embrace helped him relax and clear his mind. Nicolai began to stroke his midriff and massage his crotch. He nuzzled Thane's neck, pressing against him like a cat rubbing its head against a mate. "Don't worry," he said. "I'll keep guard here."

Thane nodded, his cock already thickening in response to Nicolai's stimulation. Their lovemaking earlier in the evening had renewed and strengthened their link. Thane felt his friend's calm presence in the strange dimension where their essences had bonded. An aura seeped from their skin and tinged the room with the color of embers in a dying fire. His skin began to tingle.

Nicolai caressed the mage's smooth chest with feathery strokes, while his other hand slid beneath the soft leather of Thane's pants. He pressed his palm against Thane's stiff cock and rubbed gently.

Golden sparks filled Thane's vision. His surroundings faded to nothing more than a remote awareness of his friend's expert manipulations. The sparks shimmered and then exploded in rainbow hues. A swirling curtain of color engulfed him.

As the dazzling light faded, the cantrip manifested itself as a web of colored threads forming a sphere around a silver box. The threads quivered, as if straining to contain expanding energy. At the top of the web sat a huge black spider. Multifaceted eyes like red jewels stared at him with cold hunger. The spider's rear legs were bent, ready to propel it into a leap.

Thane studied the vision with iron calm, keeping the warm glow of his anima concealed behind a mental shield. As he had feared, it wasn't a passive spell to unknot. Death and blood were bound up in it, yearning for a life to destroy. The cantrip looked impenetrable. The spider was poised to attack anything with a spark of life that touched the threads.

There's nothing I can do. Unless . . . could I make it spit its venom elsewhere? Cautiously, knowing that attracting the spider's attention would be fatal, Thane reached out with his mind. His surroundings slowly manifested in degrees of light and darkness. The brightest light, shining like a lighthouse beacon, was Nicolai. As long as the northerner didn't touch the cantrip, he would be safe.

Opening his mind further, he sensed a quickly pulsating green light. *The cat. Perhaps . . . no. This cantrip is too well made. It will know the cat's too small.*

He turned his attention to the last source of anima, a sickly ocher glow that pulsed slowly. *The sorcerer. Unconscious, but the right size.* It was a dangerous gamble, but Thane saw no alternative. He released a small portion of his own anima in a tightly spun thread. Attaching one end of the thread to the sorcerer was an easy task. A wave of nausea swept him as he felt the sorcerer's malignant soul; scores of innocents had died at the man's hands, and he had taken pleasure in every moment of their pain. Any lingering hesitation over what he was attempting vanished instantly.

The spider shifted on its web, waving two front legs overhead as if feeling vibrations in the air. Thane held his mind motionless, calming the disgust that contact with the sorcerer had generated. A minute passed before the spider lowered its legs.

Moving with infinite deliberation, Thane spun out the thread of anima, arcing it overhead until one end was connected with the sorcerer and the other end dangled above the web. The spider's jeweled eyes seemed to fix on him. He dropped the thread.

An explosion of sound and movement tore him out of the kei. He gasped, his mind reeling. He felt himself being dragged to his feet, Nicolai's powerful arms wrapped around his chest.

"Are you all right?" Nicolai asked urgently.

Thane's vision cleared in seconds. Nicolai had dragged him halfway across the room, away from the desk. The sorcerer's body lay on the floor in front of them. Its eyes were open, and foul-smelling smoke wafted from its mouth and nostrils. Brown charred patches discolored the dead man's clothing.

Thane wiggled out of Nicolai's clasp and knelt by the sorcerer's body. The odor of burned meat mingled with decay and sulfur. Without warning, the sorcerer's head wrenched to the side and his face twisted into a demonic mask.

Thane rocked back on his heels. "By the gods! Look at this, Nicolai. Was this creature still a man? Either he'd been twisted by his magic, or could some dark power in the kei have possessed him?" He gingerly poked the creature's mottled red face. It felt like rough leather.

"A good question," Nicolai replied. "But we don't have time for it now. We'd best finish our business here quickly."

Thane went back to the desk. No warning tingle greeted him. He pulled open the top drawer. Empty, except for a curled piece of parchment. He held it close to the candle. Nicolai looked over his shoulder, his breath warm against the mage's neck.

"Can you read it?" Nicolai asked. "It looks like tracks of a fox chasing a rabbit across the snow. Is it a code?"

"No, not a code. It's written in Old Meyherian. I studied it once, when . . . back when I lived in Lord Tolmin's house."

Nicolai pressed against him gently, knowing the pain Thane felt when reminded of the past. When only sixteen, Thane had worked for a squire who recognized his ability and tried to shape him into a tool. It hadn't taken him long to discern the squire's plans. He rebelled, and was severely beaten. He fled to Chanture and found work in Lord Tolmin's house.

The sanctuary Thane found in Lord Tolmin's house had led to boundless joy in the arms of Lucian, another of Lord Tolmin's young servants. Together they explored the mysteries of love and passion, and began to perceive realms that could be reached by channeling acute pleasure in unexpected directions. The seeds of the art sprang from their discoveries. But their two years of happiness ended in a bitter defeat. Lucian had died when he and Thane rescued Lord Tolmin's daughter from prison, where she had been taken on suspicion of treason.

Thane was too engrossed in the parchment to dwell on memories. He brought the document closer to the candle and tilted it to make the characters more distinct against the parchment's stained background.

"It's been a long time . . ." He pushed fingers through his hair, his brow creasing. "I'm not sure of some of the words. But I understand the basic meaning. These are orders."

"Orders to whom?"

Thane turned the document over and inspected the broken wax seal on its back. "See this emblem, a skull with crossed swords behind it? It's the mark of the imperial sorcerers. These must be orders to this man we just killed. His name was Zaggrat, according to this."

"Maybe that's what he was guarding! What does it say?"

Thane put the paper on the desk and leaned over it, his brow furrowed. "This is obscure. It seems to refer to something called the Kynda Fortia." He chewed his lower lip. "Fortia is an old word for force, but I don't know the other term. Could it be some new sorcery?"

"Maybe not new," Nicolai said. "Up north, the word kynda means to kindle something. Like a fire. Or new life."

"The device we destroyed in the basilica at Fochelis," Thane said. "The Leech. It might be used for that purpose."

Nicolai nodded. "You thought the zamindar planned to use it to extend his life. To kindle his life force, you might say."

"It's as we feared," Thane said. "The Leech's purpose was to preserve his life, stealing anima from others. He intends to build a new one." He rubbed his eyes and sighed. "How can this help us stop him, though? We need *more*, a way to attack."

"Maybe we should leave now, figure it out later."

"Just a little longer. Let me see what the rest of this says." Thane's finger traced the marks across the page, from right to left. His eyes widened as he read.

"This is what we're looking for! The orders tell Zaggrat to collect seventeen crystals. He's to drive the garrison commander relentlessly. The soldiers and peasants can't be allowed to rest. The zamindar wants no delay."

Nicolai looked worried. "If those crystals are the same kind we found in Fochelis, they're dangerous."

"Unless they're shielded by silver." Thane's eyes burned with excitement. "We've got to look, Nicolai. If the sorcerer was collecting crystals, he might have hidden them here. *That's* what he was guarding!" His gaze swept around the dark room.

"I'll search that chest," Nicolai replied. "You look through the desk."

The chest proved to be filled with the sorcerer's clothes, mostly robes made from silk and velvet. Several bore crusty bloodstains. The zamindar's sorcerers, though ignorant of the art discovered by Thane, were expert at using pain and terror to work spells.

Thane pulled all the drawers out of the desk, dumping their contents on the floor. He was still rummaging through the pile as Nicolai crouched by his side. "Nothing," he muttered as he poked through moldy apple cores and other rubbish with a broken stylus.

Nicolai turned a drawer over. "Nothing hidden underneath. Sorel says you should always check the bottoms of drawers when you search a desk."

"Sorel should know," Thane agreed. Nicolai's lover, while thoroughly honorable, had learned the ways of the world under the tutelage of his merchant father. It was fortunate he had found commerce so unsavory, since it had led him to defy his father and venture off with Nicolai.

Nicolai started to turn the drawer right side up. Thane suddenly put a hand on his wrist. "Wait. What's that mark on the back edge?" He took the drawer and examined it closely. Shallow indentations at the bottom edge of each side panel showed where the drawer had repeatedly slammed against something.

Thane put the drawer down and picked up the candle, then crouched in front of the desk. He peered into the space the drawer had occupied. "Look," he said excitedly. "Stops in the drawer tracks, and wood panels just past them. It looks like there's space between the stops and the front of the desk. There could be a secret compartment!" He put the candle back on the desktop, then reached into the cavity and tapped on the panel beyond the stops. Hollow thumps echoed from the desk's recesses.

Thane explored by touch. Soon his fingers brushed over a tiny lever concealed behind a wedge of wood at the joint between the desk's top and the panel. "Found it! This must release a catch—"

The panel sprang open and a burst of violet light bathed Thane's face. He fell back, his arm numb. A cloud of oily smoke boiled out of the cavity and engulfed his head. His scream came out a muted gurgle as angry motes of red light swarmed out of the smoke and converged on his eyes. He fell onto his back, thrashing and choking.

Nicolai fell on top of him, grabbing his flailing limbs. "Thane! The cantrip didn't attack me. Use my strength!"

Thane's body convulsed, and his face twisted in agony.

"*Feel our bond*," Nicolai insisted. "I'm with you!"

Though nearly blind, Thane caught a glimpse of his friend's urgent expression. Searing pain in his lungs made it nearly impossible to think. As his vision faded he sensed a cool white spark among the flaming torrent of red. *Nicolai?*

Desperately, he stretched his mind toward the white spark. It grew into a slowly pulsing globe as he neared, its light conveying the northerner's familiar feel. With the last of his strength he touched the white star's fringe.

Nicolai seized the contact. Thane felt as if he had been jerked at the end of a noose. He teetered on a magical precipice, a heartbeat away from succumbing to the attack. Then strength poured through the bond. With relentless determination, Nicolai threw all his anima into the battle with the forces released by the cantrip.

Thane's faltering consciousness dimly perceived his friend's effort. Nicolai's steadfastness focused his mind on something more important than his pain. *He won't relent. If I die, he'll die with me.* He forced himself to draw on the strength Nicolai offered. The red motes were like fire ants, each one a point of intense agony. But their strength lay in numbers, not individual power. One by one he began to snuff them out. The sparks attacked in a frenzy, but he concentrated on Nicolai's anima and used it as if washing tormenting insects off his body under a waterfall. Their bond burned with the flow of power. Finally he extinguished the last mote and opened his eyes.

Nicolai bent over him anxiously. "They're gone, I felt you destroy them. Are you all right?"

Thane took a deep breath, then nodded slowly. "Thanks to you.

I wouldn't have survived without you."

The northerner kissed Thane gently on the cheek. "None of us could survive without each other. Especially without you. I can feel it in our bond, as sure as my heartbeat."

Thane took a few breaths, then his eyes went wide and he pushed himself upright. "Something's wrong. I can't feel our bond."

"What? It's there. Strong as ever."

"I can't feel it!" Thane's surprise turned to horror. "What . . . what if I can't bond any more?"

"You just need rest. We've strained our bond too hard."

"I hope you're right," Thane said cautiously. He savagely suppressed his clamoring fears. Not being able to use the art, or to feel the touch of Ander's spirit, would be a kind of death. But he couldn't afford to think about it now. He pushed himself off the floor and retrieved the candle.

"We might as well see what they were hiding. We've paid the price." He crouched beside the desk and held the candle so its light penetrated to the back of the drawer cavity. The secret compartment lay open. A metal box the size of a deck of cards gleamed silver in the flickering light.

Thane handed the candle to Nicolai, then held his breath and reached inside the opening. His senses strained for any tremors that might signal another trap. Cool metal met his fingertips. No more traps lashed out at him. Letting his breath out with a relieved sigh, he removed the box from its hiding place and carefully placed it on the desktop.

"It's heavy," he observed. "Much heavier than you'd guess from the size. It must be nearly solid silver." Arcane magical symbols were etched in a band around its sides. The lid was hinged on one edge, and the opposite side secured with a catch. Someone had taken pains to assure the box couldn't open accidentally.

"I wonder how many crystals it holds?" Nicolai said.

Thane tapped the cool metal, his expression thoughtful. "I think we'd better not open it. If there *is* another sorcerer in Pella, we don't want to attract his attention." He looked rueful. "I've been caught once tonight. That's enough."

"You don't have to convince me," Nicolai assured him. He cuffed Thane's shoulder. "Maybe you're as smart as Sorel thinks, after all. I was beginning to wonder."

"Sorel was just being charitable. Let's leave now, before anything else goes wrong."

"What about Zaggrat?" Nicolai asked, prodding the sorcerer

with his toe. The leathery body was already stiffening.

"Trying to hide it would be more dangerous than leaving it here. If we leave the door locked and the key on his belt, the commander might think he died from natural causes."

"Or from a spell gone bad," Nicolai added. "I doubt they'd admit it, but they'll probably be glad to see him dead. Nobody likes the zamindar's sorcerers. Not even the zamindar's troops."

Thane nodded. "Their doubts should buy us some time, at least. We'll figure out a way to get the crystals out of the house tomorrow." He slipped the box into a shirt pocket.

Working quickly, they closed the secret compartment, picked up the debris Thane had dumped on the floor and replaced the drawers. They left the burning candle on the desk as they had found it. After Thane left the room Nicolai locked the door and hung the key on the dead sorcerer's belt, then climbed out the window. A few minutes later he climbed back in through the bathroom window.

They retreated to the attic, locking the door as the first hints of dawn glimmered in the spaces between slatted window vents. Exhaustion claimed them. They barely managed to get their boots off before collapsing on the mattress. Thane fell asleep quickly, but found no relief. Visions of losing the art, of losing Ander, haunted his dreams.

The attic door crashed open. Thane and Nicolai jerked upright, instinctively reaching for weapons that had been left at Lady Tay's house when they embarked on the mission. But Ivan was alone, and made no threatening moves. He merely stood at the door and shook his head with disgust. "Still asleep, an hour after dawn! Worthless whores, both of you!"

They scrambled to their feet, blinking and disoriented.

Ivan grabbed Nicolai's shoulder and shook it as if he'd rather be strangling him. "No breakfast for you sluggards. I've no time to waste on you today. Get to work!"

Nicolai pried Ivan's hand off his shoulder. "Another night without love, Ivan? Don't blame *us* for your sour mood, or for getting a late start. We'd be ready at dawn like everybody else if you didn't lock us up like your personal harem."

Ivan ground his teeth, and for a moment looked as if he would strike Nicolai. But the thought of brawling with a companion apparently repulsed him. He stepped back and glared. "You're not worth it, boy. Get to work. I don't want to see your faces until lunch." He turned and marched down the stairs.

Thane made sure the silver box in his pocket was concealed, then followed.

Thane mortared stone after stone, slowly building up the wall around the potting shed. His stomach growled, but he barely noticed. Noises from inside the house were too alarming. Ivan was shouting at the kitchen staff, and the maiden who had pursued him the day before was nowhere to be seen. Even worse, the guard around the house had been doubled.

Does Commander Stecher know about the crystals? Are they investigating a death, or a theft? In the bright light of day, it seemed likely the commander knew Zaggrat's orders and had been assisting the sorcerer. And Ivan's insistence on getting them out of the house suggested something was going on they didn't want strangers to know about.

They're searching the house, I'd wager my horse on it. What'll they do when they don't find the crystals? None of the possibilities that came to mind were reassuring.

Anxiety and hunger mingled in a sickening stew. Adding to the bitter flavor was an incessant fear that the cantrip had injured him permanently. Try as he might, he couldn't feel any hint of his bond with Nicolai. He glanced over his shoulder, saw his friend on a ladder whitewashing the house, but it was as if he watched a stranger. The missing tug of affection through their link left an aching void. He turned back to his work, heartsick.

A flurry of shouted curses from the kitchen made him jump. Crockery crashed to the floor and shattered. It sounded like they were tearing the place apart.

He troweled another layer of mortar onto the wall, then picked up a piece of fieldstone and dropped it into position without looking. The stone fell into the cavity between the two courses of rock that formed the wall. Thane peered into the dark cavity, already three feet deep. *Not worth pulling it out. I don't care if I waste the commander's damned rocks.*

"Where were you last night?" Ivan barked.

Thane whirled around, his heart pounding, but nobody was in sight. A mumbled reply, followed by a wail, drifted out a kitchen window.

They're interrogating the servants. They must know the crystals are missing. Despite the protection Ivan had inadvertently given them by locking them in the attic, the steward's frenzy worried him. He picked up another rock, his head pounding. *What if they search us?* The longer he thought about it, the more likely

76

the possibility seemed. Confidence won by success the night before faded.

Thinking of the fate that would await them in the zamindar's hands, of the secrets they might be forced to reveal, led to an unavoidable conclusion. The crystals' value lay mostly in depriving the zamindar of their power. Keeping possession of the crystals, at the risk of their lives and the lives of their friends at the Lyceum, wasn't a wise decision.

Before he could talk himself out of it, Thane turned his back on the house and slipped the silver box out of his pocket. The sun reflected on its burnished cover, seeming to suggest the power within. Much as he wanted to turn the crystals against their former owner, the safety of his comrades was more important. He put the box deep inside the wall's cavity.

Working quickly now, he placed several small stones on top of the box and returned to his masonry. Spurred by the sounds of turmoil within the house, he added another foot to the wall by the time the sun reached its apex.

Nicolai came up behind him as he knelt beside his bucket mixing another batch of mortar. The northerner surveyed the wall in amazement. "I scarcely believe it. I thought you'd be hungry enough to *eat* the rocks. Instead you're having as much fun as a Priest of Yataghan skinning a heretic. Maybe you should skip breakfast more often."

Thane looked up. His troubled eyes clearly revealed that enthusiasm for masonry had nothing to do with his efforts. "I've hidden the box in the wall," he whispered. "We need to get out of here, Nicolai. I'm not feeling well."

Nicolai crouched by his side. "What's wrong? Are the crystals affecting you?"

Thane shook his head dismally. "I don't think so. I . . . I think the cantrip did more than damage our bond."

Nicolai shook his head in bewilderment. "I keep telling you, the link's still there. I've felt it all morning."

"Well, whatever it is, I've got a problem. We need to get out of here so I can try to fix it."

"Won't it look suspicious if we leave now?"

Thane tapped the edge of his bucket with his trowel. A minute passed before he blinked and looked back at Nicolai.

"Maybe there's a way. If Ivan responds the way I think he will. Just follow my lead."

Nicolai smiled knowingly. "You can't be *too* sick. You're still sly as a snow leopard."

"Huh. Save your compliments until you see if you get out of here with your skin intact."

Leaving his trowel in the bucket, Thane stood up and led the way across the yard. The commotion in the kitchen had died down, but as they neared the door they could hear the rhythmic creak of floorboards as a heavy man strode back and forth.

They entered the kitchen and encountered a household in shambles. Three women huddled in a corner, one of them crying. Every cabinet door was open, and everything the cabinets had contained was strewn across the floor. Ivan strode on a narrow path, broken pottery crunching beneath his boots.

Thane ignored the mess and stood by the door with his arms crossed. "Where's lunch?" he demanded. "You said we'd eat at noon, and I'm hungry."

Ivan whirled and glared at him. "Get out of here. I haven't got time for the likes of you."

"I'm hungry!" Thane insisted. "You can't treat us like this. We're doing honest labor, we're not slaves. And when do we get paid?"

Ivan clenched his fists and drew himself up to full height. Even twenty years past his prime, he was an imposing hulk. A low growl rumbled from his throat, but Thane didn't move. Instead, the mage took another step into the kitchen and gestured at the disarray with a sweep of his hand.

"This is no way to run a household, Ivan. How's the staff supposed to get lunch ready in a mess like this?"

"You'll get fed when I'm ready to feed you!"

The women in the corner looked up timidly, but the oldest one's lips quirked in a smile as Ivan lost his temper.

"I don't think the commander would like it, if he knew how you're treating us," Thane replied. "Locking us up at night, trying to starve us. I plan to mention this to our usual employer. *She* won't be amused, either."

Ivan's face went from flushed to beet red. His body quivered, but he restrained himself with a visible effort and stalked over to Thane. "Outside. Now. Both of you."

Thane gave him a nonchalant glance, then sniffed. "Come on, Nicolai. They obviously don't have lunch ready yet. We might as well wait outside."

They left the kitchen, Ivan close behind. Once they were in the yard Ivan grabbed Thane by the front of his leather shirt. "You preening whore! I've half a mind to drop you down the well."

Thane pried Ivan's fingers loose. "I don't give a damn about your problems managing the kitchen maids," Thane said. "But I've taken all the abuse I'm going to take. I'm going to speak to the commander."

"You can't see him," Ivan growled. "He's very busy today."

"I'll speak to his wife, then," Thane replied smoothly.

Ivan blanched and his mouth moved silently. There was murder in his eyes. But apparently he had enough troubles without the questions a brawl would raise. He took a deep breath. "You're dismissed from service in this house. Both of you, for insubordination."

"That's fine with me," Nicolai declared. "I'm sick of whitewash. Pay us and we'll leave gladly."

"All you deserve is a whipping! You'll leave now, or I'll give it to you myself."

Nicolai was warming to the argument and looked ready to continue it, but Thane put a hand on his arm. "Never mind, Nicolai. I'm too hungry to waste time arguing." He gave Ivan an impudent stare. "I'm sure Lady Tay will speak with the commander and make it right for us."

Ivan's breath rasped, but he reached into a pocket and removed a large iron key. He stalked across the yard and unlocked the gate in the compound's outer wall. Thane and Nicolai followed, not even looking at Ivan as they marched through the stone arch and into the street. The gate crashed shut behind them.

They walked around the corner, then slumped together against a tavern wall. Thane wiped sweat from his brow.

"You did it!" Nicolai said, jubilant. "He was so eager to get rid of us he didn't even stop to question us about last night."

"He locked us up himself. I was gambling he hadn't thought about us picking the lock. Keeping him angry muddled his thinking."

"Well, it worked. We learned what the zamindar is doing, and set back his schedule. A successful mission, I'd say."

Thane pushed himself away from the wall, his head shaking. "You're forgetting my problem with bonding. If I don't get it back, I might as well be dead. What am I going to tell Ander?" Nothing could dispel that dread that shrouded his heart.

7

ANDER HAD JUST swallowed a bite of meat pie when a throb of pleasure rippled through his body. *He's back!*

He pushed his chair away from the kitchen's trestle table and raced into the main room, leaving Lady Tay's companions looking at each other in bewilderment. The cavernous room's front door swung open as he approached. Thane stepped through, followed by Nicolai.

Grinning from ear to ear, Ander tackled Thane and wrapped him in a fierce hug. Nicolai steadied them as the mage stumbled backward under the onslaught.

Thane's surprise was quickly replaced by a fervent response to his lover's greeting. He seized Ander and brought their lips together. Oblivious to their amused observers, they basked in their breathless reunion.

A soft chuckle interrupted their rapture. Ander opened his eyes and saw Lady Tayanita, her green traveling cape draped over her arm. "If I could get you to greet all our guests like that, I'd be a rich woman."

Ander blushed, but couldn't restrain his joy at Thane's safe return. "You're rich enough already, Lady. Besides, you've never had guests as fair as Thane."

"Except perhaps for Nicolai and Sorel," she replied diplomatically. "But come to think of it, you gave *them* a warm greeting, too."

Ander's blush deepened to scarlet, but Thane only laughed. "Better not joust with her, Ander. You've met your match." He turned to Lady Tayanita. "Want to hear what happened?"

"Certainly," she replied. "But not now. One of my best customers is expecting me."

"I'll talk with you tonight," Thane promised.

"More likely tomorrow. Theo believes in a leisurely pace. We usually spend more time playing cards than in bed."

"I hope you win," Thane said. "We'll be sure to stay until tomorrow. There are matters we need to discuss."

Lady Tayanita threw the cloak around her shoulders, then shook her head and sighed. "So serious. But then I guess you need to be." She touched Thane's shoulder. "Good luck yourself." She turned and swept out the door.

"Let's use her parlor," Ander said, gesturing toward the nearby door. "We need to talk *now*."

The three of them went into the dimly lit room. Ander shut the door and turned to Thane. "What's wrong? I feel your fear."

Thane's face went white. He glanced at Nicolai, then down to his feet. "Um, I . . . it might be too early to say. It might be nothing."

The anxiety surging through their bond belied Thane's attempt at reassurance. Fear squeezed Ander's heart. "Nothing? Then why are you so worried?"

Thane didn't answer, and Nicolai shuffled nervously. Ander looked at him, pleading with his eyes. Nicolai shrugged and looked away, a pained expression on his face.

Thane tousled Ander's hair before he could ask more questions. "I'll tell you later. After I understand better myself. What happened here? Did you have a chance to talk with Leif about our cause?"

Ander took a deep breath and let it drop. *If he wants time, he has it.* "I did. He hates the zamindar, for good reason. And his skill as a lover is famous. I think he could master the art without trouble."

"He isn't reluctant to bed customers, the way you were?"

"He's selective, but enthusiastic. Once he took on half a dozen Travinian horse traders who were in Pella for a festival. Travinians howl like wolves when they cum, and Leif had them howling all night! The next day they offered Lady Tay a king's ransom if she'd send Leif with them for a year."

Nicolai's eyes went wide. "I've seen Travinians. They're tough men, with the endurance of their own war stallions."

"I think Leif considered it a challenge," Ander agreed. "Besides, they were a handsome group. Wild boys, long hair cut like a horse's mane, on their first trip to the city."

"I should see him today," Thane said. "We'll be leaving tomorrow and might not have another chance."

"I'll take you to his room," Ander offered. "He might be up already, if yesterday's customer didn't keep him occupied all night."

Thane accepted the invitation, while Nicolai left to begin preparations for the trip back to the Lyceum. They stopped by Ander's room to retrieve the mage's cape and the small case of elixirs concealed in its pocket, then went to Leif's room.

Ander paused outside the door. "I'll wait in my room, if you'd like," he said. "I told him you might be coming to see him."

"I could use your help. He'll be more relaxed if you're with me."

The tension in Ander's shoulders eased. *Whatever his problem is, it's not with me.* He gave Thane a sultry smile. "If Leif's test is anything like mine was, I envy him."

"Each test is different. It depends on the person being tested." He grinned eagerly. "Let's begin. Leif was your favorite lover, so I like him already."

Ander opened the door, letting out a whiff of cinnamon incense. Amber linens covered the walls and hung from the ceiling, making the room look like a wealthy traveler's tent. The window was open a crack and a gentle breeze made the linens ripple. Keeping with the tent motif, Leif slept on a pile of cushions and furs. A candle guttered inside a stone lantern, its terraced curves evoking the same hints of the east as Leif's almond eyes. A white cat with black nose and paws napped in the corner on a pile of silks. Grapes and pears, arranged on a black lacquer tray, added a faint earthy fragrance to the air.

Leif was sprawled on a lambskin, still asleep. The tawny fleece was a close match for his skin. He lay on his stomach, arms crossed beneath his head, the heavy gold braid of his ponytail snaking between the blades of his wide shoulders. A translucent sheet of pale gold silk lay across his lower body, accenting rather than concealing his narrow hips and firm buttocks. His face was turned to the door.

"But for the eyes, he might be Nicolai's brother," Thane whispered.

"He has Nicolai's kindness," Ander agreed. "Though not his calm. Leif's an excitable creature."

Thane grinned. "Then let's get him excited. He already has me hard, just from looking! Go ahead and wake him."

Ander took a step forward, and Leif's eyes opened a fraction of an inch. "No need," the blond said, not moving a muscle. "I heard when you entered."

Ander grinned and put an arm around Thane's waist. "I should have mentioned, Leif can sneak up on a nervous cat. He's the terror of gossiping girls, always overhearing them."

Leif stretched his arms above his head, smooth curves of muscle flexing beneath satiny skin. Then he rolled onto his back and sat up, ignoring the way his morning erection tented the thin sheet. He bowed his head in Thane's direction. "I'm honored by your visit. I've been wanting to meet you, and thank you."

"Thank me?" Thane lifted an eyebrow. "Why?"

"For making Ander whole. He's my best friend, and I sense how he's changed. You've given him something, some gift beyond my power to grant."

Thane's eyes widened. "Can you feel what the change is?"

Leif's expression was a mixture of perplexity and curiosity.

"Love, certainly. But *anybody* could sense that; Ander's been longing for you since you left. There's more, though. He's no longer a boy." Leif's eyes crinkled merrily. "And he's become a better lover than ever. But I'm being a poor host. Sit, have some food. I was hoping you'd tell me what's going on."

They joined Leif on the cushions. Thane placed his cape nearby, then accepted a pewter cup. Leif filled it with water from a clay pitcher, then poured for himself and Ander before lifting his cup. "To friends well met."

Ander sipped the water. A trace of lemon tickled his tongue. He glanced at Thane, who was drinking while maintaining eye contact with their host. *Thane's the mage, but Leif has magic of his own.* After the ritual greeting, he remembered Thane's request for help in putting Leif at ease. While the young blond looked relaxed, Ander knew his formality signified uncertainty. There was one sure way to draw him out.

"You're right about Thane," Ander said. "He changed me. But remember what I told you, about how there are secrets of love you've never suspected? Thane knows them all."

The gleam in Leif's eyes showed Ander that he'd chosen the right course. The blond fixed his gaze on Thane and nodded solemnly. "When Ander hinted at your knowledge, it reminded me of something. My grandmother was born far to the east. She told me ancient legends, stories of powers long forgotten. Mysteries of flesh and spirit."

Thane leaned forward eagerly. "You must tell me, everything you remember! Any detail might have significance."

Leif bowed his head solemnly. "It seems I was right," he said. "I felt new depths when Ander and I made love. A mystery just beyond my reach. I knew, then, he had found *more* than a lover." He extended both hands, palm up. "I'm unworthy, but I offer myself as an apprentice if you'll have me. I know you're honorable. Ander would never love you if you weren't."

After a few seconds Thane seemed to reach a decision. He clasped Leif's hands. "I can't confirm your guesses. But Ander vouches for you, so I trust you. We'll show you some of what we've learned, if you choose to share yourself with us. After that, who knows?"

"No one knows the future," Leif agreed. He released Thane's hands and grinned. "And even if I'm wrong, bedding you together is a chance I'd never miss. Did you know that Ander and I never slept with a third?"

"Keeping up with *you* is challenge enough," Ander said. "But now you'll have Thane to contend with. I'm not worried."

"I'm not worried either," Leif replied. "I'm looking forward to it. See?" A quick tug sent his sheet slipping to the floor. His erection thrust up from his crotch. Its smooth shaft curved slightly, making the glans press against his flat stomach right at his navel. He pressed it forward with a thumb against its base, then let it snap back against his abdomen as he arched his back. His cock stretched across taut muscle, an ivory column topped with a purplish cockhead shaped like a heart. His balls nestled snugly against its base, firm and rounded, with only a trace of blond hair dusting the soft skin. He threw his head back, his ponytail falling free between wide shoulders.

Ander knew the invitation well. Rather than accepting it himself, he took Thane's hand and guided it to Leif's erection. Thane's fingers curled around the smooth shaft. Lightly, his fingers barely touching the sensitive skin, he traced the penis from base to tip.

Ander shed his clothes while Thane explored Leif's body. When he was naked he knelt beside them. He reached down and cupped Leif's balls, then leaned close. They kissed gently. Both were achingly aroused.

Thane rolled to his feet and stripped. His flawless body, muscular and perfectly proportioned, radiated vitality. Ander broke the kiss and turned to him. "What do you want me to do?"

"Just help me pleasure him," Thane said, kneeling beside Leif. He touched the blond's cheek. "You've guessed something of our art. But don't be concerned with mysteries, for now. Let us give you pleasure. Try to make it last."

"What about you?" Leif asked. He glanced down, smiling when he saw the long span of Thane's erection. He brushed the shaft's underside with a light stroke. "What do you crave?"

"I desire only your friendship. If anything else happens between us, it can grow from that. Just tell me what you feel, and what you want."

Leif smiled warmly. "Ander chose well. You care more for your lover's pleasure than your own."

"He's generous," Ander agreed. "Kiss me, Leif, and let him show you." He put a hand against the boy's chest and pushed him back among the cushions. The young companion stretched out, extending his legs and spreading them apart, as they renewed their kiss. Ander pressed him down, hands on his shoulders, pinning him to the cushions.

Their kiss grew more urgent as Thane moved between the blond's legs. Leif began to moan and writhe, but Ander didn't break the kiss. In his mind's eye he pictured Thane fondling Leif's cock, brushing it with whispery kisses. The handsome mage made love with single-minded intensity. Leif's body quivered, and his moan took on a desperate tone. Ander withdrew his tongue from Leif's mouth and raised his head, but kept the boy pressed down.

The blond's eyes were wild with excitement. "What's he doing? It feels like my cock's a foot long, and every inch tingles!"

Ander looked down the length of Leif's hard body. Thane crouched between the blond's legs and held his cock across the palm of one hand. A strand of spit ran from his lips to the cockhead, which was wet and shining. With his other hand he traced the length of the wide tube running along the shaft's underside. Sparkling white light scintillated around his fingertips, a minute flow of anima. Ander knew from experience how extraordinary it felt. Thane's movements were slow and controlled, and he studied the throbbing penis stretched across his hand with total concentration. The art required intimate knowledge of the body; the mage knew strokes and patterns of pressure to elicit sensation from every part. The pleasure's intensity could be breathtaking.

Ander turned back to Leif. "He's just making sure you're paying attention. But say something if you think you're about to cum. As he said, see how long you can make it last."

"Then let me taste you. I want to give, as well as receive."

Ander smiled, then lowered his head enough to rub his nose against Leif's. "Anything you want. Just ask." He swung himself around to straddle Leif's head, then extended his arms and straightened his legs. His body stretched over Leif's, lean and rigid. He lowered his hips and let his cockhead graze the boy's lips. Leif's tongue lapped the sensitive juncture between the cockhead and the shaft. Ander froze, his cock quivering, as a strand of precum oozed onto Leif's tongue. When his racing heart slowed, he lowered himself further. Leif's lips parted to admit his cock. Moving in a slow glide, his shaft sank into the wet heat of his friend's mouth.

Thane looked up and grinned. "He's doing well, Ander. Let's increase the challenge. Why don't you suck him while I make preparations?"

Ander nodded, too breathless to speak. Leif's hands went to his hips and guided his slow thrusts. His cock sank to the hilt, massaged along its length by expert throat muscles.

Ander lowered his head as Thane pulled Leif's cock upright. It was wet and shining, precum oozing from its tip. He parted his lips and let the shaft enter him. Musky flavor bathed his tongue, Leif's familiar taste mixed with Thane's spit. He eagerly sucked the upward curving cock, lashing it with his tongue and coaxing more fluid from it.

Thane touched the front of Ander's neck and felt the blond's cock move in his lover's throat. The gesture turned into a caress, his fingers brushing the slick penis as it slid between Ander's lips. Then he moved back, leaving Ander and Leif slowly writhing together. He picked up his cape and took a thin leather case from one of its pockets. Finally, he selected a piece of black silk from a nearby pile.

When his preparations were complete he crouched next to the entangled youths. He put a hand on one of Ander's hard buttocks, taking a few moments to feel the muscle move and watch Ander's cock slide in and out of Leif's mouth, before interrupting the lovers. "Enough for now, Ander. We need to speak with Leif."

Slowly, savoring the clinging softness of Leif's lips, Ander withdrew his cock. Thane wrapped his fingers around the shaft as it emerged, squeezing an additional offering of precum out of the shaft. It smeared across Leif's upper lip, and the blond's tongue flicked out to capture it.

Ander let Leif's rigid cock slide free of his mouth and rolled to his side, opposite Thane with Leif between them. He noticed Thane's leather case and grinned. "You're going to love this, Leif."

The mage's eyes sparkled with boyish eagerness. "I'd like to try something. But we need to blindfold you first." He held up the black silk. "When you're blindfolded, you become more sensitive to touch."

Leif didn't hesitate. He sat up and took the cloth. "I know what you mean. I often make love with my eyes closed." He folded the silk rag into a band, then placed it across his eyes. Ander took the ends and tied them in a knot behind his head.

"Sit behind him," Thane told Ander. "It's good to be held by someone you know."

Ander insinuated himself in the cushions, spreading his legs so Leif nestled between them, and wrapping his arms around the blond's chest. His cock pressed against the small of Leif's back. He nuzzled his friend's neck while his hands explored the muscled torso. "Just lean against me," he said. "Don't be surprised by what we do. Nothing will harm you."

Leif shivered, but Ander could tell it was from excitement rather than fear. He glanced down and saw that his friend's penis stretched against his flat belly, a strand of precum drooling down the underside of the shaft.

Thane opened the leather case. Both halves held tightly corked vials filled with oily liquids, ranging in color from clear to deep blue. He pulled out a vial of clear fluid and twisted the cork off. Eucalyptus fragrance filled the air.

Leif cocked his head and sniffed curiously. Ander chuckled softly. The prospect of taking his more experienced friend by surprise was strongly appealing.

Thane poured oil onto his right palm and moved closer to Leif, crouching on one knee between the blond's outstretched legs. "I'll tell you before I do something," he said. "We don't want to startle you."

"You're a considerate lover," Leif replied. "As I expected. A perfect match for Ander." He breathed deeply and let his weight fall back, surrendering himself with complete trust.

"Don't fear," Thane said as he lowered his hands to Leif's cock. "The feeling will be strong, but only pleasure." He cupped Leif's scrotum with his left hand, and wrapped his right hand around the straining penis. Leif tensed, then quickly relaxed.

Ander smiled knowingly. This particular oil seemed cool and slick at first, not at all difficult to deal with. But then it began to tingle. The effect was subtle at first, but grew as the flesh became more sensitized. He had gotten so hard the first time Thane had used it on him, he had thought his cock would never go down again.

Slowly, Thane slid his right hand from the base of Leif's cock to the top. He rotated his hand slightly to spread oil evenly over the smooth skin. When his thumb and index finger reached the bottom of the glans he paused. The penis throbbed in his hand as if in anticipation.

Thane leaned forward until his lips were within an inch of Leif's. "You're at the threshold," he whispered. "Cross it with me, and enter into light." As his lips met Leif's in a gentle kiss, he slid his fingers over the crown of the boy's cockhead. The kiss grew more urgent as the elixir worked its magic on the sensitive glans. After a few seconds Leif gasped, and Thane broke off the kiss.

Ander watched in fascinated admiration as Thane took the measure of Leif's cock. Precum flowed in a steady stream. The mage traced through it with a fingertip, mixing sensitizing oil with the natural lubricant. Leif started squirming.

Ander felt a ticklish throb in his own cock. *Am I sharing Leif's pleasure? But how? We don't have a bond.* He glanced at Thane, but the mage was totally absorbed in exploring their friend's body.

Thane's hand began to move on Leif's cock, sliding back down with agonizing slowness. The phallus glistened with oil, and the cockhead looked darker than before. Leif started to reach for his cock, but Ander restrained him.

"Let Thane do it," he whispered. "You want to soothe the spark, but it's not yet time. Trust us."

The blond took a ragged breath. "Then hold me tight, Ander. I've never felt like this before!"

"I know," Ander said, humor in his voice. *And Thane has just begun.* He adjusted his embrace so Leif's arms were restrained against his sides. Ander felt the tickling sensation in his own cock grow as Leif started breathing faster.

Thane released the blond's genitals, then took another vial from his case. Pale red fluid coated the glass container in viscous streamers.

Ander caught a whiff of clove when Thane twisted the cork off. *The elixir of dreams. Why is he using that one?*

Wasting no time, the mage coated both his hands with the red-tinged oil. Aromatic vapors filled the air. "Something different now," he said. "You'll feel as much pleasure as before, but you'll be able to control it better. Let your mind float. See where the currents take you."

"My cock . . . do something! It feels like I'm starting to cum, but instead the feeling keeps getting stronger!"

"That's good," Thane assured him. "Don't fight your flesh. It's showing you a new path. And it's time to take another step." He reached down to Leif's crotch and grasped his phallus with an oiled hand. Leif moaned softly, his pelvis lifting as if he was trying to fuck the air itself, but Thane didn't relent. His other hand, equally well oiled, moved lower. As he gently squeezed Leif's cock he slid his other hand's index finger into the boy's ass.

"Ohh . . ." Leif's body went rigid. His long legs curled around Thane's crouched form, muscles bunching in hard slabs. "There's a spark inside me," he groaned. "It tickles!"

"Imagine you're kissing me," Ander whispered in his ear. "Think of lying together beside the river, like we do in the summer. Feel the sun's heat on your back."

"Ander speaks wisely," Thane said. He began to slide his finger in and out of Leif's clenching channel, at the same time stroking the blond's cock with the lightest possible pressure. "Imagine you're dreaming. What about the spark you felt? Is it still there?"

"Yes," Leif gasped. "It's growing. Like a star." He threw his head back, moaning softly. "So intense! Give me release!"

Ander's cock throbbed with a pleasurable itching. He squeezed Leif tight and ground his cock between them. A pale glow drew his gaze down. Leif's cock pulsed with golden radiance. A cloud of sparkling points danced around the glans like bees around their hive. As their speed increased, they spun away from Leif's phallus and flowed along Thane's hands. Motes swirled around the mage's index finger, sparkling like rubies in the red oil, then vanished into Leif's ass. The mage was channeling Leif's pleasure back into him, compounding it with each slippery stroke.

Leif groaned again, arching his back and gasping. "It's consuming me! I need to cum!"

Thane slowed his strokes even further. "There's only one way to truly soothe that itch. You should do it for him, Ander. It's right that his best friend bring him release." He withdrew his finger from Leif's ass, a mass of sparks dancing around his hand as he broke contact, then gently released the blond's cock. It strained against Leif's abdomen, luminous and dripping with precum.

"Yes, fuck me, Ander! Now!"

Ander's inflamed cock needed no further encouragement. He released Leif and eased him onto his back. The blindfolded youth writhed on the cushions. He reached for his penis but Thane grabbed his wrists. Without releasing his grip, the mage moved around until he crouched above Leif's head. He pulled Leif's arms upward, immobilizing them.

Ander took a vial of simple lubricant from Thane's case. He unstoppered it and quickly applied a thick coating to his cock. Even the light touch of his own hand as he spread the oil along his shaft was enough to make his scrotum pull up tightly against the base of his cock. He put his hands under Leif's knees, then lifted the youth's legs and leaned forward until his cockhead nudged the well-oiled opening of Leif's ass. His erection became hard as iron at the first contact with the elixirs Thane had been using. It ached almost painfully.

"Put it in," Leif pleaded. His ass lifted and rubbed Ander's cockhead, trying to engulf it. The blond's cock pulsed visibly, and motes of light still floated lazily around the slippery organ.

"This is a new beginning for us," Ander said softly. "Let me show you a place you've never imagined." He slowly eased his cockhead through the ring of muscle.

An explosion of sensation engulfed him. His cock tingled with a torrent of sensations nearly impossible to comprehend: the slippery warmth of his friend's clenching ass, a tickling sensation as if a hundred feathers grazed his cock in fleeting touches, an itch compounded of hot lust and desperate need. A low groan wrenched from his gut as his cock sank deeper into the boy's ass.

The sound mingled with Leif's gasps in an odd harmony, as if they were a single beast caught in a storm. A pale red aura shimmered around their bodies and pulsed in time with their synchronized heartbeats.

"Good," Thane said. He crouched above Leif like some wild creature, his long phallus spearing upright between his muscular legs. He watched Leif's panting form with undisguised lust.

"Fuck me, Ander!" Leif's muscles stood out in sharp curves, and his ass clenched Ander's cock with strong squeezes.

Ander leaned forward until he supported himself on out-stretched arms with Leif's knees hooked around his elbows. Thane lifted his gaze from Leif's cock and met Ander's intent stare. They kissed passionately as Ander began to fuck Leif with long strokes.

Leif's tight channel gripped him fiercely, its slippery sides shaping themselves to the contours of the invading cock. Ander fought to control his thrusts, restraining the urge to bring release with a few short jabs of his aching shaft. His own ass clenched, feeling echoes of the intense pleasure radiating from Leif's body. Behind it all hovered Thane's strong presence, supporting Ander through their bond, sustaining him on the brink of orgasm stroke after stroke.

Suddenly Leif stopped squirming. The blond held himself motionless, muscles taut, his mouth open in rapture, with Ander's cock buried in his ass to the hilt. Ecstasy blossomed within him and his cock spat its first long streamer the length of his body. Streaks of light raced along his cock and torso like fireworks. He let out a throaty wail as jet after jet of semen drenched his chest.

Ander growled deep in his throat. An overpowering jolt of energy poured through him, first along his cock and then through his groin and the rest of his body. An explosive orgasm hit him like lightning. His hips bucked and he threw his head back as his cock spewed its seed deep inside his partner. Again and again his cock convulsed and fountained hot semen.

Thane released Leif's wrists and scooped up some of the boy's cum. He smeared the pearly fluid over his cock, then leaned back, propping himself up with an arm thrust behind him. He pressed his thick phallus upright with the other hand and presented it to Ander.

Though his orgasm still racked his body, Ander lowered his head and took Thane's cockhead in his mouth. The flavor of Leif's semen mingled with Thane's precum. He pressed his tongue against the bottom of the glans and lashed it feverishly. He was rewarded with a gush of Thane's cream. It filled his mouth, flooding him with its earthy potency, dribbling from between his lips as more and more pumped out of his lover's powerful body.

At last, his mind reeling, Ander slowly withdrew his still-hard penis from Leif's ass. Milky semen coated its full length, and dribbled out in a small stream when his cockhead emerged. He let Thane's cock slip from between his lips, then lowered Leif's legs to the floor and eased himself down. Their lean bodies pressed together, Leif's copious ejaculation smearing their skin. Their bodies still glowed with a faint red halo that slowly faded as their breathing returned to normal.

Thane stretched out next to them, then removed Leif's blindfold. The blond looked at him with awe.

"So the legends are true! There's something beyond the pleasure, isn't there? I felt—"

Thane put a finger to Leif's lips, touching them gently. "Not here. These things shouldn't be spoken of unless we're sure of our privacy." He gave Leif a knowing grin. "I've been in more houses of companionship than you might guess. More than once, there was an ear on the other side of the door. Is this house any different?"

Leif rolled his eyes. "You're right. Tannis hasn't stopped talking about you and Nicolai since you got here."

Ander tugged his ponytail. "You've probably been taunting her, little monster. I know how much you like dangling beautiful boys she can't have in front of her."

"Who, me?" Leif's pious expression was utterly unconvincing. "I'd never be so cruel, Ander." He managed to hold his dignified expression for five seconds while Ander looked at him sternly, then broke into a wide grin and giggled. "Well, maybe I mentioned that Thane's your lover, and she doesn't have a chance against *you*."

"I can say this much," Thane said. "I can tell you're skilled enough to become an apprentice. Would you like to join us?"

Leif's smile widened, his happiness radiant as the sun. "I'd give anything for the chance. Much as I like Lady Tay's house, it hasn't been the same since Ander left."

Loud pounding at the door made them jump.

"Thane? Are you in here?" Nicolai's tense voice immediately dispelled their relaxed happiness.

Ander sprang up and went to the door. He turned the lock and opened the door a crack. Nicolai stood alone in the corridor, his hair disheveled. Ander let him in, then closed the door again.

Nicolai's tense expression softened at the sight of the three athletic youths and the smell of sex. "Leave Thane alone a few minutes and look what happens. It never fails."

"What's the problem?" Thane asked. "You sounded worried."

Nicolai nodded, though his appreciative gaze never left Leif's sleek form. "Lady Tayanita just sent word. She heard a rumor that the city gates are going to be closed at sunset. She fears there's going to be a search. If we don't leave now, we might be here a long time."

Thane reached for his pants. "We'll go immediately. If the rumor is true, the commander is desperate. We'll certainly be taken in for questioning if they catch us." He paused with one leg thrust into his pants, looking at Leif with a thoughtful expression.

"Leif, I know you want to come with us. But it might be better if you wait until any search is over. We might get stopped on the way out of the city. It'd be safer if you weren't with us. And you might learn something valuable after we're gone."

Leif nodded solemnly. "If I'm to be an apprentice, I'll act like one. I'll stay and listen if that's what serves you best."

Ander picked up his shirt, then bent over Leif and gave him a quick kiss. "Until you join us at the Lyceum, then. It'll be worth the wait, I promise."

Leif's smile returned. "Of that, I have no doubt."

8

CONFUSED AND frustrated, Ander slumped in his saddle. *What can it be? Nicolai knows, so why would Thane hide it from me?* He bit his lip and restrained himself from raising the subject again. Whatever the problem was, Thane refused to talk about it. The night before he had lapsed into silence, holding Ander tightly beneath the blankets they shared with Nicolai. Their lovemaking had been fierce. Ander ached to help, but expressing his love and support only seemed to make Thane feel worse.

The mage had moved ahead of the others. He rode with a stiff back, discomfort showing in the rigid set of his shoulders and his stony silence. Nicolai rode beside Ander, and merely looked disgusted. The northerner's attempts to lighten Thane's mood had failed miserably.

Ander sighed and looked around the forest. They'd reach the Lyceum by nightfall unless the snow got heavier and started drifting. Landmarks along the trail were already becoming familiar. A pile of boulders on their left meant they were within a mile of the timber bridge crossing the Wildwood Gorge. Soon they would pass a stone obelisk marking the Battle of the Iron Arrow. From there it was only a few miles to the boundary of Thane's estate. *Maybe if I change the subject. If he starts talking, he might relax.* He spurred his horse forward. Thane gave him a sidelong glance, wary.

"I hope Leif can come to the Lyceum soon," Ander ventured. "Erik and Skorri will test his endurance, I wager."

"Only a fool would bet against you on that," Thane replied. His shoulders relaxed slightly. "But Leif might surprise them. For someone who doesn't know the secrets of the art, he has great control."

"Leif has some secrets of his own," Ander said. "His mother taught him that sex is the purest and most subtle of all skills. He took it to heart."

A smile tugged at Thane's lips. "To the heart, and beyond. Skorri and Erik might find their *own* endurance strained."

Ander returned the smile, elated at seeing Thane's mood lift. "It'll be interesting, forging a link with him. Sometimes he goes wild during sex. I've always wondered what he's feeling when it happens."

Thane's smile faded as quickly as it had appeared. His face paled, and his eyes shifted back to the frozen trail. Their horses walked patiently through the rocks and decaying pine needles, their calm a startling counterpoint to the tension that suddenly crackled in the air.

Ander waited in vain for an explanation, but none was forthcoming. An exasperated snort made him twist around. Nicolai had moved up to join the conversation, and was just behind them. His weary expression was tinged with irritation.

"Sometimes there are disadvantages to Thane being stuck at nineteen," Nicolai said. "When he's determined to feel bad, you're not going to talk him out of it."

Ander ground his teeth in frustration. The young northerner's unhappiness was plain. Nicolai's natural inclination was to soothe, using his strength to protect his friends in times of trouble. Ander wanted to press him, plead for his help, but knew the youth's loyalty was as strong as his compassion. He might let his disapproval show, but he'd never break a pledge to Thane.

Ander resigned himself to the silence and wrapped his cloak more tightly around his body. Gray clouds loomed above them and snowflakes danced in the breeze. Nicolai was oblivious to cold, and Thane too preoccupied to notice it, but Ander shivered and pulled up his cloak's collar. Soon they were clattering over the timbers of a high bridge. Snow fell more heavily, wet flakes blending into the cataracts thundering through the narrow chasm beneath them.

Ander's cloak was soaked by the time they reached the obelisk. His leathers still kept him dry, but the cloak's insulating properties were lost. He began to shiver as dusk fell. They rode through shadows, the only sound the occasional howl of a wolf deep in the forest. The castle finally came into sight, its windows glowing warmly in the darkness. They crossed the bridge into the old fortress and entered the courtyard.

A door at the round tower's base swung open. Golden light spilled onto the snow. Sorel bounded out and ran toward them, his breath puffing in white clouds. He stopped beside Nicolai's horse and gave his partner a pat on the thigh. "I felt you coming. I felt your disquiet, too. What's wrong?"

Thane dismounted, landing heavily on legs stiff from too long in the saddle. "Now's not the time, Sorel. We're cold and hungry. The news will wait."

Sorel took the reins to Thane's horse while the others dismounted. "I'll take the horses to the stable. Go ahead to the library and warm yourselves. I've got a fire going."

"That's my Sorel," Nicolai said affectionately as he handed his reins over. "Always ready with the pleasures of the body."

"I trust that's not a complaint," Sorel answered cheerfully. "You've never objected to creature comforts before." He pressed a hand against the mound at Nicolai's crotch, then collected Ander's reins and led the horses toward the stable.

Ander followed the others to the tower, numb with cold. His flesh began to tingle as soon as they entered the foyer at the tower's base. A spiral staircase at one end of the entry hall led to upper floors and a tall oak door, already ajar, opened onto the Lyceum's library. They hung their cloaks on pegs beside the front door, then went into the library.

A roaring fire filled the massive fieldstone hearth. Everything had been restored to its rightful place following the recent search. Ander crouched in front of the fire and extended his hands toward the flames. Nicolai settled contentedly on the leather sofa that faced the fire.

After a moment's hesitation, Thane sat cross-legged on the floor next to Ander. Light from the fire glinted off the planes of his high cheekbones. The angle of the light turned his eyes a dark gray. He watched Ander intently, his expression unreadable. A minute passed in awkward silence. Unanswered questions hung between them like a sheet of ice, impenetrable and painful to touch. Finally, Thane lifted a hand and touched Ander's cheek fleetingly before hanging his head and looking at a spot on the floor in front of his legs. "I'm sorry," he whispered. "I was hoping I'd think of something, find a way to make everything all right. I . . . I'm afraid, Ander. It's hard for me to admit."

Ander gulped, alarmed by the ache in his lover's voice. He moved closer and put an arm around Thane's shoulders.

"I'm going to go look for Sorel," Nicolai said as he slid off the sofa. "See you later." He left the room in a few long strides, closing the door softly behind him.

"What is it?" Ander asked, his voice tight. "What happened at the commander's house?"

Thane closed his eyes. His lips pressed together and his breath rasped. Ander rubbed his neck, massaging tense muscle. As Thane dropped his defenses their link burst open and throbbed with turbulent emotions: fear, grief and a torrent of insecurity. Despite his thirty years of experience in life, Thane doubted himself with all the intensity of any youth of nineteen. The art had preserved his spirit, as well as his body, at the moment in time when he and Lucian had first immersed themselves in the kei.

At first Ander was too overcome to speak. He tightened his hug and tried to send reassurance back through their link. Thane's failure to respond increased his concern to near panic. "Whatever it is, I'll stand by you," he said. "You *know* that. You feel my heart, just as I feel yours. There's no way you could doubt it."

Thane looked up, eyes brimming with tears. "I never doubted you, Ander. But I'm afraid of what might happen if I . . . change. If I become someone different from who you love now." He looked down again and rubbed his eyes with the back of a hand.

Ander was bewildered. "Change? What kind of change?"

Thane took a ragged breath. "What if I wasn't a mage? Or at least, not a very good one?"

Ander blinked. "I'd love you no matter what. But how could you not be a mage?"

Letting his breath out in a rush, Thane pulled Ander close against his side. "I got caught by a cantrip. If it weren't for Nicolai, it would have killed me. He freed me from the trap but that wasn't the end of it. Afterward—"

A loud thunk signaled the door latch opening. Anna marched in, a determined look on her face. "It's a good thing you got back tonight. We have a problem."

"Can't this wait?" Ander asked. "We've had a long trip and we're both exhausted." He could feel Thane's dismay at the intrusion, and the mage's struggle to compose himself.

"No," Anna replied as she took a chair near the fire and pulled it around to face Thane. "It's the weather spell. We've used it for years to keep severe weather out of the valley, but I don't think it's a good idea anymore. We've never had the zamindar's sorcerers looking for us before. They might be able to detect the spell's effect on the kei."

Thane straightened and squared his shoulders, but didn't get up. His discipline and dedication, always in evidence in his work, prevented him from neglecting duty's call. "You could be right," he said tiredly. "But what about the gardens? Some of the plants won't survive if it gets too cold."

"The really tender plants are all in the greenhouse. And *none* of us will survive if we let the zamindar's sorcerers find us!" She stood and beckoned for Thane to follow. "We need your help to dismantle the spell, or I would have done it sooner. You're the only mage who understands its complexities."

Thane nodded, then gave Ander a brief hug before struggling to his feet. "Don't wait up for me," he said. "She's right. We can't afford the risk of discovery."

"Can I help?" Ander asked. The sight of his anguished and exhausted lover going off for yet more work made him ache.

"Not for this," Thane said softly. "Go to bed, jirí. We'll talk in the morning."

Ander felt lightheaded as they turned and left. *Jirí. Beloved.* Though he already felt Thane's love to his core, it was the first time the mage had used the term of endearment in front of others. He went to bed with the feeling that some unseen corner had been turned.

A cool breeze brushed Ander's cheek, rousing him from slumber. As he stretched, his arm slid across Thane's smooth torso. The slow rise and fall of the youth's chest told him that his lover still slept. He yawned, wondering what time Thane had come to bed, and opened an eye just enough to see where the cool breeze came from. Morning sun poured through an arched window in the east wall. Snow crusted the edges of diamond shaped panes. He shivered and snuggled closer to Thane to better share their warmth.

Thane's eyes opened and his body stretched sensuously. He rolled onto his side, pulling Ander against him. "You're still here," he said, his eyes filled with wonder. He ran a hand through thick hair at the nape of Ander's neck. "Sometimes I fear I'll wake and find I've been dreaming."

Ander returned the hug, felt Thane's heart thudding against his chest. "Maybe we haven't been fucking enough," he suggested. "*That* should convince you I'm real."

Thane smiled and gave him another squeeze. "Maybe that's exactly what I need." He took a deep breath, then continued in a rush. "I can't put it off any longer, Ander. You have to know what happened in Pella. About my accident." He looked miserable.

"Go ahead, tell me," Ander urged.

Thane rolled onto his back and looked at the ceiling. His breath left frosty wisps in the cold air. Finally he grimaced and met Ander's gaze. "It's our bond. I can't feel it. Or *any* bonds with other mages." His voice dropped to a despairing whisper. "I haven't felt this alone for many years."

For a moment Ander stared, incredulous. "But . . . the bond's *there*, Thane! I feel it, as strong as ever!"

"I know. Nicolai says the same thing. But I still can't feel it, Ander. Do you understand what that means?"

Ander's eyes got wide as he considered the question. Though he was only an apprentice, he knew that all the higher forms of magic relied on shared anima to energize spells. Only mages who shared a bond could combine their anima. Thane, the first and strongest of all the mages, would be crippled. *And he can't feel my heart, or share my pleasure when we make love.* The reason for Thane's reluctance to reveal his infirmity was painfully clear.

"The bond's still there!" Ander insisted. "Something must be interfering with your perception." He rolled on top of Thane, straddling the mage and pressing their bodies together. "Tell me what happened."

There was no escaping the demand. Thane took a deep breath and recounted how they had searched and discovered the crystals. Ander held him tightly, as if afraid of losing him.

By the time the story was told, Ander shivered from the anxiety pouring through their bond. "Nicolai's guess is probably right," he said. "Residue from the cantrip must have clung to you. Is there some way we could tell?"

The question distracted Thane, acting like balm on his ragged nerves. He stroked Ander's back from rounded buttocks to broad shoulders as he pondered the question. "I can think of some things to try," he said at last. "If the spell left a taint, some of the crystals in the workroom might react to it. They've been prepared to function in magic. A malignant spell might leave an aura that would affect them." He gave Ander a strong squeeze. "It's worth a try."

Ander returned the hug, then slipped out from beneath the quilt and reached for the clothes he had left on the floor next to their cushion the night before. "Do we have time for breakfast first?" He started dressing. "It's damned cold in here this morning. A few minutes by the hearth would be welcome."

Thane pulled on his pants and boots. He frowned at his leather shirt, which glistened with a thin layer of frost, before gritting his teeth and pulling it over his head. "We'll get breakfast soon," he promised. "Just a quick stop in the workroom first. I thought of something to try, it'll only take a moment."

Ander finished dressing, hungry but gratified by Thane's enthusiasm. The hope he felt through their bond was more satisfying than any breakfast he could have desired.

They entered the corridor between Thane's chambers and the workroom. Nobody else had rooms on the tower's highest floor, and all was quiet.

Sun filled the workroom, pouring through prisms set in the windows and painting the walls with color. Water in the granite pool at the room's center was crusted with an icy fringe. Ander opened a valve that allowed hot water from the springs beneath the castle to flow into the pool.

Thane went to a trestle table positioned between two tall book-cases. A cabinet with dozens of small wooden drawers filled the table's back hall. He reached up high and removed a drawer in the next-to-top row. Ander joined him and helped push aside a stone mortar containing dried leaves and flower blossoms. Aromas of lilac and pine bark lingered in the cold air.

Thane placed the drawer on the table's scarred surface. It held a large crystal, shaped like a thick-bodied spear, that shone in the morning light with an azure luster. "A Blood Stone," he explained as he tilted the box to make light glint on the crystal's facets. "They're used to find places where blood magic has been performed." He turned the box upside down and dumped its contents on the table. Then, his hand shaking slightly, he touched the crystal.

Thane gasped and staggered backward, eyes wide with shock and pain. The crystal had turned from pale azure to a livid purple.

Ander felt the mage's nausea. He swallowed the bile in his throat and reached out, catching Thane as his knees buckled. After a few seconds Thane regained his balance.

"What happened?" Ander asked. "What did it mean?"

Thane licked his lips, still looking sick. He leaned forward and put his hands on the table. "I'm not sure," he admitted. "But one thing I *do* know. The cantrip I triggered wasn't completely dissipated when Nicolai helped me fight free. What I felt just now was like the beginning of the attack in Pella." The pain vanished from his expression as a new idea seized his attention.

"The Blood Stone absorbs anima when it's created. It takes three mages using a potent elixir, it's a strong spell. There must have been enough anima in the stone to awaken whatever traces of blood magic still cling to my body." He shivered with disgust. "I feel like I'm covered with spiders. I want to get the zamindar's damned spell *off!*"

"We'll find a way. At least you know it's a spell, not some kind of injury," he rubbed Thane's shoulder soothingly. "Are there any spells for purification? What about the magic we used when Nicolai got sick on the trip to Fochelis?"

"That's different. He was—"

A sharp crack, followed by a crash, made them whirl toward the window. Muted screams followed moments later. They rushed to the window. Ander opened the latch and swung the heavy frame outward. A blast of icy air hit their faces.

Initiates were already running into the courtyard. The creak of tortured wood drew their eyes to the greenhouse in a clearing behind the castle's walls. At first a cloud of swirling snow obscured their view. As it settled, they saw a sickening pile of twisted timbers and crushed vegetation. One end of the greenhouse, nearly a third of the massive structure, lay in ruins.

Ander's heart raced to his throat. "The snow! It's too much for the greenhouse roof!" Thane sprinted for the door with Ander at his heels. They careened along the stone corridor and down the spiral staircase, then outside.

Two dozen initiates were already in the courtyard, running toward the gate that led to the greenhouse. They parted to let Thane and Ander through the tunnel-like portal. What Ander saw when they emerged into the clearing made his heart sink.

The greenhouse, a beautiful structure of ornately carved wooden beams and sweeping sheets of glass, shuddered beneath a thick coat of snow. A third of the building was destroyed. Through the collapsed portion of a wall he saw broken remains of the tender plants that filled the building. Thousands of specimens collected through years of effort, the ingredients for elixirs and potions that increased awareness and gave the art its power, would have died almost instantly when the icy air reached them. The magnitude of the loss was incalculable.

Nicolai was among the crowd already on the scene. As they approached, the northerner threw a rope at the protruding end of a beam just below the roof line. The toss was true, and a loop at the end of the rope snagged the log. He tugged the rope to tighten the knot.

Sorel dropped to a knee and held the end of the rope steady as Nicolai swarmed up. In seconds he reached the beam and swung himself up to straddle it. He began using his arms to sweep the roof. Bystanders jumped back as sheets of wet snow rained down.

Suddenly a freezing wind swept the clearing, followed by a loud groaning noise. The standing portion of the greenhouse seemed to shudder. Nicolai immediately slid back on the beam that supported him, then reached down and found the rope. Timbers began to snap as he swung beneath the beam. Halfway down he released the rope and dropped to the ground, landing in a snowbank.

The greenhouse trembled as wind whistled through its broken walls. A great pane of glass twisted free of its damaged mooring and crashed into the debris below. Those standing nearest the building hurriedly moved back.

Suddenly a bloody figure crawled from the wreckage. He collapsed face down in the snow while only halfway out.

Sorel was twenty yards from the youth. He rushed forward, ignoring the danger from the teetering building, and pulled the figure from the rubble. Ander and Thane skidded to a halt next to them. Erik blinked at them. His handsome features were dazed, and blood matted his dark brown hair.

"Move him back," Thane said. "The greenhouse could fall any second. We're too close."

"Wait," Erik gasped. "Skorri's inside. Trapped . . ."

"I'll go," Sorel said. He turned and dashed through the gap in the wall. Moments later Nicolai arrived.

"Has Sorel gone mad? Did he just go inside?"

"Take care of Erik," Thane told him. "Get him inside, gently. He could have broken bones."

"What about Sorel?" Nicolai insisted. "I'd better see what he's doing before he gets himself killed."

"This is my fault," Thane said. "Now go. Erik can't wait. I'll help Sorel."

"Me, too," Ander said. "You're not going in there alone."

Thane looked like he wanted to protest, but after a moment he nodded. "Let's go."

They followed the path Sorel had taken into the shattered greenhouse. Cold air was heavy with the smell of wet earth and dying vegetation. Hotsprings beneath the castle had been used to keep the greenhouse at a tropical climate; moisture from the humid air had turned to ice and coated everything with a thick layer of frost. Shattered panes of glass were strewn about the wreckage like huge knives, their edges sharp as razors.

The section of greenhouse they entered had contained a bamboo forest, interwoven with exotic orchids and vines of tropical flowers. The blooms that hadn't been crushed beneath falling glass were already dusted with snow. Splintered bamboo waved in front of them like the spears of an approaching army.

They found Sorel crouched beside a foot-thick timber near the center of the wreckage. Skorri lay unmoving, his legs pinned beneath the timber. Chunks of glass and fragments of bamboo flew as Sorel uncovered the rest of the young blond's body. The greenhouse vibrated like a reed as icy wind howled through its fractured walls. Another glass panel fell from the ceiling fifteen feet to their left. It sliced through a stand of bamboo like a scythe, but was deflected away from them. Ander and Thane joined the effort. In seconds they had freed Skorri from all the wreckage except the massive timber. The boy still lay motionless.

Ander couldn't see any blood, which only made Skorri's stillness more alarming. He straightened and examined the beam. It had been wrenched from a wall as the roof collapsed. The far end was still connected to the framing, and the wall was so badly twisted he couldn't fathom how it still stood.

Thane grabbed the broken end of the timber. "Sorel, help me lift the beam while Ander pulls him out."

Sorel positioned himself on the other side of the beam while Ander got his hands beneath Skorri's shoulders. Then Thane and Sorel started to lift. The beam shifted, the end connected to the wall screeching like a mad cat as wooden pegs squeezed out of their holes. Snow fell from the broken roof in sheets as the wall twisted, and an ominous vibration shook the ground.

Thane and Sorel put their backs into the effort and the beam lifted another few inches. It was all Ander needed. As soon as the weight was off Skorri, he pulled the limp body out from beneath it. The boy groaned and shook his head weakly.

"Hurry!" Sorel urged. "Get him out of here. The beam's slipping out of my hands!"

There was no time for delicacy. Ander knelt and gathered the youth in his arms. Skorri's pained cry raised his hackles, and a surge of panicked energy brought him to his feet. He carried Skorri toward the hole in the wall, his heart pounding, as his friends started to ease the timber back to the ground.

Escape was only three steps away when another shudder shook the building. Sorel shouted as the wall beside them buckled and the beam twisted out of his hands. The force of the sudden movement threw him backward into a pile of broken glass and ruined foliage. Thane ran to his side and helped him to his feet. They staggered together, following Ander, as splintered wood and glass crashed down around them.

Initiates rushed to Ander as he emerged. He sank to his knees, struggling not to drop Skorri. Thane and Sorel were right behind him. They were covered with an alarming amount of blood.

Two initiates, a pair of black-skinned men no older than Ander, laid out a blanket. They helped him lower Skorri onto it. Then Katy joined them and each took a corner of the blanket. The young blond was motionless again. Ander feared the worst as they carried him across the frozen field and into the castle compound, then into the dining hall.

A fire burned in the fireplace, and tables were cluttered with unfinished breakfasts. Erik sat on a bench near the fire, receiving treatment for his injuries. His shirt was gone and his eyes were closed while Nicolai used a cloth to wipe blood from a gash on his forehead. Matted hair and bruises made him look like he'd been beaten. He opened his eyes as Ander and his helpers lowered their burden to the floor. Once he saw Skorri's motionless form he lurched off the bench and knelt at their side. Terror filled his eyes. "Skorri?" He bent low, his face nearly touching his lover's tight golden curls. He put a hand on his partner's shoulder and nudged him gently. "Do you hear me, Skorri?"

"Careful," Ander warned. "We had to bring him in from the cold, but it's dangerous to move him."

Erik looked up, his eyes brimming with tears. "How bad is he hurt? I . . . I couldn't help him. I tried, but couldn't."

Ander put an arm around his shoulders. "You did the right thing, going for help. He woke for a moment when we were pulling him out. That's a good sign."

Erik's breath rasped and tears streaked his face. Ander felt him quivering with barely suppressed panic and held him more tightly. A girl brought over another blanket and draped it across Skorri's body, leaving only his face exposed.

A soft curse from Nicolai made Ander look up. Thane was entering the hall with Sorel staggering beside him. Both their shirts were soaked with blood, and Sorel's face was ashen.

Nicolai rushed to Sorel's side and took his weight off Thane. "You need some stitching, from the looks of this. Do you want me to do it?"

Sorel grimaced as Nicolai eased him to the floor. "A noble offer, but you'd feel the needle as sharply as I. Aside from not wanting to cause you pain, I don't want your hand to shake while you're poking a needle through my side. No, let one of the women do it."

Nicolai settled by Sorel's side and held one of his hands. "All right, I'll let Anna sew you up. But I'm not leaving. I can share my strength with you while it's done."

Sorel nodded gratefully. "It's not necessary," he said softly. "But I welcome your comfort."

Bending down, Nicolai gave him a gentle kiss. "My comfort is always yours. My very life, if you ever need it."

"I know," Sorel said softly. "Now get Anna over here to do the deed before the rest of my blood runs out on the floor. Let's be done with it."

"I saw her in the courtyard," Thane said. "I'll fetch her in." He left the room at a run while Nicolai picked up a knife and began to cut Sorel's shirt away.

A sudden jerk brought Ander's attention back to Erik.

"He moved!" Erik pulled away from Ander and bent over his partner with rapt attention. A few seconds later Skorri's forehead creased with pain and his eyes fluttered open.

"Stop feeling like that," Skorri mumbled. "You're going to make me sick." He pulled a hand from beneath the blanket and reached up to touch Erik's wet face, looking at the tears with bemusement. "What happened? How did we get in here?"

Erik's radiant joy must have poured through their bond like the sweetest nectar. Skorri's eyes widened in surprised delight as Erik wrapped him in a tender embrace. Ander took a moment to bask in their happiness, then went to join Nicolai and Sorel.

Bloody rags littered the floor around Sorel. He lay on his back, his lips drawn tight. Nicolai had cleaned the long gash in his side and now held a cloth against the wound. Despite the pressure, thick blood oozed around the edges of the cloth as Sorel took labored breaths.

Sorel nodded slightly as Ander sat on the floor. "Skorri's awake?"

"I think he'll be fine," Ander answered. "If Erik doesn't smother him with kisses, that is."

Sorel chuckled softly. "If I know Skorri, that's the best cure. Give him two minutes, and he won't have anything on his mind except getting into Erik's pants."

"An understandable obsession," Nicolai said. He brushed a lock of hair back from Sorel's eyes, then gave his nose a playful tweak. "I'll never forget that time in the stable when you and Skorri took turns fucking Erik while he was hanging from a ladder. His cock was big enough to make the stallions envious."

"The stallions hardly got a chance to see it," Sorel replied. "As I recall it rarely escaped from between your lips."

"True," Nicolai agreed. He smiled at the memory. "That ladder turned out to be useful. We'll have to show Ander its possibilities one of these days."

Nicolai's distractions were interrupted by Thane's return. Anna was right behind him. She carried a spool of catgut and a large needle. Ander felt a twinge of queasiness at the sight of the tools, but knew there was no alternative. Even the art, if they dared to use it, wouldn't have been enough to mend the gash in Sorel's side. Nicolai removed the bloody cloth and Anna looked at the wound.

"You're lucky," she concluded after a quick examination. "Thane said you were knocked into splintered glass. You could easily have been impaled."

"A cheerful thought," Sorel said. "I feel better already."

"Better not tease her," Thane cautioned. "Remember who has the needle."

Anna grunted, then gestured for Sorel to get up. "Stretch out on this table," she instructed. "It'll be easier and faster."

Ander and Nicolai helped him move, while Thane went to the kitchen for a bottle of brandy. Anna threaded catgut through the needle's eye while waiting for him to return. Sorel watched her with surprising calm.

"I hope it's not too bad," Ander said. He felt awkward and at a loss.

Sorel reached over and touched his hand. "Don't worry, I've been sewn up before. I know what to expect."

"But you don't have any scars," Ander blurted. He started to blush. "I mean, none that I've seen."

Sorel chuckled, though the movement made him wince. "The art does more than keep you from aging, Ander. It heals your body, too."

"You should have seen him when we met," Nicolai said. "He was a real hellion and had the scars to prove it." He grinned wolf-ishly. "But we've practiced the art a *lot*. The scars are long gone."

Thane returned from the kitchen with a bottle of honey-colored brandy and a clean cloth. After soaking the cloth with some of the liquor he handed the bottle to Sorel. "Might as well have a drink. It might help."

Sorel accepted the bottle and took a swig, sputtering as the fiery liquid went down. Then he nodded to Thane. "Go ahead and do it. No point waiting."

Thane moved the alcohol-soaked rag along the wound in short strokes, making sure there was no debris in the wound. Sorel's breath escaped in a low hiss. The muscles of his arms and torso tightened hard as boards, but he didn't protest. When the task was done he took another swig of brandy, a long deep drink, then handed the bottle to Ander. "Take care of it. I might want more later."

Ander accepted the bottle and stepped back. Anna took his place and began to close the wound with quick precise stitches as Thane pressed the edges of the cut together.

Nicolai held one of Sorel's hands in a tight grip. The bulge of muscle at Sorel's shoulder revealed the pain he was suppressing. Sweat beaded his forehead, and his gaze remained locked with Nicolai's. The few people in the dining hall fell silent, acutely aware of Sorel's ordeal.

In less than five minutes Anna straightened up. She wiped her forehead with her forearm, then touched Sorel's shoulder. "It should heal well," she assured him. "The cut was clean. But you'll have to rest a few days or it'll tear open."

"Rest sounds good," Sorel said through clenched teeth. "But now isn't the time. The greenhouse is a shambles. Most or all of the plants are dead. Do you realize what that means, Anna?"

"We all do," Thane said bitterly. He sat on a bench, looking at the blood on his hands as if his own lifeblood was draining away. "We have enough elixirs and oils to last a few weeks, a month at the most. But now we lack the ingredients to make more." He looked exhausted and defeated.

"You built the greenhouse once," Nicolai protested. "You created the botanical collection. You can do it again."

"That was before the zamindar was looking for us. Before he was building that damned Leech." Thane took a shuddering breath. "I'm not sure we *can* do it again, Nicolai. There might not be time."

"We have to try!" Ander said. He handed the brandy bottle to Sorel, then seized Thane's hands and pulled him to his feet. "Think how hard everyone has worked, how hard they've fought. You, more than anyone! You owe it to yourself to try."

Thane's expression shifted to confusion. Ander had seen that look before, especially when he stood up to the mage. *I'm reminding him of Lucian again. When will he stop looking at me and seeing a dead man?* Memories of Lucian could plunge Thane into wrenching grief. Ander resolved to pull him back from that dangerous brink.

"Where did you get the plants in the collection? You could send initiates out to get replacements. There are more people to do the work now than when you started."

Thane nodded, his expression still shuttered. "Many specimens came from Lord Tolmin, my patron. Some of the basic elixirs are derived from plants I brought with me when he gave me this estate. But the greenhouse is wrecked, and we couldn't move plants during the winter anyway. There just isn't time."

Ander felt Thane slipping, felt fatigue and despair beginning to pour through their bond. Thane's youthful spirit had two sides. His enthusiasm and energy could be boundless. But the pain of loss could engulf him just as intensely. Grief over Lucian's death had nearly killed him once.

On impulse, Ander grabbed him by the wrists and pulled his hands forward until they were outstretched before him. Thane looked down at his hands. He stood as if paralyzed. Silence stretched thin, broken only by the crackle of the fire. The turmoil in his face was painful to watch, but Ander maintained his grip and didn't waver.

When Thane spoke his voice was a husky whisper. "You're right. There's blood on my hands. The blood of my friends. I can't rest, can't give up." When he looked up again his eyes shone like steel. "I'd rather die than fail you. Thank you for reminding me, jirí."

Ander held Thane's hands another moment, then released him. Sound and movement returned as the tension in the room ebbed. "Does Lord Tolmin still collect plants?" he asked. "Would he be willing to help?"

"He'd do anything for Thane," Nicolai said. "The last of his family would be dead, but for Thane."

"And Lucian," Thane said, his gaze resting on Ander. He took a deep breath, then shook himself. "I'll ask Lord Tolmin for his help. He'll understand the urgency. If the zamindar rebuilds his Leech and gains supremacy in the kei, all our lives are forfeit."

Ander shivered at the cold in the mage's voice. Thane was right. They were locked in a race, and only the winners would survive.

9

WISPS OF A dream, oddly tenacious, curled around Ander's mind as he woke. He vividly remembered a pair of eyes, a sense of menace, and the feeling of being in Pella. Also a sense of confusion, of feeling like he was already forgetting something vital. He pushed the dream aside; reality was far preferable. The last traces of confusion left his mind and he sighed with contentment.

The road to Chanture was fairly well traveled, and they had found accommodations every night during the four-day trip. Each inn was better than the last as they traveled further south. The establishment where they stopped the night before, their last stop before reaching the famed city of pleasures and indulgence, was the finest of all. Three stories high, and made of yellow stone, it might have once been a squire's mansion.

Their bed was large and warm. Thane still slept soundly to his right. Ander turned his head to his left, where Skorri pressed against his side. The youth's eyes were open, gazing through a window at richly colored clouds that glowed with the rising sun's rays. Reddish light poured in, making the boy's blond curls look like ringlets of fire haloing his head. Ander slid a hand over to Skorri's thigh and caressed it gently. "I know that look," he said softly. "Don't worry, Erik will be fine. He just needed to rest. I'm sure Sorel will look after him while you're away."

Skorri turned away from the window and grinned. "Oh, I'm sure Sorel will take good care of him. Though it might not be restful. I just regret Erik couldn't come to Chanture with us. Neither of us has seen it."

"Then you'll have to fill him with stories," Ander replied as his hand moved higher up Skorri's leg. "I've never been to Chanture, either. It's hard to believe it's as beautiful as Thane says." The blond quivered as Ander's fingers brushed his inner thigh. As Ander had learned the first day of their trip, the boy responded quickly to a caress. He was only eighteen, and his enthusiasm for sex was boundless.

Turning on his side, Skorri reached over and traced the ridges of muscle layering Ander's torso. He peered into Ander's eyes with sultry intensity. Suddenly, quick as a cat, he leaned forward and licked the tip of Ander's nose.

Ander shook with surprised laughter. Skorri grinned mischievously as he reached down and stroked the length of Ander's hard cock.

The laughter woke Thane. He stretched like a powerful cat, then opened his eyes and gave Ander a sunny smile before embracing him. Their tongues explored, and Thane's long phallus throbbed against Ander's side. They didn't break the kiss until both were breathless. By then the young blond had reached between them and was fondling both their cocks.

"Skorri's getting frisky again," Ander said.

"Part of his charm," Thane said as he rubbed their bodies together sensuously. He rolled on top of his lover and reached out to draw Skorri into the embrace. The blond responded eagerly, straining to press his lips against Thane's. Ander's cock ached with sweet anticipation as he watched the two beautiful youths kiss, their hard cocks pressing against him. Their cheerful lust was breathtaking.

Thane finally stopped playing tag with Skorri's nimble tongue and grinned. "I'm beginning to believe all those stories Erik told me. You really *are* insatiable."

Skorri moaned and shoved his cock against Ander. "We have time for one more tumble, don't we? It's been *hours!*"

"Such hardship," Thane said in mock sympathy. "But morning's here, and there's much to be done." He rolled out of bed and picked up his shirt. There was no point arguing with the mage when duty called, so they left the warm bed and gave each other sponge baths in preparation for their arrival at Chanture.

The smell of baking bread wafting from the inn's kitchen greeted them when they went downstairs. The dining room was crowded with prosperous merchants, many dressed in the rich velvets and brocades popular in the kingdom's southern reaches. They settled at a table near the slate hearth for a breakfast of sausages, pastries and tea.

A winsome serving boy, no older than Skorri and seemingly entranced by the three travelers, attended to them with shy eagerness and many furtive glances. Skorri looked at him mournfully as they departed, an expression mirrored on the servant's face.

Ander bubbled with amusement at his friend's lusty appetite as they saddled their horses in the adjoining stable. "Were you thinking of bringing him home as a present for Erik?" he joked. "He would have come willingly, I think."

Skorri nodded. "I think you're right. I was just thinking how Erik and I have talked of going on searches, like Nicolai and Sorel do." He gave Ander an appreciative head-to-toe glance. "We'd like to visit the brothels and see if there are more like *you* to be found. But Thane hasn't yet taught us how to test for mage potential."

"In good time," Thane said as he swung into his saddle. "For now, you and Erik will have to content yourselves with other initiates. You need to study, learn more about the ways of the world, before going out alone."

Skorri sighed dramatically as he slung panniers over his horse's back. "I know. That's why I wanted to make this journey even though Erik couldn't come. It's a pity we have to hurry, though, when a beautiful boy yearns for us to linger."

"Perhaps you'll visit here again," Ander said. "Maybe with Erik next time. Think how pleased the serving boy would be by that!"

Skorri's eyes widened, the erotic possibilities of the suggestion firing his imagination. He swung into his saddle and nodded eagerly. "I'll study all the harder," he promised. "And I'll make Erik study too!"

Ander doubted how long Skorri and Erik could keep their mind on studies when they were in the same room together, but made no comment. As they continued along the southerly road, he pondered the path that had brought the young lovers to the Lyceum.

Skorri and Erik had grown up in a village far to the north. They spent their time hunting and fishing, and telling stories around fires in the round sod halls their people shared, everyone living together in a few large buildings. There was nothing unusual about friends sharing a sleeping mat, but privacy was no more than a blanket hung between sleeping alcoves and the main room. Their passion was eventually discovered, and earned their elders' wrath. The local religion condemned any form of love that omitted the possibility of offspring to increase the tribe's size and influence.

Erik and Skorri were banished, cast out with nothing but the clothes on their backs. That night, as they huddled in shock outside the village, one of their friends slipped out and gave them a hunting knife and blanket. The gifts saved their lives. They made their way south, living off the land and relying on each other for warmth. Good fortune finally brought them to the port city of Bieron, where an initiate arriving with new specimens for the Lyceum saw them stealing fruit in a market. An offer of a hot meal bought their story. Sensing their passion and their empathy, an invitation to visit the Lyceum was extended and accepted. The youths soon won themselves a new home, a home where their love for each other was cherished.

Ander smiled as he watched Skorri badger Thane with questions and observations. The young blond had an exuberant spirit, and was accustomed to a village where there was little to do for entertainment other than talk. Thane bore it patiently. While the mage would never admit it, Ander suspected the questions provided a welcome distraction from lurking grief. Chanture was where Thane had found love with Lucian, and where Lucian had died. Painful memories were inevitable.

Morning passed pleasantly. There were few travelers on the road, and bandits rarely ventured this close to Chanture. Ander relished the lack of snow. Even in midwinter, this part of the kingdom remained green. By noon they emerged from the winding forest road. The soaring buildings and terraces of a vast city appeared in a bowl-shaped valley before them. They reined their horses in and stopped to look at the sprawling metropolis below.

"Chanture," Thane said softly. "It would be a paradise, but for the zamindar."

Ander and Skorri were mute at the sight of the ancient city. A great river rolled through the valley, but didn't cut the city in half. Instead the waters split into scores of canals that laced through the city like gossamer threads. Towers rose from islands in lakes where canals intersected, and high-arched bridges were everywhere. Even at a distance, Ander could see colorfully painted boats gliding through the maze of waterways.

The city followed the valley's contour as it sloped up from the river basin. Terraces thronged the valley's walls, especially where the slope was steep. Some were devoted to rice paddies and vineyards; others contained elaborate estates filled with gardens and fanciful mansions surpassing anything Ander had ever imagined.

Thane gazed at the scene, his expression frozen as a mask, but couldn't stanch the flow of feelings through the bond with his partner. Ander felt a tumultuous mixture of bittersweet nostalgia, the sharp ache of first love and its loss, fierce anger. He yearned to comfort Thane, and tried with all his might to offer solace through their bond, but the mage was oblivious to the effort. The magical contamination interfering with their empathic link still had not softened its grip.

They began the descent into the city, weaving back and forth on switchbacks as they traversed the steep part of the valley's wall. The estates of the wealthy were even more impressive up close. The city's aristocracy and prosperous merchants strove to outdo each other in the sophistication and splendor of their gardens. Even in winter there were shrubs and climbing vines in bloom, a riot of color that shocked the eye after days of traveling through muted forests. Fragrances floated through the air like perfume.

Soon the trail widened enough for them to ride abreast. "Is it always this warm?" Ander asked. "I know we've come south a long way, but it's like springtime here. They don't use sorcery to keep it warm, do they?"

"It's the valley," Thane answered absently. "It shelters Chanture from the winter winds. And the river keeps the city pleasant in the summer. The mild seasons are the reason the wealthy built their estates here in the first place."

"They're not *all* rich, are they?" Skorri asked. "How could you have a city where everybody's wealthy?"

"You don't," Ander answered. "But ask any companion where they want to open a brothel. Merchants, companions, artisans, entertainers, craftsmen, it's the same for all of us. The wealthy can afford our services, so we follow wherever they go."

"And even the wealthy need to eat," Thane added. "The cooks in Chanture are the finest in the kingdom, and the food has to be fresh." He swept his arm outward, encompassing the vast valley. "Nearly every foot of land is used. And of course they import goods from everywhere in the kingdom and beyond. Which reminds me, Skorri. Do you remember what I told you about dealing with Petr?"

"Of course I do!" Skorri said indignantly. "I know all about haggling, just ask Erik. I won't settle for less than one gold drinar for each vial, more for new perfumes we've never before sold in Chanture."

"And don't answer any questions about the Lyceum," Thane reminded. "Petr would like nothing better than to learn our ingredients, or the secrets for blending and curing. Perfumery is a very profitable venture in Chanture. And competitive."

"I'll remember," Skorri assured him. "I'll tell him I'm just an agent, and don't know anything of perfume making." He gave Thane a wicked grin. "And I can distract him if need be. You said he has an eye for boys?"

"And girls too," Thane replied. "He must be nearing thirty now, but I'll wager he's as eager as ever. It's been five years since I sold him perfume myself. He offered me a generous bonus if I'd demonstrate an intimate perfume for him. Like many in Chanture, an enticing fragrance increases his passion."

"You declined the offer?" Ander asked.

Thane shrugged. "Chanture holds too many memories for me. And while Petr is a decent man, I have no real love for him." He gave Ander an understanding look. "Like you, I wouldn't have made a good companion. Especially now that I've found true friends again."

And pleasures of the flesh are far greater when you're linked with your lover, Ander reflected. He resolved to renew his efforts at overcoming that barrier.

They left Skorri at the corner of the avenue where Petr's shop was located. Though Thane would've liked to have seen his old acquaintance, the meeting would have been too dangerous. Five years ago, Thane had looked like a ruggedly sensual nineteen-year-old when he met the perfume merchant. Petr would likely have remembered his masculine beauty, and his unchanged appearance would have been frighteningly uncanny. It was far safer to leave the task of selling perfume to Skorri, who needed the experience anyway.

Lord Tolmin's estate was in the lower part of the city, among the canals and forested avenues favored by the old aristocracy. They wove through the crowded streets, Thane leading the way, taking frequent detours as canals crossed their path. Ander soon lost track of their route and marveled that Thane could still navigate the maze so effortlessly. He contented himself with ogling the fine shops and cafes lining the street, the elaborately carved walls of the great estates they passed, the colorfully lacquered boats that swept beneath them when they crossed over canals.

Within an hour they came to a broad avenue lined with huge oaks and maples. Stately mansions stood back from the road, partially hidden by formal gardens and elaborate fountains. Ander didn't need to be told when they arrived at the mansion belonging to Lord Tolmin. The central hall was flanked by tall greenhouses, and even its balconies were crammed with plants in clay pots. An air of genteel decrepitude permeated the grounds. Despite its unconventional nature, Ander found the place relaxing.

They dismounted and tied their horses to rings at the cobblestone street's edge. Thane was quiet as they walked along a brick path, through a garden crowded with heathers and tall spiky flowers with blue blooms. He came out of his reverie when they reached the front door, turning to Ander and smiling ruefully. "Eleven years ago I wouldn't have needed to knock. I had the run of the house. Even though I was a servant, Lord Tolmin treated me like a son."

"How much does he know about the art? Has he seen you since giving you the estate?"

"Oh yes. I visit him almost every year. He knows about the art, and the suspension of aging, though he doesn't know any details. He knows it grows from passion, and that the lovers have to be the same sex." He chuckled softly. "Tolmin was never that interested in sex. You'd understand, if you'd had a chance to meet his wife. She was a frivolous woman with no interest in science. He could scarcely think of anything to say to her. And he never had an interest in men. But I don't think age bothers him. He was never vain, and he's willing to let nature take its course."

"He's a philosopher as well as a botanist," Ander observed as Thane rang a small bell mounted beside the door. "Most men fear death."

"He probably views death as something new to experience," Thane replied. "And I think he's tired. He's been chafing under the zamindar's tyranny for too long." Before Ander could reply the door swung open.

A young servant dressed in green hose and gold shirt looked at them imperiously. "Deliveries are made in the back," he said dismissively.

Thane sighed. "New here, aren't you? Just tell him Thane is calling. And I've brought a friend I'd like him to meet."

The young man looked affronted. "You expect me to believe Lord Tolmin knows *you*? Not likely. Lord Tolmin is a gentleman and a scholar. He'd have no business with the likes of you."

Thane's face clouded, but Ander put a hand on his shoulder. He reached into a pocket and pulled out a silver coin. "For your trouble," he said politely. "Just let Lord Tolmin know Thane is here. Believe me, he'll be displeased if he learned you sent us away unannounced."

The servant scowled for a moment, then held out his hand. As soon as Ander dropped the coin into his palm he nodded curtly. "I'll return with your answer shortly."

Thane's fists were clenched, but Ander treated it lightly. "Another form of magic, that's all. Nicolai taught it to me when we visited Fochelis."

"Nicolai has always been sensible. You did well to learn from him. I should try to do the same." He slid a hand around Ander's waist and gave him a squeeze. "Forgive me. I'm just nervous. This place is full of ghosts for me."

Ander didn't need to be told which particular ghost was haunting his beloved. He returned the squeeze, wishing Thane could feel his empathy, but knowing the mage was blind to their link and feeling lonely.

The door flew open. A wiry man, smudged with dirt but dressed in fine clothes, rushed out and embraced Thane. Wispy white hair floated like a cloud around his head. The enthusiasm of his greeting left Ander blinking. After a quick hug the man stepped back and put his hands on Thane's shoulders. He looked at the mage and shook his head in amazement.

"Still unchanged, as handsome a rogue as ever! Just looking at you makes me feel ten years younger!" The old man turned to Ander, his blue eyes sparkling. "And who's your friend? Are his looks as misleading as yours?"

"Gregory, this is Ander. He's new to the art, and no older than he looks." He put his hands on Lord Tolmin's forearms and squeezed them gently. "He's someone special. Let's go inside and I'll tell you."

Lord Tolmin clasped hands with Ander, giving him a penetrating but friendly examination in the process. He smiled approvingly at Ander's firm grasp and unwavering eye. After a moment he stepped back and held the door open. "You're most welcome in my home, Ander. Any friend of Thane's is *my* friend."

The manor's entry hall, a cavernous room paneled in cherry, felt more like a jungle. Light poured through windows of colored glass, painting a bewildering array of potted plants in myriad colors. Thane surveyed the profusion with amusement.

"Your new greenhouse is already full, Gregory? I thought you said it would last you the rest of your life."

Lord Tolmin shrugged helplessly. "You know how the damned plants are, Thane. They just won't stop *growing*. It's not my fault, really."

Thane snorted. "I'll wager you wasted no time expanding your collection. Admit it, Gregory. You have some new treasures, don't you?"

"A few," Tolmin admitted grudgingly. A grin broke out on his face. "Well, seven score, to tell the truth! Come, let me show you!"

"I'd like that," Thane replied. "But first let me tell you what brings us here. We've had a problem at the Lyceum."

"Tell me about it on the way," Tolmin said as he headed for a doorway at the room's far end. "Come, come." He gestured as he walked, not waiting for them.

Thane and Ander quickly caught up with the elderly aristocrat. The mansion's wide corridors were brightly lit with rows of windows running from floor to ceiling. The air was damp and surprisingly warm. Thick stone walls captured the sun's heat and gave it back to the riotous vegetation that filled the house. Ander could see why Thane had been fascinated by the place when he took a job here as a boy.

Thane walked abreast of Lord Tolmin and put a hand on his shoulder. "I'm eager to see your new specimens, Gregory. But I have to tell you, our mission here is urgent. Our greenhouse was destroyed in a snowstorm. Nearly everything was lost."

Tolmin came to an abrupt halt, his eyes were wide with horror. "No! What about the Passion Fruit vine? And the Poisoner's Delight? And that new succulent I sent you, the—"

"All gone," Thane said grimly. "You know what it means, don't you? For our struggle with the zamindar?"

"The zamindar!" Tolmin's face registered dismay. He pushed the fingers of both hands back through his wispy hair. "How could I have forgotten? I've gotten a strange letter, Thane. From Ossia. She's up to mischief again. I've been wanting to speak with you about it, but didn't want to send word in writing." He peered at Thane owlishly. "There are spies everywhere these days. Did you know that?"

"I'd heard," Thane confirmed. "Tell me about Ossia, old friend. Then we'll tell you about the storm."

Tolmin took a deep breath, his face pained. "Forgive me for speaking of her intrigues, Thane. I regret the grief she's caused you. I've tried to make amends."

"No need for apologies," Thane said softly. "The zamindar's men killed Lucian, no one else. Your kindness saved me, Gregory. I'll always be grateful. And now Ander is healing my heart."

Lord Tolmin turned and regarded Ander carefully, a new respect in his eyes. "Then I'm truly honored to meet you, Ander. You have my thanks, and whatever else I can offer."

Ander blushed, surprised at suddenly becoming the center of attention. He bowed slightly. "Thane's love is all I desire, Lord Tolmin. But anything you can do to help our cause would be a great service."

"Our cause," Thane said, a faraway look in his eyes. "The truth is, Ossia and I fired each other's defiance." He shook himself, then looked Lord Tolmin in the eye. "I share responsibility for what happened to her, Gregory. If she needs help again, I gladly offer it."

Lord Tolmin clasped him on the shoulder. "Brave as ever. But it's not escape from a dungeon she needs this time. She asked for my help deciphering a letter. Some of her friends took it from an imperial messenger who got drunk in the wrong place at the wrong time. It was pure luck, but her friends were able to make off with his panniers. They found a single letter, its seal bearing the zamindar's own mark. I'll show you. It's in the west greenhouse with my other papers."

They continued along the corridor and soon arrived at the greenhouse that composed the mansion's west wing. It was smaller than the greenhouse at the Lyceum, but far more luxurious. Instead of timbers, the soaring framework was composed of black iron with ornate decorations where the bars connected. The huge glass panes sparkled, and the air was pleasantly warm.

Ander marveled at the vast collection of plants, but Lord Tolmin had temporarily forgotten about his new acquisitions. He led them to a table near the back of the structure. Potting materials and tools for propagating plants were scattered around its surface. He opened a drawer and rummaged through a pile of papers. In a few moments he extracted a battered envelope.

"Here it is," he said with satisfaction. "I've had it for a week now, but I'm having trouble reading it." He handed it to Thane. "It seems closely related to the Qingdao dialect. But it has nothing to do with botany, so most of the characters are meaningless to me. I thought you might be able to help me with it." He sighed and ran fingers through his hair. "I think it deals with politics, but I'm not sure. I don't attend to politics as much as I should, I'm afraid."

"You never did," Thane said with a smile. "As you always said, botany makes far more sense than politics." He examined the broken seal on the back of the envelope. His eyebrows went up. "This wax was impressed with the zamindar's own ring! I'm surprised Ossia's friends were able to get it. Was the messenger traveling alone?"

"Apparently he was," Lord Tolmin answered. "Perhaps the zamindar didn't have enough soldiers to provide an escort. I've heard the imperial guard is keeping busy these days."

"Perhaps," Thane mused as he pulled a piece of creamy white parchment from the envelope. He held it up to the light. "The paper bears the zamindar's watermark. It looks authentic, though I've never heard of an imperial messenger being intercepted before."

"Study it while I collect some seeds for you," Tolmin said. "It's useless to try taking anything else until the weather warms. How long will it take to repair your greenhouse?"

"We'll make the glass ourselves," Ander answered, since Thane was absorbed in the letter. "The rest of the work is just felling timber and carving it into beams. Two or three months should be enough, unless the winter turns bitter."

"Good, good," Lord Tolmin muttered as he started toward the foliage behind them. "I'll start some seedlings, have them ready. Let's see now, where did I put my trowel . . ."

Ander turned to Thane, looking over his shoulder as Lord Tolmin vanished into the vegetation. The document was unlike anything he'd seen before. Tiny drawings, mostly long and short bars that crossed each other at various angles, filled the sheet. "What is it?" he asked. "Some kind of code?"

"In a way, it's even better than a code. This is a kind of writing used far to the east." He pointed to a row of little drawings. "These are stylized pictures, each one means a word. I can make out a bit of it. Lord Tolmin asked Lucian to teach it to him so he could study eastern botanical texts, and I learned it too. But I haven't used it in years." He held the parchment closer.

"Why use such an obscure language for an imperial message?"

Thane shrugged, his mind absorbed in deciphering the document. "Maybe the intended recipient is from the east. I think it's instructing someone to prepare for a great event." He squinted at the paper a few more seconds, then frowned. "Strange, it's addressed to someone named Alaric. Not an eastern name." As he continued reading, his eyes went wide. "Whatever the event is, it'll happen in Fochelis. And soon! That much is clear." He jabbed a finger at a complex symbol that appeared repeatedly in the letter. "This is the mark for next month. Whatever it is, it's going to happen in the next few weeks. It could even be within days!" He looked at Ander intently. "Our only hope is to take them by surprise. We'll have to use everything we've got, make our attempt *now!*"

Ander nodded. "I'll find Lord Tolmin, tell him we have to leave immediately."

"We'll take any seeds he can spare, but that's all. Even at our best speed the Lyceum is three day's ride, and Fochelis two more after that. We'll barely make it before the new month."

And what will we do when we get there? Ander wondered. "We'll be in time," he said with more confidence than he felt. He turned to search for the elderly aristocrat, leaving Thane to finish with the zamindar's letter.

10

THE STREET outside Petr's perfume shop was crowded with merchants, shoppers, rogues, entertainers and animals. Vendors had set up carts and lined the street with food and displays of cloth, jewelry, weaponry, birds, nearly anything a person could want. Sizzling meats on charcoal grills and flatbread cooking in portable clay ovens masked the smell of dust. There were even companions lounging under striped awnings, looking sultry and available. Thane went to fill their water skins and buy food, having decided they lacked the time to stop at inns on their return trip.

Ander went into the dimly lit shop to retrieve Skorri. He paused near the door to let his eyes adjust to the shadows. The shop's proprietor was leaning across a counter and conversing in hushed tones with a richly dressed matron. Dozens of small bottles lined the shelves behind him. The colored fluids filling them seemed faintly luminous in the muted light. Rich fragrances filled the air, like a rose garden on a humid summer day.

Ander was about to approach the proprietor when he saw Skorri standing in a dark corner, close behind a handsome youth with flowing black hair. A large cabinet, covered with finely carved panels, hid them from the shopkeeper and his customer.

Ander smiled as he guessed the nature of their discussion. He crossed the room silently, coming to a stop two yards behind them. As his eyes adjusted to the light he saw that the raven-haired youth's shirt was unbuttoned and that Skorri's hand moved slowly beneath the loose cloth. "Take a deep breath," Skorri murmured in the boy's ear. "See how warm skin releases vapors from the oil?" The youth tilted his head back and rested it on Skorri's shoulder as his chest rose slowly in a deep breath. His eyes were closed, his lips slightly parted. Skorri pressed against him, reaching further beneath the shirt. "See how well it spreads across the skin?" he asked. "Especially on skin as smooth as yours." The youth shivered slightly and turned his head to nuzzle against Skorri's neck.

"It's as I said, isn't it?" Skorri whispered. "The fragrance is an aphrodisiac." His hand slipped lower and the shirt fell open, revealing a tantalizing glimpse of the young clerk's muscular torso. Skorri's hand cupped one of the large, sloping pectorals. He squeezed gently, at the same time letting the length of his body press against the boy's back. Lowering his head, Skorri's lips brushed his new acquaintance's ears. The boy's chest heaved as a shuddering sigh escaped. He was a long-haired beauty; Ander thought fleetingly how Lady Tayanita would have coveted his services.

"The perfume suits you," Skorri whispered. His other hand circled the boy's waist, pulling them firmly together. "You're irresistible when you wear it. You'll inflame anyone who's near. Do you feel what you do to me?" He ground his crotch against the boy's buttocks, at the same time moving a hand down to cup the large erection straining beneath the youth's pants. Both were breathing hard and fast.

"I'm sold," Ander said. "I'll take two bottles."

Skorri jumped like he'd stepped on a hornet. For a second he looked at Ander in a daze. When he regained his bearings he blushed crimson. The mound at his crotch verified the truth of what he had been telling the perfumer's apprentice. The young man, still flushed, quickly buttoned his shirt.

Ander put a hand on Skorri's shoulder. "You'll make a fine merchant." His gaze shifted to the apprentice, giving him a friendly glance from head to foot. "Though I can see the inspiration for your effort. Who's your new friend, Skorri?"

The perfumer's apprentice bowed slightly, obviously relieved that Ander wasn't an irate customer. His eyes widened as Ander's virile beauty registered. He smiled and extended his hand. "I'm Stian, apprentice to Master Petr." He and Ander clasped each other's wrists, holding the clasp longer than was customary.

"And I'm Ander. Unfortunately, Skorri and I have to leave. Other business has arisen, and can't be delayed."

Skorri rolled his eyes. "You've got to stop doing this to me, Ander. Leaving Stian now will break my heart."

"It's not your heart that's aching," Ander ventured. "You'll survive."

Stian leaned toward Skorri and kissed him on the cheek. "Just as well we wait for another time," he said softly. "You deserve more than a quick tumble in the back room. Come see me next time you visit Chanture. I'll make your acquaintance properly, and show you the city." He grinned and briefly rubbed the soft leather covering Skorri's erection. "I think you'd like Chanture. And I'm certain you'll be warmly welcomed here." He nodded in Ander's direction. "As would your friend."

"We'll look forward to it," Ander said sincerely. "But for now, we must go." They left the perfumer's shop, pausing only long enough for Skorri to shift his engorged cock into a more comfortable position. Outside the shop the sun beat down from a burnished blue sky. Noise and bustle surrounded them and quickly dispelled Skorri's lust. The curly-haired blond was soon his usual frisky self, helping Ander scan the crowd for Thane and commenting enthusiastically on the city's sights.

They found the mage haggling with a street vendor over the price of hunter's sausage. As soon as the transaction was completed Thane stored the purchase in his saddle bags with apples, cheese and hard rolls. The trio mounted their horses and began to weave their way out of the city's center. Skorri gazed over his shoulder as they left the city behind.

Thane's mind, though, was occupied with the zamindar's plans. He set a fast pace until they were clear of the valley that cradled the city. As they approached the Taiga Forest he slowed enough for Ander and Skorri to ride abreast with him.

"The letter must mean the zamindar's almost ready to act," Thane guessed. "I wonder if they found the crystals I hid in Pella?"

"Maybe they had more," Ander said. "If the zamindar has found a method to achieve immortality, he'll have spared no effort in collecting everything he needs."

"Or in defending it," Skorri added. "Whatever you did to him last time, I wouldn't count on it working again."

"We attacked the Leech through the kei itself," Thane said. "It was a desperate tactic. We had no choice."

"But it worked," Ander added as he dodged a branch. They had chosen a different route back to the Lyceum, shorter but more difficult. The stone road was already narrowing. Soon the stone would turn to dirt, and the road would be little more than a trail winding through dark green pines and silvery aspen. Though the sun was still high, the air had cooled quickly when they entered the forest.

By late afternoon they entered a clearing. An inn beckoned, the fragrance of hickory smoke and a baking ham hanging in the air as they passed by. Skorri pressed a hand against his rumbling stomach and looked at the inn longingly, but another hour of light remained so Thane decided to press on.

"You're learning about deprivation on this trip," Ander told Skorri as they left the clearing behind. "I expect it's good preparation for when you and Erik start going on missions for the Lyceum."

"That's not what Sorel says," Skorri muttered. "He says they get the best of everything when they're on trips. The best food, the best boys, *everything*." His nose wrinkled as he made a face. "All I'm getting is hungry and horny."

"That's no surprise. You're *always* horny, as far as I can tell.

Probably that's why Thane likes you so much."

Skorri grinned merrily. "Well, Erik and I like Thane too! I envy you, getting to bed him every day. We're lucky if we can get him into a tumble once a week, lately."

Ander glanced at Thane's tense body. The mage was concentrating on the trail, seemingly oblivious to the growing darkness and increasing cold. He clearly needed respite from his worries. "Let's start looking for a campsite," Ander suggested. "Thane's in a hurry, but he'll have to stop sooner or later."

Skorri nodded doubtfully. Thane's determination was legendary at the Lyceum; not even Ander could talk the mage into resting when a task compelled his attention.

Ander took his own advice and searched for good campsites. They were far enough into the mountains that they were unlikely to encounter other travelers during the night. The trail twisted like a snake around scree and fallen trees, and boulders littered the forest floor like a child's marbles. Thane pressed on, silent and intent.

As the fading light started to make the trail treacherous, Ander glimpsed a curving line of boulders through the trees. A small path, marked by the imprint of horses' hoofs, led away from the main trail toward the boulders.

"Hold while I check this trail," Ander called to Thane. The mage was a short distance ahead, but reined in his horse and turned to look as Ander pointed out the path.

"There's still enough light to ride," Thane said. "We could go for another half an hour, at least."

"We'll need some light to set up camp," Ander replied. He pointed to a gap in the branches. The sky was turning indigo, and stars were beginning to twinkle. "We've had a long ride, and tomorrow will be longer. We need to eat and rest."

Skorri nodded fervently, but didn't complain. Like the other initiates, he would make any sacrifice for Thane. Still, his tired and hungry expression spoke more eloquently than words.

Thane sighed. "All right, let's take a look."

Ander turned his horse to the side trail, which worked uphill. As he climbed he realized the boulders were larger than they had appeared from below. He soon emerged into a clearing at the foot of a scree slope. Several large boulders had been rolled together at a flat spot to form three-quarters of a circle, and remnants of pine boughs still covered much of the makeshift hut. A stone-lined fire pit, charred black, was placed a few feet out from the gap in the circle.

Skorri and Thane had followed. Stars gleamed like diamonds against deep blue velvet as the sun set. Skorri set about collecting firewood and fodder for the horses, while Thane and Ander found boughs to patch the gaps in the roof. By the time they finished their tasks the forest lay shrouded in darkness.

Skorri used a flint to start a fire. They spread saddle blankets over the pine needles inside the hut, then went outside and sat cross-legged around the fire to share the provisions Thane had bought in Chanture. Though the fare was rustic, their appetites were voracious. After eating their fill they passed around a goat-skin filled with good wine. A gentle breeze whispered through the forest, but the fire and their cloaks kept them warm.

Thane stared pensively at the fire. Ander was pondering the best way to divert him when Skorri pulled a small clay pipe out of his saddle bag. He glanced at Ander and winked. The handsome young blond looked much less hungry than he had before, but no less randy.

"I brought some dreamsmoke leaves from the Lyceum," he announced. "It's good for keeping you from getting stiff after a long ride." Opening a small leather bag, he took out a pinch of sticky brown leaves and rolled them into a loose ball. He tamped the material into the pipe's bowl, then stuck a twig in the fire until it was alight. His eyes full of mischief, he held the pipe toward Ander. "Would you take some smoke with me? It's always more fun to share it with friends."

Ander accepted the pipe and sucked air through it while Skorri lit the dreamsmoke leaves. In a few seconds the sweet smoke poured into his lungs. His eyes widened in surprise and his head began to swim. Skorri's dreamsmoke was an unusually powerful variety. Holding his breath, taking care not to reveal the smoke's potency, he handed the pipe to Thane.

The mage looked up from the fire. His gray eyes were unfathomable, his tanned skin like bronze in the firelight. He could have been a creature from the forest, sleek and strong, unpredictable. At first Ander feared he might refuse the pipe. But after a few seconds a corner of his mouth lifted in a wry smile. "You two don't fool me for a second, you know," he said as he took the pipe. "You're as bad as Sorel and Nicolai, always trying to cheer me up. I'm grateful, though. I guess I need it." He took a draw on the pipe. Like Ander, his eyes widened in surprise.

Skorri broke into a grin as he reclaimed the pipe. "It's a new variety. Erik and I did some cross-breeding. Like it?"

"You and Erik are dangerous," Ander said. He let the rich

smoke escape with a slow hiss. He felt light-headed after only one taste. "Are you sure you use this for preventing stiff muscles?"

Skorri was already drawing on the pipe, his eyes narrowed and nostrils flaring. Instead of answering he opened his leather pouch and took out another wad of leaves. By the time he needed to breathe he had the pipe ready for another round. Grinning like an imp, he handed the pipe to Ander again. "Among other things. It's good, isn't it?"

Ander nodded, his lungs again full of the intoxicating smoke. He felt flushed, and his cock began to stiffen as he gave the pipe to Thane. Skorri noticed and put a hand in his own groin, cupping the leather-covered mound of hard flesh.

Thane's features relaxed as he took his second breath of smoke. He handed the pipe to Skorri, then turned to gaze at Ander. Their eyes met and held. The sultry invitation in Thane's gaze left no doubt that the zamindar had been forgotten, at least for the moment.

Ander leaned toward the mage and pressed their lips together. Thane's tongue tickled his lips into opening. Before he knew what was happening, a strong flow of dreamsmoke blew from Thane's lungs into his own. The mage held him by the shoulders, tight and motionless, and continued the kiss even after Ander's lungs were full.

"Let's go inside the hut," Skorri suggested, his voice low and husky. "The night is getting cool, but the boulders are still warm from the sun."

His companions didn't need further prodding. The three youths crawled into the makeshift hut, bringing the goatskin of wine and Skorri's pouch of dreamsmoke leaves with them.

Entering the hut was like stepping from winter into summer. Heat from the boulders warmed the air, which was trapped by the thatch roof. There wasn't enough room to stand, but there was ample space to stretch out.

They took their cloaks off and emptied the interior pockets so the garments could be used as blankets. Each of them carried a thin black case of vials containing oils and elixirs used in the art. An assortment of daggers, powders wrapped in folded paper and magically altered gem stones completed the collection. They stored the equipment at the back of the hut, then sat in a circle and passed the pipe around again.

Ander held his breath and tried not to sway as his mind seemed to pull away from his body. He watched Skorri deliver a smoky kiss to Thane. They seemed to move as if under water. Ander blinked slowly. When his eyes opened again, Thane and Skorri were on their sides with arms and legs entwined. Hot arousal flowed from Thane, coursing through their bond, returning his attention to the demands of his own flesh.

Carefully, feeling almost disconnected from his body, Ander emptied the pipe on a patch of bare dirt and smothered the embers. He put the pipe with Skorri's other possessions, then turned back to his comrades.

Thane welcomed him into their embrace. Ander soon found himself in a tangle of arms and legs, his mouth pressed against Thane's. Immersed in the kiss, his eyes closed and his senses absorbed by the eager intrusion of Thane's tongue into his mouth, he barely felt Skorri's fingers working at his belt. It wasn't until he felt his pants sliding down his hips that he realized what the young blond was doing. He opened his eyes just in time to see Skorri start to work on Thane's belt.

Thane pulled away from Ander, giving Skorri access to his belt buckle. In moments Skorri tugged the pants down and Thane's erection sprang free, nine inches of smooth flesh, rigid and potent. Ander stared at it in a lustful daze until the mage touched his cheek and renewed their kiss.

Ander felt as if he floated, that only the link with his lover kept him from drifting into the clear night sky. He watched through half-closed eyes as Skorri slipped out of his clothes. The well-muscled blond, illuminated by the campfire's wavering flames, was a perfect embodiment of sleek symmetry. His smooth chest, divided by a deep cleft between sloped pectoral muscles, danced with light and shadow. His shadow prowled around the boulders as he moved to the other side of the hut and opened a case of elixirs. As he squatted on his haunches his cock stood up at a sharp angle from his groin. Its foreskin had pulled completely back and the dusky helmet of his glans glistened wetly in the dim light. Lean muscle shifted on his abdomen as he twisted to put the opened case at his side.

Warm hands against his sides brought Ander's attention back to Thane. Their cocks were pressed together from root to tip and Thane's gentle thrusting motions made them rock against each other. Their leather shirts had worked halfway up their chests, leaving taut abdomens bare for caresses.

Skorri scooted close and touched Ander's arm. He held a vial of clear oil in his right hand. "Can I fuck you while you suck each other?" he asked, his boyish voice husky with desire. "I've been thinking about it all day!" His upthrust cock twitched and swayed between his strong thighs.

Ander grinned and nodded, quickly peeling his shirt off. Then he tugged Thane's shirt up. The mage cooperated, lifting his arms and letting the garment slide over his head.

Ander turned and straddled Thane head-to-toe. His long black hair hung forward, obscuring his face, as he looked over his shoulder at Skorri. His firm buttocks clenched enticingly, and the muscles of his broad shoulders flexed in complex patterns. "I'll make it good for you," he promised. "Fuck me, Skorri. Show me how you do it with Erik."

The young blond smiled widely as he twisted a cork out of the vial. Aromas of vanilla and musk filled the hut as he poured oil into his other hand and started spreading it over his cock.

Ander took a moment to marvel at his lover's body. Thane had reached a peak of physical perfection when he stopped aging at nineteen. Powerful muscles formed graceful curves, and his long legs looked like a dancer's. His body showed the effects of hard labor in the Lyceum's gardens. Only his cock and balls, and a narrow band around his waist normally covered by a loincloth when he worked at tending plants, remained white. The rest of him was a golden brown. Ander found the contrast intensely erotic.

Still in a daze from the dreamsmoke, he lowered his head. For a moment he let his cheek rest against the belly of Thane's cock, feeling its heat. Despite their passionate lovemaking in the short time they had been together, he felt more aware of Thane's animal vitality than ever before.

He was jarred out of his reverie when Thane grasped his cock and angled it downward. With his other hand he urged Ander to lower his hips. He tilted his head back and let Ander's cock slide into his throat in a long, smooth glide.

Ander gasped, momentarily shocked at the moist heat inside Thane's body. The rush of pleasure made him hunger to return the sensation. He took one lick along the slick underside of Thane's glans, enjoying the musky flavor, then took the cockhead between his lips. Taking a deep breath, letting his throat relax and open, he pressed down. The long shaft slid into his throat. He growled softly and his body tingled. The thick shaft slid even deeper, until his nose pressed against Thane's balls.

The lovers took up a slow rhythm, repeatedly plunging each other's cocks into their mouths down to the root, using the mild sense of detachment produced by the dreamsmoke to control their trembling bodies. They moved like a single creature, their bodies in perfect unison. The firm mounds of Ander's ass moved up and down as his cock slid between Thane's lips.

The flexing of Ander's rounded buttocks and the smooth cleft between them held Skorri entranced. He poured more oil into his palm and leaned forward, placing his hand above the cleft and letting oil dribble between Ander's buttocks. Then he slipped his fingers between the globes of muscle and used his fingertips to coat the smooth skin. His oily index finger found the tight opening and tickled it gently as Ander continued to fuck Thane's mouth.

Ander moaned in delight. The young blond had a delicate touch. Despite Skorri's excitement, clear from his heavy breathing, he caressed Ander's ass a full five minutes before his finger wiggled its way through the well-lubricated hole.

Ander went rigid, Thane's cock filling his throat, as Skorri began to twist his finger. He worked it in and out while using his other hand to pour more oil. His fingertip found the sensitive spot just inside the ring of muscle and gently stroked it. The stimulation brought a dizzying surge of pleasure, but Ander focused on Thane's straining body and resumed deep-throating the youth's glistening shaft.

When the opening was sufficiently relaxed Skorri eased another finger in. He worked the hole carefully, watching Ander's ecstatic face as he pleasured Thane and had his cock sucked in return. The young blond waited as long as he could, barely touching his drooling cock as he finger-fucked Ander. Finally he couldn't stand it any longer. "Roll on your side," he said, his voice strained. "I need to fuck you, really bad."

Ander lifted his head and let Thane's cock snap back against his belly, then turned to look at Skorri. The boy was nearly panting. His hands and genitals, coated with clear oil, gleamed in the firelight. He was on his knees, and his penis speared up in virile demand.

Ander rolled onto his side and lifted his left leg, exposing the cleft of his ass. Skorri reclined behind him and used one hand to guide his cockhead to Ander's ass, the other to hold Ander's leg up. The helmeted tip found its mark; he gave a slight push and his glans slipped inside.

Ander stretched, keenly aware of the athletic bodies surrounding him, then turned his head to accept Thane's penis. His partners moved as if they had a single mind; two stiff cocks slid into him at the same time. The sweet sensations made him want to groan, but Thane's thick shaft completely filled his throat. Skorri's cock was slick and smooth, slithering in and out with slow thrusts. He tried to grip it with his ass muscles, reveling in its curving hardness and the soft flaring at its tip, but it was impossible to get a purchase on its slippery surface.

Skorri complemented his fucking by nuzzling Ander's neck and shoulders. The young blond was breathing hard, and Ander could feel his heart pounding. The boy's body trembled with the effort of restraining himself. Sweat beaded his skin, glistening on smoothly flexing mounds of muscle.

Dreamsmoke still baffled Ander's senses. One moment he would forget everything except the carefully controlled slide of Skorri's cock. Then the taste of Thane's drooling penis burst to the forefront, making him salivate and marvel at his lover's masculine potency. Thane's expert sucking sent shivers through his body. Then Skorri would distract him by nibbling at his ear, murmuring endearments, panting with lust as his rampant cock explored the warm sheath of flesh that clenched it like a slippery glove.

Ander allowed himself a few more moments of delirious pleasure, then let Thane's cock escape from his mouth. "You've taught Skorri well," he said. "He fucks like a fine companion."

Thane let Ander's spit-soaked shaft rest against his cheek. "So I see," he answered. "Though Erik's done more than I to teach him, lately."

"You two have been tight as newlyweds after a two-day feast," Skorri commented. He rocked his pelvis forward and sank his cock in a deep thrust that made Ander moan happily. "Though I can see why you don't want to let each other out of bed."

Ander glanced over his shoulder at the rutting youth. "The art should be shared. I've been too selfish with Thane's love. Why don't you fuck him, Skorri? Show him what you've learned."

The blond grinned, obviously pleased by the idea.

Thane nodded eagerly. "Fuck me, Skorri. Let me feel your hardness."

Skorri pushed into Ander one more time, rubbing their bodies together sensuously, then eased back. His slippery cock pulled free of Ander's ass and snapped up against his hard belly. Ander's pang of regret at losing the intimate contact was offset by his anticipation of Thane's enjoyment.

Skorri released Ander's leg and scrambled to his knees. He paused to brush his lips over Ander's neck, then picked up the vial of oil and moved behind Thane. Ander watched, feeling as if he was dreaming, while Skorri spread oil over the entrance to Thane's ass. The boy was rapt, his features intent with lust, as his fingers gently massaged the tight opening.

The mage reached for Ander and pulled him close. The hot wetness of Thane's mouth on his cock brought Ander's mind back to their lovemaking. His lips slid down his partner's shaft at the same time Skorri's index finger wiggled into Thane's ass.

Disorientation swept through Ander as the blond worked first one finger and then a second through the slippery ring of muscle, and the sensation of penetration flowed through his bond with Thane. His cock twitched, along with Thane's, as Skorri's fingers probed. The youth took his time, working his fingers in and out, adding oil until the hole was thoroughly coated.

Finally Skorri took position. He nestled behind Thane and lifted one of the mage's legs, then placed his cockhead in the concave depression between his buttocks. His phallus was still coated with a thick sheen of oil; scents of vanilla and musk were strong in Ander's nostrils. Skorri nudged his cock forward. His cockhead slipped smoothly into Thane's ass and the rigid penis eased in to its base.

A whiff of smoke drifted in from the dying campfire. Flames still licked at the charred logs and cast wavering light through the makeshift hut's entrance. The light made Skorri's body look as if it were made of gold. Ander was mesmerized as the blond took up a steady rhythm in his fucking. The boy's cock was within inches of his face, yet he felt as if the slick phallus stretched his own ass. The confusion of sight and physical sensation was dizzying, and was compounded by the expert sucking his cock was receiving from Thane. Pleasure ravaged him, yet somehow the dream-smoke allowed the sensations to keep building without triggering the climax that felt only a heartbeat away.

Ander managed to retain a shred of restraint, forestalling his orgasm, but he could see that Skorri was quickly losing the battle. The young blond's slender hips moved more quickly, his cock plunging in and out of Thane's ass with increased urgency. His balls were pulled up tight against the base of his cock and his breath came in short gasps.

Suddenly Skorri's body stiffened. He froze, his cock full in Thane's ass, his leg muscles standing out in hard definition. Then he gasped.

Ander felt the spasming of the boy's cock, felt the hot spewing of cream deep inside Thane's body. He held himself motionless, Thane's cock down his throat, and watched in fascination as Skorri's cock jabbed in short strokes. He felt the hard curve of Skorri's stiff flesh as if he were impaled on it himself. The oily cock fountained again and again, filling Thane's ass to overflowing.

The feel of Skorri's release nearly triggered Ander's orgasm, but

Thane had stopped sucking when the young blond began ejaculating. Ander teetered on the edge of orgasm, sure he would succumb but miraculously he managed to ride it out.

Skorri pulled out and rolled onto his back, his chest heaving. His cum-streaked cock glistened in the dim light.

Thane gently released Ander's penis, then eased back from their head-to-toe embrace. He knelt above Skorri and looked into the handsome boy's face.

"Erik is very lucky," Thane said. "As am I." He lowered himself to hands and knees and kissed Skorri deeply. The blond's cock, still tumescent, began to twitch and stiffen again. When they broke the kiss Thane looked at Ander.

The invitation in his gaze was unmistakable. Ander moved next to Thane. As the mage and Skorri resumed their kiss, Ander put one arm around his lover's waist and let the fingers of his other hand trail lightly down the crack of his ass. Milky semen drooled from the stretched hole. He ran a finger through it and traced circles around the winking rosette. The circles grew smaller and smaller until his finger rested on the opening. He pressed gently and his finger slipped inside. A new freshet of Skorri's cum seeped out.

As Ander's finger explored inside the hole, he felt Skorri's oily hand encircling his rigid penis. The blond stroked its length, twisting his hand to spread the oil smoothly, all the while jousting with Thane's tongue in his mouth.

When Ander's phallus was covered with oil, Skorri put a hand on Thane's shoulder. "He's ready for you. Hard as a ram, too!"

Thane playfully butted heads with Skorri, then looked over his shoulder at Ander. "How do you want to do it?"

"Fuck him on his back," Skorri suggested. "You can get deeper that way."

"Trust Skorri to know," Thane said with a grin. He rolled onto his back and spread his legs wide. The smooth flesh of his inner buttocks presented an inviting target.

Ander crouched between his partner's long legs and pressed his cock down until the glans lined up with Thane's hole. A gentle push, slurping through the thick semen Skorri had deposited, and he was inside. The intimate contact reinforced their bond. As he eased his cock in deeper he felt the slow penetration of his own ass as clearly as if being fucked himself. He was able to gauge his penetration to perfectly match Thane's needs. Soon his penis was fully engulfed in the slick channel, sliding in a coat of oil and Skorri's ejaculation.

He leaned forward and pressed his chest against Thane's. They clung together, hardly daring to move, as they adjusted to their surging sensations. Ander felt an echo of his own sensations flowing back through the bond. He realized that despite Thane's fears, the mage wasn't completely cut off from his lovers. Hope buoyed him, making him grin.

"What is it?" Thane asked, his eyes opening wider as he noticed Ander's sudden smile.

Best not to distract him with it, Ander decided. *For now, he needs love.* "Later," he said. He slid his cock out a couple of inches and then back in. They both shuddered, and Thane's cock twitched between their bellies. A warm smear of precum coated the hard muscles of their abdomens.

Ander lifted himself up, then slid his hands down Thane's body to behind his knees. He lifted and pressed the youth's legs wider apart. Carefully, wanting their lovemaking to last at least as long as Skorri had managed, he began to slide his rock-hard shaft in and out of the clenching hole.

Skorri sat next to them, his cock again fully erect, watching intently. He leaned forward and slipped his fingers beneath Thane's cock, hefting the thick shaft. A strand of precum draped between the cockhead and the tan skin of Thane's belly. Skorri let it coat his finger, then wiped the clear fluid over the glans.

Ander nearly came when Skorri's finger slid over the point where Thane's cockhead joined the shaft of his penis. He held his breath, every nerve afire, his cock twitching. Skorri saw how close he was to coming and stopped caressing the mage's cock. Looking at Ander mischievously, he pushed Thane's throbbing cock upright.

"Want me to suck it? I wager you wouldn't last long then!"

"No wager," Ander gasped. "Even without your lips I'll not last. I'm sliding in your seed, Skorri, and I've never felt anything finer!" He resumed his slow thrusts, repeatedly penetrating full length and then pulling out until just his cockhead remained inside the hole. He leaned forward again and nuzzled Thane's neck as his thrusts quickened.

Skorri's hand remained between them. The blond pushed Thane's cock against Ander's abdomen and rubbed it back and forth. The slippery motion of Thane's penis against his belly, unexpected and intense, was more than Ander would withstand. He grabbed Thane's shoulders, plunged his cock in to the balls, and erupted in a convulsive orgasm. His body bucked with the ferocity of his climax. As soon as it started Skorri tightened his grip on Thane's penis and slid his oily fingers around the crown of the glans. Thane gasped, his body stiffening, and a flood of semen spewed out.

They clutched each other in desperate pleasure, their long cocks releasing volley after volley of rich cream. The scent of cum filled the hut, overwhelming even the dreamsmoke. Skorri kept his hand between them, pressing Thane's penis against the hard muscle of Ander's torso, tense with excitement as he watched their strong bodies writhe.

At last Ander collapsed in exhaustion. The simultaneous experience of his own orgasm and Thane's, the relayed feeling of his own cock ejaculating deep in his body and of Skorri masturbating Thane's cock, left him breathless. As his heart slowed he realized they had achieved this peak without using the elixirs and sensitizing balms employed in the art. Heartfelt passion had magic of its own.

A soft gasp made Ander open his eyes just in time to see Skorri bring himself to climax a second time. The boy still had one hand between their bodies, holding Thane's cock, but with his other hand he stroked his own stiff penis feverishly. In seconds another ejaculation shot through the air. It splattered against Ander's side, hot and sticky, adding to the thick aroma of sex. Skorri closed his eyes for a moment, his face blissful, then sighed and pulled his hand out from between Thane and Ander. "Making up for lost time," he said. "Watching you fuck Thane made my blood hot. I wouldn't be able to sleep without coming again."

Ander grinned, then lifted himself off Thane. His cock emerged from his lover's ass coated with his own and Skorri's semen. He picked up a cloak, then gestured for Skorri to join them. The boy slid into place next to Thane, his head resting on the mage's shoulder, and Ander drew the cloak over the three of them.

11

Dawn was glorious, painting the clouds with red and gold. The night had been mild and they warmed quickly as they saddled their horses. Thane wanted to finish the trip to the Lyceum in a single day, though they were only a third of the way back.

Ander had no objection. He had grown accustomed to long rides, and didn't relish the prospect of camping once they got higher into the mountains. He gnawed a piece of smoked beef and pondered the past night as they rode. If Thane still suffered from an inability to perceive his partner's sensations through a bond, it wasn't apparent in his enthusiastic lovemaking. And Ander certainly hadn't felt any impairment; the sensations flowing from his lover had been intense.

As the day wore on Ander forgot everything but the journey's demands. Thane set a grueling pace, and the narrow trail they followed was treacherous. It required all his concentration and skill to keep up. The time they were saving was paid for in danger and strain. Sun on his back, together with warm leathers and boots, kept him warm even as they got higher into the mountains and the temperature dropped. By the time night fell the trail reconnected with the road at the mouth of the valley where the Lyceum lay. Though he was sore and exhausted, Ander breathed a sigh of relief. The Lyceum was still hours distant, but the prospect of a hot meal and soft bed now beckoned.

The sky had remained clear. Stars sparkled like diamonds, their reflections shimmering in the black sheet of river beside the road. The air warmed as they descended from the pass into the valley. Snow from the recent storm had mostly melted, leaving only drifts on the shaded side of trees and boulders. Profound calm filled the forest. Numb with exhaustion, Ander allowed his mount to follow the others home.

At last they rounded the final bend in the road and the old fortress materialized out of the forest. Its tower and walls reflected in the river, making it appear more a dream than reality. Lanterns glowed by the main gate and candles flickered in windows, fragmented by the diamond-shaped panes.

They rode into the courtyard and roused a groom to attend to their horses. Skorri left to join Erik in the dormitory used by initiates while Ander and Thane trudged to the tower. It was nearly midnight and nobody was about to greet them.

"I'm too tired to bathe," Ander said as they started up the circular staircase. "Even to eat. I feel like I could sleep for a week."

Thane nodded, fatigue showing in his slow steps and drowsy eyes. He put a hand on Ander's shoulder as they reached the third floor landing. "Go on to bed," he said, pausing on the stairs. "I want to see Sorel and Nicolai first, though. They need to know what we learned, get ready for tomorrow's work."

Ander blinked slowly, feeling lightheaded, again surprised by Thane's determination. Some inner force drove the mage onward even though his body was on the verge of collapse. Ander's heart went out to him. He took a deep breath and straightened his stance. "I'll stay with you," he said. "Sleep can wait a bit longer."

Thane gazed into Ander's eyes. A gentle smile made him seem boyish. "Faithful Ander. I don't know how I'd continue without you."

"That's nothing you need fear. I'll always be at your side. You know it as well as I." He felt a quickly suppressed surge of doubt through their bond. *Lucian was faithful too, yet Thane lost him.* He gave the mage a quick hug, then took his hand and tugged him toward the corridor. "If you're determined to wake Sorel and Nicolai, let's get it done. The night deepens."

They left the staircase and entered a corridor that curved away in both directions, dimly lit by widely spaced oil lamps. The ancient stone seemed to waver before their tired eyes, but they soon arrived at the door to their friends' chambers. Thane tapped on the door. A few moments later they heard a muffled response. They took it for an invitation and entered.

Moonlight poured through a large window, and the embers of a fire still glowed in the fireplace. As with most personal chambers in the Lyceum a large round cushion covered in black leather dominated the room's center. The rest of the room reflected the lives of its occupants. Half the chamber was kept empty for Nicolai's exercises. While the athletic blond no longer needed to make a living as an acrobat, he enjoyed the demanding stunts and was proud of his skill.

The other side of the room displayed Sorel's more inquisitive and complex disposition. Two mahogany bookcases filled with leather-bound volumes flanked a writing desk that was littered with parchments and obviously got frequent use. A man-shaped target was propped up next to the door. Several of Sorel's throwing knives protruded from its neck, heart and groin. While Sorel was a consummate lover, he was no less adept as a fighter.

Sorel and Nicolai lay together on the black cushion. Their cocks were thick and heavy, glistening with oil; they looked as if they had only recently finished their lovemaking. Nicolai brushed thick hair from his eyes and yawned, but Sorel looked at them appraisingly, his sensual features alert. "You're back early," he observed.

Thane's expression was grim. "We came across information in Chanture. It foretells peril. There's no time to waste."

Sorel sat up, his eyes wide. "Is the Lyceum in danger?"

Thane wavered slightly, then shook his head and held up a hand. "No, not yet. Not that kind of danger. But the zamindar . . . he's getting ready . . ." He caught himself, took a deep breath. "We have to get to Fochelis. The zamindar—"

"How long have you been riding?" Sorel demanded. "You're both about to fall down."

"We're all right," Thane said, but his body belied the claim. He was swaying again and his eyelids drooped.

"Sorel's right," Ander said softly. His own fatigue made him thick-tongued. "There's nothing more we can do tonight. We should rest."

"No, there's too much to do—"

Sorel rose from the cushion and went to Thane's side. He put his hands on the mage's shoulders and looked him in the eye. "Listen, Thane. We're not in immediate danger, and you'll get nothing of value done tonight. Get some rest, or tomorrow will be wasted."

Nicolai joined them and touched Ander's hand. "Sleep with us tonight. The fire's been out in your chambers for days, it'll be cold as a tomb. You'll sleep better here."

Ander turned to Thane, agreement with Nicolai's offer plainly written in his face.

At last Thane relented. He smiled faintly and clasped Sorel's hand. "I was right to come here, though I had the wrong reason."

Sorel and Nicolai made quick work of disrobing the travelers. Soon the four of them were nestled together on the soft cushion. Ander pressed against Thane's side, an arm across his chest, with Sorel's warm body behind him. Peace swept through him and he succumbed to dreams.

The rustle of clothing roused Ander. He still held Thane against his body, but Nicolai and Sorel were already up and nearly dressed. He stretched, amazed at the soreness of his muscles. His movements jarred Thane awake as well.

Sorel looked at them and grinned. "So you're alive after all. We were beginning to wonder."

Thane groaned and rubbed his eyes. "What time is it? Why

didn't you wake us?"

Nicolai tossed a leather shirt at him from behind, neatly dropping the cold garment on Thane's bare chest. "Don't worry," the northerner said. "You're still early enough for breakfast, if you keep your hands off each other. We've sent word to Anna. She'll meet us in the dining hall in half an hour."

"We're eager to hear the news from Chanture," Sorel added. "And there've been developments here you need to know about. But first wash. The way you smell would alarm the new initiates."

"That reminds me of a story Skorri told us," Ander said. "About how you and Nicolai smelled like pine trees for a week when you tried a new oil and couldn't get it to wash off. Is it true it turned your cocks green, too?"

"I think I'll ignore that question," Sorel said with an air of affronted dignity. "There are some aspects of the art you aren't ready for yet."

Nicolai laughed and prodded Sorel out the door. "Leave them be. Who knows what else Skorri told him? You'll probably be happier not knowing."

Ander and Thane dressed quickly, then went to the washrooms beneath the tower. Hot water and fragrant soaps were an intoxicating luxury after the rigors of the journey, but they didn't linger. They bathed and dressed again, barely making it to the dining hall across the courtyard within the half hour Sorel had specified.

Anna had already arrived. She sat with Sorel and Nicolai at a table near the huge fireplace at the hall's far end. A dozen or so initiates still were at their meals. The smell of baking bread and cooking ham made Ander's stomach rumble. He was suddenly ravenous. They took seats next to Nicolai.

Anna had already completed her meal. She leaned forward, her elbows planted on the tabletop. Despite her gray hair she radiated vitality. She looked at Thane and Ander, shaking her head in disbelief. "Eighteen hours in the saddle and you're already recovered. I wish I had stopped aging as young as you two."

Thane grinned back at her. "What do you mean, young? Ander's an old man of twenty."

Anna snorted, then straightened her back. "Nineteen or twenty, you're both too frisky for my taste. But it's probably lucky you're so durable. You're going to need it." Their breakfasts were served, and Anna poured herself more tea while they started eating. "Repairs to the greenhouse haven't gone well," she said. "There are unexpected problems."

Thane looked up from his plate, his eyes questioning.

"It's the weather," Sorel explained. "We've always made glass in the courtyard, during the summer. That doesn't work in the winter. Every time we pour out a sheet, it shatters as it cools. We're having to convert one of the stables into a workshop, which takes time. And we're having trouble finding enough dry fuel for the fires. We have to make a *lot* of glass."

The mage pondered the report, then put down his fork and shook his head. "Maybe it doesn't matter. When we were visiting Lord Tolmin, we learned the zamindar is preparing something in Fochelis. Maybe he had enough crystals to rebuild the Leech without the crystals we hid in Pella. We don't have time to reestablish the gardens, Sorel. We have to go to Fochelis and stop him *now*."

Silence descended as the news sank in. Ander glanced around the table. Anna and Nicolai looked shocked, but Sorel wore his calculating look. The sultry youth looked surprisingly mature when he turned his mind to political matters. "What exactly did you learn?" he asked.

Ander and Thane took turns recounting the visit with Lord Tolmin and the contents of his letter from Ossia. By the time they finished their meal, the tale was told and Thane was stiff with anxiety.

"We don't know exactly when it will happen," Thane concluded. "But it will be soon. All we can do is go to Fochelis and try to find an opportunity. If we're fast enough, maybe we can take the zamindar by surprise."

Sorel tapped his fingers on the table, his expression thoughtful. "We took him by surprise once. If you were the zamindar, what would you learn from that experience?"

Thane looked up sharply. "I'm *not* the zamindar. He's a bloodthirsty madman."

Sorel shook his head sadly. "Bloodthirsty, yes. But mad? He's no more mad than most men, Thane. He's only smarter, stronger and more ruthless."

"What are you saying?" Thane asked, incredulous. "You know everything he's done!"

"I'm not defending him. I'm only saying that he's managed to control the kingdom for twenty years because he's no fool. In fact, he's probably the most devious bastard alive. That's why I don't take anything he does at face value."

Thane looked exasperated. "We saw the letter ourselves, Sorel! It was stolen from an imperial messenger, and was written in a tongue almost nobody could read."

Ander shifted uncomfortably. Thane was raising his voice, and all the initiates still in the dining hall were turning to look. He could see by the bunched muscles in Thane's shoulders that the mage had no patience for this argument, and he remembered Thane's desperate urgency the day before. But Sorel had staked his ground and wasn't about to retreat.

"The letter only makes me more suspicious," Sorel argued. "If it's such a rare language, why did it fall into Lord Tolmin's hands? He's one of the few people in the kingdom who'd be able to decipher it. And for an imperial messenger to get drunk and allow himself to be robbed in a tavern? Too many coincidences, Thane. Especially where the zamindar is involved."

Thane's clenched fists banged down on the table. "DAMN IT, Sorel! What would you have us do? Sit here by a warm fire while the zamindar seizes the kei?" Anger burned in his eyes, anger tinged with hurt.

Sorel surged to his feet, tight lipped. He glared at Thane a few seconds, then turned and stalked toward the door at the other end of the hall. The dozen initiates still at breakfast watched, silent and wide-eyed. Skorri and Erik were just entering the room as Sorel left. They looked at each other in bewilderment as the youth stormed past without a word.

Nicolai groaned softly, while Ander blinked in stunned silence. He let out his breath slowly, not realizing until then that he had been holding it. Pain and confusion flowing from Thane through their bond had hit him like a fist in the stomach.

Anna pushed back from the table. "I'll speak with him," she said. The cold tone of her voice felt like a lash.

Thane turned his back to the dining hall and faced the fire, lowering his head and staring at the floor. His aching frustration must have touched everyone who shared even a shred of bond with him.

Ander reached toward Thane, but Nicolai caught his hand. He turned, saw the suffering in Nicolai's eyes. The northerner shook his head slightly and gestured for Ander to follow him.

Ander was torn. Thane's turmoil was overwhelming, but Nicolai had known the mage for years. Uncertain whether his efforts would help or only fuel his lover's anger, Ander decided to trust the northerner's judgment. He nodded, then followed Nicolai from the room. Thane remained motionless as they left.

They left the dining hall and emerged into the crisp air of the courtyard. Nicolai put an arm around Ander's shoulders and gave him a gentle squeeze. "He's been so much happier since you got here," he said. "I had hoped this wouldn't happen again."

Ander's eyes were wet with tears. He rubbed at them angrily. "What's wrong with him, Nicolai? He usually listens to Sorel's counsel."

Nicolai removed his arm from Ander's shoulder. They started walking toward the gate leading to the greenhouse. "It's not Sorel he's angry with," he said. "It's himself. He feels powerless and threatened." The northerner paused, the sadness in his face nearly enough to bring back Ander's tears. When he spoke again his voice was soft as the wind. "It's the way he felt when the zamindar captured Lucian. He was powerless to stop the torture, and believed he was responsible. He nearly went mad with grief, Ander. And now he fears it's going to happen again."

The words were chilling. Ander knew the wound left by Lucian's death was deep. He had often suspected that Thane's relentless energy was a desperate attempt to divert his mind from grief that still tore at him.

"How can we help him?" Ander whispered.

"First, we have to give him time. He can't be comforted when he's in such pain. All he can hear right now are the cries in his memories."

"What of Sorel? I think Thane hurt him."

Nicolai snorted. "Sorel's got a temper, but he loves Thane as much as the rest of us. And he knows the argument's true cause. He'll cool quickly." A smile tugged at his lips. "In truth, he's probably already looking forward to making up with Thane. Those two glow like the sun when they put their minds to pleasuring each other."

They arrived at the wrecked greenhouse. Slush and mud covered the ground. Most of the building's framework had already been rebuilt with massive timbers, though the beams lacked the smooth finish and intricate carvings the old framework had displayed. Half a dozen initiates were already at work on the framing. Worst of all were the empty beds where only a few days ago lush gardens had bloomed.

Nicolai pointed to a corner of the structure. "See those bamboo poles at each corner? They're hollowed out. Katy has them connected to a hot spring in the basement. We'll be able to run warm water over the roof to keep the snow off, until it's safe to use weather spells again."

There was regret in Nicolai's voice. It was clear he didn't expect the threat from the zamindar's sorcerers to be eliminated anytime soon.

"Can I help?" Ander asked. "I'm pretty good with hammer and saw."

"That's nearly done. The big job now is finding enough dry wood to make the glass." He pointed to a trail on the clearing's far side. "Check out that way, toward the ravine. Look for fallen trees and mark where they are. We'll send out teams with horses later in the day to bring in the logs."

"Shouldn't I stay closer? What if Thane needs me?"

Nicolai slapped him on the back. "You're already helping him, by letting him work this out by himself. You're barely past nineteen yourself. You know what it's like when you can't help feeling bad and everybody tells you to stop it."

Ander smiled ruefully. "All right, I'm convinced. I'll come back around noon." He hiked across the clearing while Nicolai went to work with the carpenters.

The forest along the trail had already been thoroughly scoured for firewood. He decided to leave the trail and hike west, using the sun to reckon direction. In only a quarter of an hour he found the first fallen tree. He marked the location and continued westward.

In the next two hours he found two dozen more fallen trees. But the shady forest was cold and depressing. A clearing beckoned to his right, bright sun reflecting off rocks and snow drifts. *A few minutes won't do any harm. Just until I warm up.* He turned toward the light.

A dazzling vista emerged as he left the forest. A ravine fell away to the left, billowing with mist rising from frothy cataracts. Snowbanks filled the clearing except where boulders made islands in the sea of whiteness. Sun and wind had created rippled patterns in the snow, like breakers rolling onto an ocean shore.

Ander entered the clearing and climbed onto a sun-warmed rock. He squinted at the brilliant points of light reflecting off rippling drifts, marveling at the scene's pristine beauty, then surveyed the forest around the edge of the clearing. Two fallen trees were visible within fifty feet of where he sat. He shielded his eyes, trying to block the glare, and peered deeper into the surrounding trees. His stomach began to flutter. Disorientation, similar to dreamsmoke but less severe, made him close his eyes for a moment. When he opened them again he saw what appeared to be a stump that he hadn't noticed before.

It moved.

For a heartbeat he sat motionless. *Bandits? Wolves?* Then his reactions took over. He rolled off the rock without getting to his

140

feet, landing on all fours in two feet of snow. A quick scramble and he was behind the boulder. His heart hammered in his ears, every nerve straining. He silently cursed himself for venturing into the forest without a weapon.

A minute passed without a sound other than wind whispering through pine boughs. Goose bumps rose on his neck as he tensed for an attack. But instead of an arrow or a lunging wolf, he staggered under another wave of disorientation. Moving as if under compulsion, every muscle tight, he cautiously peered around the boulder. At first he couldn't see into the forest's shadows. Then a flicker of motion caught his eye.

Rippling light, reflected from the textured snowbanks, shimmered and coalesced into the figure of a naked youth: lithe but strong, tawny skinned, with thick black hair flowing down his back. The figure turned and looked toward Ander, slanted eyes lending an eastern cast to princely features.

Lucian! He had seen the ethereal remnants of Thane's first love only once before, in a shrine high in the hills above the Lyceum. Composed of echoes and fragments of anima left in the kei when Lucian and Thane had explored the magical realm, the ghost could barely manifest itself in the physical world. Only Thane's love, and the longing that still burned in the mage ten years after the death of Lucian's body, prevented the ghost from dissipating into the kei.

Ander stumbled to his feet and faced the ghost. Even as a shade, Lucian's beauty was remarkable. Thane claimed that Ander resembled him, but Ander found it hard to believe.

The ghost raised an arm in greeting. The spectacle of a nude youth in the winter forest, oblivious to the cold, added to the dreamlike feel of the encounter. Ander plowed forward through deep snow. As he reached the edge of the clearing a feeling of rapport began to develop. Before long he felt the gentle touch of Lucian's mind. But this time the mental contact tingled with urgency.

"What? Did you—" Ander stopped and blinked, trying to make sense of the sudden whispering inside his head. Desperation, that much was clear. But the words were indistinct. A hundred questions flooded his mind.

He opened his mouth to speak. Lucian held up a hand and shook his head vigorously. Then he steepled his fingers, his thumbs linked, centering his hands over his heart. Ander recognized the gesture; the space between Lucian's hands was shaped like a candle's flame. Then he remembered. Leif had once explained the eastern paths to enlightenment his grandmother practiced. *Calm air lets the candle burn, allows the light to shine. Clear the mind and illumination will blossom.* Though he was filled with questions, he forced himself to remain still.

Lucian gazed at him somberly. As Ander's breathing slowed, the ghost's form solidified. He could have been flesh and blood but for the faint golden aura surrounding his lean body. The tide of questions dropped and left a calm pool in Ander's mind. Lucian nodded approvingly, and Ander again felt the feathery touch of the spirit's mind.

"We must be quick. There is danger, and I am weakened."

"I know! Something soon in Fochelis, we saw—"

Lucian's eyes narrowed to slits, his expression pained. He held up a hand to stop Ander's outburst. "I was dreaming, but Thane's pain wakened me. I saw what was in his mind. He's wrong, Ander! Be still and listen!"

Renewed questions clamored, and Lucian's form began to waver. Ander reached forward desperately, his hand passing through the ghost's shoulder. A ripple of strangeness passed over his skin and Lucian vanished in a blink. Aghast, he stumbled backward and fell in the snow. He burned with disappointment.

As he got to his feet the air around him shimmered like a golden curtain rippling in a gentle breeze. Lucian rematerialized, less solid than before. Ander could see the faint outline of trees and branches through the ghost's torso. His hands were pressed to his head and his eyes were closed.

"Deception, Ander. Treachery. Pella, not Fochelis! Danger in the kei. You must tell Thane."

Ander hesitated, fearful that anything he did would make Lucian vanish again, perhaps permanently.

The exotic youth opened his eyes and gave Ander an entreating gaze. "I'm just a shadow, but I still love him. Yet he mustn't know I exist. He carries too much grief already. Love him for me, Ander. Give him peace. Only then can I rest." Lucian's yearning could be felt even more clearly than his words could be heard. Tears glistened on the ghost's cheeks.

Ander was dumbfounded. He had never imagined that ghosts could cry. "I *do* love him," he whispered.

Lucian reached toward Ander, achingly beautiful and sad. Suddenly the world was bathed red. Lucian's expression turned to agony, torment that Ander felt as intensely as a white-hot brand. Then Lucian vanished and the pain cut off as if severed by a knife. The red haze disappeared at the same instant.

Ander's feet felt like they were frozen to the ground, and he began to shiver; whether from cold or from reaction to Lucian's agonizing disappearance he couldn't tell. He could sense the ghost wouldn't be coming back. The clearing felt cold and empty. He turned and headed for the trail to the Lyceum.

Lucian's guidance posed more problems than it solved. The ghost clearly shared Sorel's doubts about the role Fochelis played in the zamindar's plans. But Ander didn't see how the information could be used. Thane wasn't likely to abandon his plans based on Ander's mere suggestion, especially when he couldn't even reveal why he was making the suggestion. Things seemed to be falling apart and he couldn't see a way to stop it. Then a new thought made him stop in his tracks. *Should I tell Thane about Lucian's shade? But what if the knowledge renews his grief, as Lucian fears?* A desperate gamble, but nevertheless a chance. He resumed walking, wondering if it was a gamble he dared take.

Should I ask Nicolai and Sorel what they think? They'd keep the secret, if asked. It was tempting, but he remembered Lady Tayanita's cynical advice about secrets: it's possible for as many as three people to keep a secret, provided that two of them are dead.

Distracted by the dilemma, Ander found himself back at the Lyceum no closer to a solution than when he had left the clearing. Still uncertain what to do, he went looking for Thane. A few inquiries led him to the workroom at the top of the castle's tower. He found the mage leaning on a trestle table with his head bowed, poking morosely through a pile of crystals.

Thane looked up and blushed as Ander crossed the chamber. "I'm sorry," he said. "I'm a fool. There's no excuse for hurting my friends. It shames me."

Ander put an arm around Thane's waist. "I think they understand. Have you spoken with Sorel since breakfast?"

The mage returned Ander's squeeze, pulling him tight. "An hour ago."

"Is he all right now?"

"We shared a mug of mulled cider and talked. Then Nicolai came in, all cold from working on the greenhouse, and coaxed us into a tumble. We just finished a few minutes ago." He smiled faintly. "Nothing brings out the comradeship in Sorel faster than passion."

Ander glanced at the crystals Thane had been examining. They were the same stones he had been experimenting with as a remedy for his impairment. *Poor Thane. He must still be blind to magical bonds.* He tightened his hug. The young mage took a deep breath and rested his head on Ander's shoulder.

143

How do I persuade him not to go to Fochelis? He stood still for several seconds, cradling his lover's strong body, reluctant to re-open the subject that had sparked Thane's argument with Sorel. But there was no avoiding the problem, and delay would only make it harder.

"Thane, when you spoke with Sorel, did—"

The workroom's door flew open, swinging through its arc to crash against the chamber's stone wall. Ander and Thane sprang apart and spun to face the door. But the frenzied figure in the door-way was only Katy, her unruly hair even more wild than usual.

"You've got to come down to the library! A boy just arrived from Pella, says he needs to see both of you. *Now.*"

"Did he give his name?" Ander asked, his heart pounding.

Katy wrinkled her nose while she searched her memory, remind-ing Ander of an otter. In two seconds she nodded decisively. "Leif."

Thane was already out the door. Ander followed, filled with dread.

12

THEY FOUND Leif in the library, slumped on a sofa facing the fire. Sorel knelt at his side and held a cup to his lips, but Leif's head lolled forward as if he was drunk. His skin, usually honey brown, was pale and tinged blue. Ander slid onto the sofa next to him. The young blond blinked at him and reached out with a clumsy hand. "I came as fast as I could. Rode all night . . ." Ander grasped the wavering hand; it was ice cold. Leif's riding leathers were wet and stiff.

"He practically fell off his horse," Katy offered. "And then he couldn't stand by himself. Sorel had to carry him in."

"You're right to warm him," Ander said. "He's numb from cold. But a fire isn't the best way. One of the companions at Lady Tayanita's house knew healing. He says a warm bath works best." He glanced at Thane, who had been trying to warm Leif's other hand between his own. "The baths beneath the tower would be best. Do you know if anybody is using them?"

Thane released Leif's hand and sprang to his feet. "I'll look. If anybody's there I'll clear them out." He turned and loped out of the room.

"Help me lift him," Ander asked Sorel. They put their hands beneath Leif's arms and carefully lifted him. Between the two of them, the boy seemed to weigh almost nothing. They draped his arms over their shoulders, then carried him out of the library and down the circular staircase. Katy followed until they reached the arched threshold to the men's chambers beneath the tower. Not even Katy would violate the injunction against entering an area reserved for the other gender's magical practices.

Ander supported Leif while Sorel swung the thick door shut. They crossed an antechamber, then entered the vaulted room containing the men's ritual baths. Thane was closing a valve that allowed water from a hot spring to flow into the uppermost of the three terraced pools. As the flow was cut off the waterfalls between the pools slowed to a trickle. Leif looked around in a daze. The marble-lined chamber was lit only by an oil lamp in a corner, and it felt like a humid summer night. They eased him onto a bench. Sorel knelt and began removing Leif's boots while Ander peeled his shirt off. The leather, thick and lined with fleece, was soaked inside and out. Ander dropped the garment and put his hands on Leif's shoulders. The youth's eyes were nearly closed, his breathing raspy.

"Listen, Leif. Remember what Alred said when he told us about snowchill? It might hurt when your feeling starts to come back." He shook his friend gently, trying to focus his attention. "Do you understand? Are you ready?"

Leif licked his lips. "Need to talk, Ander. Important."

"We'll talk later. First we have to get the chill out of your bones." He slipped his arms under Leif's armpits and lifted him. Sorel unfastened Leif's belt and the leather trousers slid off. Ander carried him across the chamber and up the short flight of stairs to the middle pool where Thane waited.

"I'll hold him while you get your clothes off," Thane said. The mage was already nude. He lifted Leif out of Ander's arms.

Ander surrendered his burden, then quickly stripped and turned to help Thane. Stepping carefully, they carried Leif into the warm water. One end of the pool, where water fell from above in a broad sheet when the inlet valve was open, was only ankle deep. Steps beneath the water led to greater depths. At the pool's middle, one could sit comfortably in water that rose to the middle of a man's chest. Ander sat with his back against the pool's side, then Thane eased Leif down to recline against him. Ander cradled his friend so he was submerged in water up to his neck, the long braid of his ponytail floating on the dark water like a golden serpent. Thane settled next to Ander, and Sorel sat against the pool's opposite side.

"We might as well get him clean," Thane suggested. He and Sorel scooped soft soap from a niche, and Ander supported Leif's body so it floated just beneath the water's surface. Thane spread the soap over Leif's chest while Sorel lathered the boy's smoothly muscled abdomen. Eucalyptus fragrance filled the air.

The warm water and gentle stimulation roused Leif from his stupor. His eyes opened, registering surprise as he became aware of the palatial surroundings and the handsome youths bathing him.

"Just relax," Ander said, noticing his friend stirring. "Let us take care of you. You're going to be all right. Now, tell us why you came."

Leif nodded, though his eyes were still sleepy. "Remember Pavol? The guard I've been seeing the past few months? The boy with plowhorse shoulders and a grin like a puppy?"

"I remember. Your only customer who's in the guard. I've never seen a boy so enamored of a companion."

Leif smiled. "It wasn't hard. His family strictly follows the doctrines of Yataghan. Sex for pleasure was a revelation to Pavol. And besides, he's truly a kind boy. It's not his fault his father indentured him to a military crony."

"You learned something from him?" Thane asked, his soapy hand barely moving along Leif's chest.

Leif nodded. "We spend a lot of time talking before sex. He likes to cuddle."

Ander gave Leif a squeeze. "I know better. *You* like to cuddle, and make your partners pant with lust before even touching their cocks."

Leif's dark eyes opened wider and sparkled, animation starting to return to his features. "Well, it works, doesn't it? Pavol gets slick from tip to root before I even touch him below the waist. Makes him far more tasty."

Sorel chuckled softly, deep in his chest. "I'm starting to believe the stories Ander tells about you. What did this Pavol have to say?"

"I'm sorry, my mind wanders when I'm sleepy. First, even before Pavol's gossip, some new sorcerers appeared. They showed up a few days ago. They've been standing in the marketplace all day, holding silver orbs. The townspeople are terrified, think they're picking victims for new tortures. But I don't think so."

"Why not?" Sorel asked. He began unbraiding Leif's ponytail in preparation for washing the luxuriant hair.

"For one thing, they don't seem interested in the townspeople. Their eyes never leave the orbs." Consternation pulled Leif's eyebrows downward. "It's like they're searching for something and expect to see it in the orb. Some people think they're trying to find travelers carrying gold. But I don't know why the zamindar would do that. He can always raise taxes if he wants more gold."

"You're right," Thane said, frowning. "I'd guess they're searching for the crystals Nicolai and I took."

Sorel finished unbraiding Leif's hair and started working soap through the golden strands. "Let's hear what else he knows. Maybe there's a pattern that will help us understand."

Leif yawned. Warm water, combined with exhaustion from his ride, were taking their toll.

"Can you tell us more?" Ander asked. "Or do you need to rest?"

Another yawn, even bigger than the last, then Leif shook his head. "There's more. Pavol said discipline is so strict, he could barely get a single night off duty. *All* leaves are canceled beginning next month. They've been told there will be patrols all day and night. Guards on the guards. Whippings for the slightest infraction."

Ander stiffened. *Lucian was right! Whatever's happening will be in Pella!* His arms clasped tightly around Leif, bringing a sur-

147

prised grunt from the young blond. Excitement at the confirmation of the ghost's warning made him shiver.

"Pella's a backwater," Ander said. "There's never been anything like this before. I think Sorel's right about Lord Tolmin's letter being a diversion. The zamindar wants his enemies in Fochelis, while he does something in Pella."

Thane looked baffled by the outburst. Ander blushed, but didn't retract his statement. His discomfort grew as silence stretched, but he didn't explain the real reason for his conviction.

Sorel watched both of them with unblinking attention. His sensual beauty often led people to assume he possessed a shallow mind, but Ander knew better. Before being disowned by his merchant father, Sorel had observed negotiations with some of the wiliest men in the kingdom. He had a keen understanding of people and their use of words, and could sense deception like a cat smells a mouse.

Ander forced himself to relax. He shrugged slightly and returned Thane's gaze. "I grew up in Pella. Believe me, this is remarkable. That's why Leif rode all night to tell us about it."

"It does fit together," Sorel agreed. "The sorcerers' orbs make me especially curious. It's as if they're trying to tighten both military *and* magical protections around Pella."

"A new convoy with crystals might be arriving in Pella soon," Thane guessed. "After losing the last set, they'd want to make sure it doesn't happen again."

Ander chewed his lip, forgetting to hold Leif up. The blond's body settled gently, leaving only his head and shoulders above the water. His long hair floated on the surface of the water following the curve of Ander's chest.

"Where do we go, then?" Ander asked. "Pella, or Fochelis?"

They mulled the dilemma, pondering the disastrous consequences if they chose wrongly. Unexpectedly, it was Leif who broke the silence. He spoke softly, without opening his eyes.

"One more thing. Lady Tay's influential customers have been keeping their mouths shut. But one had too much to drink, and babbled about gaining imperial favor. Lady Tay wanted me to tell you. She thinks the zamindar himself is coming to Pella."

Lady Tayanita's opinion was enough to tilt the balance. "We'll go to Pella," Thane said. "I'll ask Anna to investigate in Fochelis."

Relief swept Ander. Thane had made the right choice, and the secret of Lucian's existence still held. As his anxiety dissipated, his attention returned to Leif, who seemed to have fallen asleep in his arms. He tightened his hug. "How are you feeling?" he asked softly.

Leif's eyes opened to slits. "The chill is gone. There's no pain. Alred said that means there's no frostbite. I just need to sleep now."

Thane leaned over Leif and kissed him gently on the cheek. "Welcome to the Lyceum. I'm sorry your arrival was so painful. We'll make it up to you after you've rested."

Leif gave Thane a tired smile. "I hope I can return your gift in kind."

Ander stood, lifting Leif with him. "You're going to like it here," he predicted. "But first you're going to rest." Leif didn't argue. He started nodding off as they dried him. They wrapped him in a warm robe, then took him upstairs and laid him on the leather cushion in Thane and Ander's room. Sorel fed the banked fire in the hearth while Ander covered his friend with a quilt.

"Rest as long as you need," Ander said, brushing hair from his friend's eyes. "One of us will wake you when it's time to eat."

Leif nodded, his eyes nearly shut. He was asleep before Ander's hand completed its caress. They left him to his slumber, closing the door softly.

13

THANE SAT motionless, surveying the gray city and nearby encampment with foreboding. Rain beaded on the heavy gray wool of his cloak. Ander, Sorel, Nicolai and Leif waited in the woods behind him. Long before they sighted Pella, they had known something was wrong. Even Leif could sense the edgy tension in the air.

Finally he turned his horse to the shelter of the forest canopy. As soon as he was among the trees he threw back his hood. Cool spring rain soaked his short brown hair and ran down his face, unnoticed.

"You and Ander were right," he told Sorel. "He's here. There's an encampment near the east gates. It's hard to see in this rain, but there's a tent flying the imperial pennant. And the stench we smell in the kei must be coming from the zamindar's personal sorcerers. It's far too strong to be the product of some backwoods wizard."

Ander pushed back his hood and met Thane's eye. "Are we too late? Does this corruption in the kei mean the zamindar has already succeeded?"

Thane's eyebrows pulled down. "Maybe. But there's no way to tell from here. We'll have to go into the city."

The anxiety in his friends' eyes did nothing to bolster Thane's confidence, but he held himself straight and pulled his hood back over his head. He turned his horse toward Pella and led them out of the forest.

They approached from the west, the side opposite the zamindar's encampment. The rain tapered off as they descended from the foothills, but the air thickened with a cloying tension. Thane recognized it as the stench of blood magic. They rode into the city without being challenged, though the guard at the gate was double its normal size.

Once inside the city walls they breathed easier. The streets bustled with merchants, children, animals, the usual noise and pungent scents of a rough city. Though the zamindar's guards and sorcerers kept a tight grip on order, the imperial visit had clearly been good for business.

When they reached a wider avenue, Ander came abreast of Thane. "It's strange. It doesn't *feel* like Pella."

"The kei is thick with spells," Thane agreed. "You saw the sorcerer above the gate?"

Ander nodded, his nose crinkling with distaste. A cascade of hair, unruly after their long ride, fell over his eyes. Thane felt a pang. *He's too young for this danger. Hardly older than Lucian was.* But he knew that Ander, like Lucian, would have refused to stay behind.

"We'll have to be cautious," Thane continued. "Any use of the kei is sure to be detected."

"Then we'll stop them without using magic," Ander said, absently brushing hair out of his eyes. "You'll find a way. You've beaten the zamindar before. You can do it again."

Thane looked away, his face burning. *Am I being a fool? Am I betraying them, leading them in a hopeless cause?* Doubts tormented him, but he concealed them with fierce determination. They were committed, and his friends had faced danger courageously many times before. Still, his lack of a plan made the desperate mission seem foolhardy.

The zamindar's personal guard grew more conspicuous. Worse, even though they avoided the marketplace where the zamindar's sorcerers had stationed themselves, a nagging sense of being observed strengthened as they rode deeper into the city. Thane brought them to a halt before they entered the gaudy precinct where Lady Tayanita's House of Companionship and Refreshment stood.

"I don't like it," he told Ander. "It's been bad ever since we passed through the gates. But around here it's enough to make you gag. Someone's watching the kei."

"I feel it too," Ander agreed. "Like a cat ready to pounce."

Thane made an abrupt decision. "It's too dangerous here. We'll find somewhere they're not watching as closely. We'll contact Lady Tayanita when it's safer."

"It might even be Lady Tayanita they're watching," Sorel said. "She's been arrested before, on suspicion of treason."

"Where do we go, then?" Nicolai asked. He glanced around cautiously. "We'd best not linger in the street."

"I know an inn that's not too far," Leif suggested. "It's popular with husbands cheating on their wives. The innkeeper asks no questions, pretends to be blind. Everyone knows better, so they don't try to cheat him, but they're grateful for the fiction."

Thane nodded. "Lead the way."

Leif took them around the long way to avoid the marketplace. But with the zamindar's entourage in town, even the side streets were crowded. Men and women dressed in rich robes, many of them accompanied by personal guards, pushed their way through the more plainly dressed natives. Thane kept as much distance as he could from the visiting aristocrats. The cruelty of their expressions, the arrogance of their demeanor, fueled an anger he knew he couldn't afford.

They soon reached the inn. "Remember, pretend like he's blind," Leif said as they unsaddled their horses in a stable near the inn. They left their mounts in the care of an ostler, then threw their saddlebags over their shoulders and crossed the narrow street.

Leif opened an unmarked door and they entered a dimly lit dining room. As Leif had said, the inn and its customers put a premium on discretion. The few couples in the room, whispering over tankards of ale, didn't even look up as Thane and his wet companions walked across the room to stand near the fire. A few moments later a slender middle-aged man emerged from the kitchen. He traversed the room without difficulty, though his eyes were closed.

"Greeting, Sergi," Leif said. "I hope you're well."

The man bowed. "Leif. Welcome." He cocked his head sideways, as if listening. "You've brought many friends today. Four? How can I serve you?"

"We'll be needing a room," Leif answered. "How about the one with the enormous bed? Is it available?"

"Fortune smiles on you," Sergi said. "The room's empty." A sly smile played about his lips. "Your popularity grows too great for the beds at Lady Tayanita's house."

"We'll go on upstairs, then. We've been traveling and need to get dry."

"I'm honored to serve you," the innkeeper said with a small bow. "It's good to hear you again, Leif."

Leif touched him lightly on the arm, then picked up his saddlebag. "I'll show them the way," he said. Sergi nodded and returned to the kitchen. Leif led the way up a narrow staircase to the second floor. A hallway provided access to a series of rooms. He opened the door nearest the stairs.

Wavy glass panels filled two small windows, admitting silvery light. Plaster walls were painted a rosy gold, and a fire burned in the small hearth. One object dominated the chamber: a massive bed, covered with blankets and furs, occupied more than half the room's space. It could accommodate all five of them, albeit snugly.

Thane dropped his saddlebags and sank onto the mattress. "I see why you favor this room," he said. "Do you often need this much space?"

Leif grinned. "There's a pair of boys who're fond of me. Handsome twins with hair gold as the sun. Their father visits the ladies at Lady Tayanita's. They don't want him to know they're lovers, so we come here instead. Sergi has an arrangement with Lady Tayanita."

Sorel put a hand on Leif's shoulder. "Now you've done it. You've given Thane a new idea. We've never tested twins before. They'd likely have deep rapport, and make exceptional mages."

"I should have thought of it before," Thane mused. Then he took a deep breath and shook his head. "It'll have to wait. Sorel, Nicolai, see what you can learn about the zamindar's encampment. Numbers, guards, patrols, whatever you can learn. The rest of us will try to find out *why* they're here."

Nicolai looked at the huge bed and sighed. "A pity we can't try out the furniture first. It looks so comfortable."

"Don't worry," Thane assured him. "We'll wait till you're back. This bed is big enough for acrobatics, and you're the best of us at that. I think Leif will be amazed."

Nicolai grinned. "Then Sorel and I will be quick. Meet here for dinner?"

Sorel slapped his partner on the back. "Dinner it is. Come on, beast. We'd best leave before your cock gets hard and all your thoughts turn to love."

"Wise counsel," Thane agreed. "I think Ander and I should start our search as well." He turned to Leif. "Do you want to come with us? Or do you think your friend Sergi might have news he'd be willing to share?"

"I might as well start with Sergi," Leif decided. "I can help him in the kitchen. He'll tell me whatever he knows, as long as it doesn't involve his customers."

"Good. Until dinner, then."

The sun was still an hour from the horizon when Thane and Ander returned to the inn, cold and weary. They entered the dining room and found Leif sitting at a table in the back. The young blond clearly retained the innkeeper's favor; the table held a pitcher of hot mulled wine, five glasses, and a platter of bread and sliced meats.

"Have you seen Sorel and Nicolai?" Thane asked. He settled onto a bench and poured wine for Ander and himself.

"Not yet," Leif said. "But it's still early. They're probably waiting to see when the patrols are relieved."

"Did you have any luck with Sergi?" Thane picked up a slice of baked ham. He was ravenous, but forced himself to eat slowly.

"More than I expected," Leif replied. "He seemed relieved to find someone to talk with. He's worried."

"We noticed the same thing," Ander said. "There's a lot of muttering in the plazas, people whispering in the wellhouses. Everyone was cautious, though. I didn't see anybody I know, and nobody wanted to talk with strangers."

Leif drank some wine, then put his glass down. "No wonder. Sergi says twenty of Pella's foremost citizens are being held in the zamindar's camp. He calls them guests, but everybody knows they're hostages. Their lives are forfeit if anybody starts trouble. And did you hear about the sorcerers walking the streets at night?"

Thane's appetite disappeared. "No. What did you hear?"

"They've started barring the city gates at night, as if we were at war. Once the gates are closed the sorcerers start walking the streets. Each has a guard, and each carries one of those silver orbs I told you about."

Ander stopped eating as well. "That's all? They just walk around?"

"Sergi says they stare at their orbs like they're in a trance. The guards have to clear the road, otherwise the sorcerers would stumble over anything in their path."

"They're searching," Thane said. "They've probably been hoping somebody would try selling the crystals in the bazaar."

Ander nodded. "That's where a thief would go to find a buyer. The sorcerers haven't found the crystals there, so now they're starting to search the rest of the city."

Thane frowned. "You could be right. But the crystals were in a shielded box, the sorcerers must know that. What if they're doing something else entirely? Something in preparation for whatever the zamindar has planned?"

Ander shrugged. "I admit I'm just guessing. There's no way to know."

"Perhaps there is," Thane said. "If I get close enough to one of those orbs, I might be able to feel what it's doing to the kei."

Ander put a hand on Thane's forearm. He didn't say anything, but Thane saw the entreaty in his eyes. He put his hand on top of Ander's. "Don't worry, I won't interfere. Just watch and learn. Besides, we don't have much choice. We have to do *something*." He turned to Leif. "Do you know what streets they'll be on tonight? Do they follow a pattern?"

"Sergi said they start from the city's gates and walk all the main avenues. Even some of the back streets and alleys. If you're near a gate around sunset, you'll see one."

154

Thane straightened, looking determined. "There's no time to waste, then. It's nearly dusk. Where's the closest gate?"

Leif looked smug. "The Minstrel's Gate. We could be there before dark. And I've got a lair there, on a balcony overlooking a garden. Pavol and I sometimes meet there for a quick tumble when he can't get off duty. There's even a key to the garden, hidden behind a loose rock in the wall."

Ander rolled his eyes. "You're incorrigible, Leif. You climb into a *balcony*, near the gate, to fuck with on-duty guards? Does Pavol like danger?"

"It's not so dangerous," Leif said airily. "The garden's overgrown, and the doors from the house to the balcony are boarded up. It's old Lady Trygvesson's mansion. I doubt she's even opened the curtains for ten years."

"Perfect!" Thane pushed back from the table. "We should leave now."

Ander sighed, resigned. "I know I can't talk you out of it. You're sure we don't have time to finish eating first?"

Thane hesitated, not missing the phrasing of Ander's question. Though he didn't want to show it, Leif's plan wasn't without risk. "Ander . . . I don't think all three of us need to go. Someone should wait here for Sorel and Nicolai."

"Leif can do that. If he's lucky he might even talk them into a tumble."

"But Leif knows the garden, how to get to the balcony. He knows where the key is."

Ander snorted. "You can't fool me, you know. I know exactly what you're feeling. You think it's dangerous. That's all the more reason I should go with you."

Thane didn't try to deny the accusation. "Please, Ander," he said softly. "If you're with me, I'll worry for your safety. I'll need to concentrate on the kei. Worrying about you would get in the way."

Ander flinched, hearing the truth in Thane's words. After a few seconds he reluctantly nodded. "Be careful, then. I won't rest easy until your return."

Thane put an arm around his shoulders and hugged him fiercely. "Don't worry, jiri. We've been sleeping on the ground too many nights. I'm eager to have you in a warm bed again!"

Ander returned the hug, then turned to Leif. "You be careful too."

Leif raised an eyebrow. "Me? I'm *always* careful. How do you think I've kept two steps ahead of Tannis all these years?"

"Cleverness and caution aren't the same thing," Ander warned.

"And Tannis isn't the zamindar."

"True," Leif admitted, suddenly serious. "We'll take care."

Leif was polite to call this overgrown, Thane thought as he peered at the ancient garden through an iron gate. The old mansion, a stone's throw from the Minstrel's Gate, was in severe disrepair and the garden looked as though it hadn't been tended in decades. Trees had taken root in the flower beds and grown unchecked. Evening light slanted through skeletal branches.

Leif pulled a loose piece of fieldstone from the wall and retrieved a key. He opened the gate and let Thane into the gloomy garden. "Pavol keeps the hinges well oiled," he whispered. "Lady Trygvesson probably couldn't hear a thunderclap in her own bedchamber. But you never know who might be on the street."

Thane prowled deeper into the foliage, holding his cloak tight around his body, looking around warily. "We'll be able to see what the zamindar's sorcerer is doing from here? It's like a bramble patch."

Leif pointed up. "See that balcony? It's an easy climb, there are boards nailed to the oak by the wall. You can't see them from the street." His white teeth flashed briefly as he grinned. "Pavol and I aren't the only ones who sneak into this garden." He held up the key. "But we won't be disturbed. Anybody else who comes by looking for the key will know the balcony's in use. Besides, it doesn't get used much at night. Too cold."

Thane started for the tree. "Let's go, then. The sorcerer could start his rounds any time." The climb was quick and easy. Thane jumped lightly onto the balcony, landing without a sound. The balcony was only about a yard wide, but extended for ten feet. Its iron railing was covered with boards that provided a shield against both wind and prying eyes. He crouched behind the makeshift wall and saw that Leif had been right. They had a clear view of Minstrel's Gate.

Leif crouched next to him, then tugged a board a few inches to the side. "We can watch through the gap," he said. "We'll be safer that way." He grinned excitedly, obviously caught up in the adventure.

Thane crouched behind the wall, testing the view through the gap. "You're sure nobody can hear us inside the house?" he asked.

"Lady Trygvesson is frail," Leif answered as he sat beside Thane. "I doubt she ever leaves the ground floor." He shivered and looked at the darkening sky. "But then, Pavol and I never came here to talk. We never sat around in the cold, either."

"My cloak is big enough to cover both of us," Thane offered. "Would you like to share warmth?"

"That's the best proposition I've had all day," Leif said. Thane held his cloak open, and Leif nestled snugly against his front. The mage pulled the cloak around him, then let Leif hold its front edges together. He lowered his arms and wrapped them around Leif's lean midriff.

The heat of their bodies, trapped by the heavy wool cloak, soon warmed them. A few travelers still passed through the Minstrel's Gate, but the sun had already dropped below the top of the city's wall. The gate would be closing soon.

They leaned together comfortably. Thane was surprised at how quickly he had adjusted to Leif's presence. The exotic boy already seemed like an old friend. "You feel like Ander, in a way," he said. "It's a sign that you're close." He spoke softly, his lips nearly touching Leif's right ear. A faint aroma of straw and smoke lingered in the thick blond hair.

Leif nodded, almost imperceptibly. "Close, yes. Not in the same way as *you* and Ander, but still strong. He's always been my best friend. And my most intimate lover."

"He cares deeply for you, too. He trusts you completely."

Leif leaned his head against Thane's shoulder. "Ander is fiercely loyal. But you already know that, don't you? You can feel each other's thoughts?"

"Oh, yes," Thane said. "And more. When you form a bond with a lover, you can experience everything he experiences. Especially when you're using the art."

"When you're making love." Leif shivered with anticipation. "Will . . . will I have to wait long before learning how?"

Thane squeezed him and playfully tickled his ribs. "I'm sure you'll learn quickly. It won't be long before you're ready to attempt a bond. And you've got an advantage."

"My experience as a companion?"

"That helps, but your friendship with Ander is even more important. You'll bond with him more easily than with someone you don't know as well."

Leif sighed happily. "I'm glad Ander will be my first. Will I get to bond with you too, after I learn how?"

Thane chuckled softly. "I think I see where Ander got his randy mind." He moved a hand lower, to Leif's crotch. The boy's cock was hard and long. Thane pressed his hand along its length, feeling it pulse and stiffen even more under his touch. "Don't worry. I'm looking forward to teaching you the art. You're as beautiful as

Ander, in your own way."

Leif squirmed under Thane's fondling, his cock achingly hard. "Could I bond with you and Ander while the two of *you* make love? Would I feel what both of you feel? I'd like to watch and feel at the same time, if—"

Suddenly Thane leaned forward. "Look!" he whispered, his body taut. "Soldiers at the gate."

Leif released the cloak and moved aside, giving Thane a clear view. The mage moved forward and peered into the street below.

Eight soldiers had assembled inside the gate. They stood in a square formation with a space in the middle. Then another figure emerged from the shadowed gatehouse.

Air seemed to swirl around the ancient sorcerer. His red robes, the color of blood, writhed around his frail body as if alive. He held a silver orb in his wizened hands. Slowly, he lifted it until its unearthly glow lit his face with pale light. He looked like a cadaver.

It seemed to Thane that the sky darkened in a heartbeat. He felt the cold pulse of the sorcerer's blood, and a mind like a hungry crocodile's. The search party started forward.

A sharp pain stabbed at Thane's gut. He fell back, gasping and pressing his hands to his belly. He blinked, stunned.

"What is it?" Leif hissed, grabbing Thane by the shoulder. "What's wrong?"

"The kei," Thane gasped. "It's afire!" He winced again, doubling over and groaning.

"What should I do?" Leif asked urgently.

Thane crawled back to the edge of the balcony and forced himself up enough to look through the gap between boards. The patrol had stopped moving. The sorcerer, holding his orb at arm's length, slowly turned through the four points of the compass. His face, when Thane could see it, stared with feral intensity.

"I don't understand," Thane moaned. His arm jerked spasmodically, and his head throbbed. "The sorcerer is searching. But I don't know why—" His face contorted and a groan wrenched from his throat, rising in pitch as another surge of agony pierced his heart.

"*Quiet,*" Leif hissed. "They'll hear you!"

Thane leaned against the balcony railing and peered blearily through the crack. The sorcerer was facing their direction. He held the orb above his head. Golden motes danced around it like agitated fireflies. His skeletal grin was triumphant.

"He knows I'm here," Thane said. "I don't know how, but he

does." He gulped painfully, trying to force his mind to work. "Can we get into the house from here?"

"No. The doors are sealed fast. That's why this is such a safe lair."

"It's safe no longer." A loud crash made them both jump. Thane looked down and saw two guards battering the garden's gate with their shoulders. The neglected lock wouldn't hold for long. He felt as though the air were being squeezed from his lungs. "Tell the others what happened," he gasped. "Wait until you're sure everyone is gone." He sat up and unfastened the clasp that held his cloak. "Make sure Ander gets this. It contains secrets, has to be protected." He thrust the heavy garment into Leif's hands.

"What are you doing?" Leif demanded. "They'll kill you if they catch you!"

"If I stay here they'll kill both of us." There was another crash from the gate, and the groan of metal anchor pins pulling free of rock. He clutched Leif's hand, his knuckles white. "The others can help! There's no time to argue!"

Leif gave a quick nod, scowling fiercely.

Satisfied, Thane got to his feet. Pain ripped through his side; it felt like a knife was slicing him open. Struggling to stifle a scream, he climbed over the balcony railing and grabbed one of the boards nailed to the nearby oak.

The trip down the tree was torment. Each step was a blur of pain. Five feet above the ground he lost his footing and fell into a clump of weeds. He struggled to his feet, then staggered toward the far corner of the garden. At the same time the gate finally yielded to the guards with a grating screech.

Four guards charged into the garden with their swords drawn. The sorcerer remained at the gate with the other four guards, his orb still held high. He shouted three incomprehensible words and the orb pulsed with a red flash.

Thane felt as though flames engulfed him. He screamed, paralyzed with pain, as he collapsed. Within seconds the guards found him, shaking and nearly unconscious. They dragged him to the garden's gate and dropped him at the sorcerer's feet, then stepped back. The sorcerer lowered his orb and looked at Thane with undisguised glee.

"So we've finally run the fox to ground. The zamindar will be pleased." He nudged Thane with the toe of his boot, none too gently. "Whoever you are, you'll soon rue the day you were born."

Thane forced his eyes open. "It's a mistake," he managed to gasp. "I've done nothing!"

The sorcerer's sneer managed to make his sunken face even more hideous. "Lies are useless, fool. You're stained with the traces of a spell. A spell you triggered when you stole the zamindar's property."

"I have nothing," Thane moaned. "You have the wrong man."

The sorcerer grinned maliciously. "Oh, I believe you don't have the zamindar's baubles. We'd have found them by now if they were still in the city. Since we couldn't find them, we looked for whoever stole them instead. And now you'll help the zamindar get back what belongs to him."

Argument was useless, and Thane's mind and body were too abused to maintain the effort. The sorcerer uttered another spell. A searing jolt of pain coruscated through his body, followed by merciful darkness.

14

THANE SWAM up from nightmare infested darkness, pulled by his body's agony. Sharp metal bit his wrists, and his shoulders ached. He lay face down on a rug, his arms wrenched behind his back and bound by shackles. Strained muscles demanded relief but his mind, even clouded by pain and sorcery, forced his body to remain still. He heard voices.

Barely opening one eye, he peeked through his lashes. Two men stood nearby. One, a tall man with stooped shoulders, long gray beard and red robes, could only be an imperial sorcerer. It was a few moments before Thane could identify the other, even though he seemed familiar. Hard eyes, widely spaced on the round face of an overweight old man. Thin lips compressed in a frown. Rich clothes in the imperial colors of black and gold.

A rush of heat was followed by sick dread. He realized why the man was familiar. His likeness, in a highly distorted and flattering rendering, appeared on every imperial coin. Thane lay in chains at the zamindar's feet.

The zamindar spoke again, harsh and skeptical. "You're becoming an old fool, Najja. This creature can't be important. He's barely a man. He'd fetch a high price in a house of companionship, but no more. Throw him to the guards for their amusement and get back to the search."

"Your words are wise, as always," the old sorcerer said in a fawning tone. But his eyes were calculating. "Still, youth and beauty can be deceptive. He might be nineteen or twenty. Think how much *you* were capable of at that age."

The aging despot nodded thoughtfully, his eyes narrowing. "I'll grant you, he looks strong and quick enough to make a good thief. But what about the cantrip? You said your own mages couldn't survive it, even if they knew of it and prepared themselves. How could a young thief defeat the spell?"

Najja scowled, displeasure and fear mingling on his dour face. "This magic we've encountered, it's completely unlike our own sorceries. Perhaps the mages who wield it are likewise different."

The zamindar snorted. "Or perhaps your magics are getting as feeble as your mind. Don't waste your time on goose chases, old man. I won't abide another failure." The threat in the zamindar's voice was unmistakable.

The sorcerer frowned, but didn't protest. Then his eyes widened slightly. "As I said, this one is more than he seems. He's awake.

He's been listening to us." He took a step forward and whacked the end of his staff against Thane's ribs.

Thane's eyes snapped open. His jaw clenched to restrain a shout as pain shot through his chest; breath hissed sharply between his teeth. He struggled into a seated position.

They were in a vast tent, lit by flickering oil lamps. In a glance he saw painted silks hung as shimmering curtains, ebony chairs and tables inlaid with gold, tightly woven rugs of incredible detail. But the luxurious tent held no interest. His gaze fixed on the zamindar as sudden rage made his heart pound. *Lucian's murderer. The butcher.* Years of grief and burning anger clamored in his mind. To find himself in chains when he finally confronted his enemy left him shaking.

"Doesn't look like much of a menace to me," the zamindar said. "You caught him by one of Pella's gates, you say? What was he doing?"

The sorcerer lashed out with his staff again, thumping Thane on the upper arm. "You heard the question! You'd best not hold your tongue, if you want to keep it in your head!"

The bruising blow cleared Thane's mind. His encounter with the zamindar was perilously close to being short, and fatal. The bored look in the zamindar's eyes told him he didn't have much time.

"I . . . I was waiting for someone at the gate," he stammered. "That's all. A visiting friend."

"I already warned you that lying is useless," the sorcerer said, raising his staff as if to swing it against Thane's head. "Tell us about the crystals, fool! We know you took them. Tell us how you survived the spell that still stains your hands."

Thane cringed, but the blow didn't fall. Though the zamindar seemed skeptical of his role in the theft, the ill-tempered sorcerer plainly had no doubts. A gamble on the old man's curiosity seemed the only option.

Bowing his head, Thane signaled his defeat. "I didn't know it was the zamindar's property, I swear it! The man who paid me said the stones belonged to him, that the garrison commander had taken them without authority."

"A virtuous thief?" the zamindar snarled. "Don't waste my time, boy. Tell us the truth or you'll surely regret it."

Thane licked his lips and glanced around the tent. Outside, a campfire cast the shadow of two guards on the canvas flanking the tent's entrance. And the zamindar himself was armed with both a short sword and a jeweled dagger. Escape was impossible.

Thane bowed his head in submission. "I beg forgiveness. If I wronged you, it was from ignorance. I haven't even profited from it, I've yet to be paid. That's . . . that's why I was waiting by the gate."

"I don't believe him," the sorcerer said flatly. He jabbed Thane in the chest with the end of his staff, making the young mage wince. "Look at him. There's no fear in his eyes. And he has no explanation for surviving the cantrip. He's trying to deceive us!"

"No!" Thane protested. "I swear! The man who hired me gave me a potion to drink. It tasted vile, like spoiled wine. He told me where to find the stones. He's to pay me as soon as he returned from delivering the goods to a customer. He should be back soon, that's who I was waiting for!"

"A glib tongue," the sorcerer muttered, frowning through his gray beard. "You're quick, but ignorant. The sorcerer you killed was the only man other than myself who knew where the crystals were hidden. His soul belonged to me, he couldn't have betrayed us." His eyes seemed to glow softly with red light as he peered at Thane. "I sense this whelp is hiding something."

"A problem easily cured," the zamindar said. He returned to a cushioned chair and picked up a golden goblet. "He'll feel less impudent after we've opened his back with a lash." He took a sip of wine, then gave Thane a cruel smile. "Soon you'll beg to reveal your secrets. My torturers' reputations are well deserved."

A lump rose in Thane's throat, but he said nothing. Memories of the torture Lucian had endured made him break into a cold sweat. The pain, shared through their bond, had nearly killed him. Only Lucian's death, drowning in blood after deliberately chewing off his own tongue, had brought a kind of release.

The imperial sorcerer stepped back to join his master. His red robes swirled around his scrawny body, but he still radiated power. He bowed stiffly in front of the zamindar.

"You're right, lord. We'll have to rip the knowledge out of him. But I suggest giving him over to the sorcerers instead. We're less likely to accidentally kill him."

The zamindar paused, then nodded curtly. "As you wish, Najja. Just don't fail me again."

The sorcerer bowed more deeply, then turned back to Thane. This time there was no mistaking it. His ancient eyes glowed like rubies in a skull.

The door slammed open and Ander jerked up from the book he had been studying. Sorel and Nicolai rolled apart, their half-clad bodies tensing for action. Leif burst through the doorway.

"They captured Thane!" he gasped. "At the gate, the sorcerer somehow knew he was there!" He collapsed on the bed between Nicolai and Sorel, his chest heaving.

Ander closed his eyes and felt for his bond with Thane. Even at a distance there should have been a discernible thread of connection. Instead, there was only emptiness. "He's not there," he said in a horrified whisper.

Sorel leapt up. "Was he hurt?" he demanded. He took his shirt off the chair where it had been draped and pulled it over his head.

"I . . . I couldn't tell," Leif stammered. "Something was wrong with him. But he was awake, arguing with the sorcerer. Until the sorcerer used a spell, then Thane collapsed. He was still breathing, though. I was watching from the balcony, saw everything."

Ander's body ached, every muscle rigid. Nicolai put an arm around his shoulders and squeezed tightly, trying without success to reassure him.

Sorel tossed Nicolai's shirt onto the bed, then turned to Ander. "Listen to me," he said. "Thane was alive the last time Leif saw him. We have to concentrate on keeping him that way."

"You're right," Ander said, his voice shaky. He took a deep breath. "What can we do?"

Sorel crossed his arms over his chest and scowled. "I see two options. One is to try bribing a merchant to get us into the zamindar's encampment, making a delivery. It'd be a blind gamble. We don't even know where they're holding him. Or we could try to learn something in the kei."

"But I can't *feel* him!"

"A problem," Sorel admitted. "Maybe it's because the spell he's under is blocking his bond. We might be able to find a way through it. The kei is still a vast mystery, Ander. We make discoveries all the time."

Suddenly Ander sat up straight, nostrils flaring. *Could Lucian help?* If anyone knew the mysteries of the kei, it would be the ghost. But it would be impossible to attempt contacting the shade without revealing his existence. Ander realized he was holding his breath and exhaled slowly.

Sorel's head cocked to the side. "What is it, Ander?"

Ander gulped, at a loss. Lucian had sworn him to secrecy, but Thane's life hadn't been in danger then. Thane's capture changed everything. "I need some fresh air," he said softly. His gaze locked with Sorel's, and he tried to convey his desire for discretion. Though he had started to develop a bond with Sorel during his training, the link was weak compared to the profound joining he experienced with Thane.

Sorel's reputation for keen perception was justified. "I'll walk with you," he said. "You shouldn't be alone at a time like this." He turned to his partner as Ander stood. "Nicolai, why don't you and Leif decide what merchants we might approach?"

"All right," Nicolai agreed. "We'll wait for you here."

Ander followed Sorel downstairs. Several customers lingered over their meals; aromas of roast beef and hickory smoke lingered in the air. They slipped out the door unnoticed and walked to a dark alley between the inn and a stable.

Sorel put a hand on Ander's shoulder. His handsome features held sympathetic concern. "It's time for you to tell me," he said gently. "Whatever it is, you know you can trust me. That's not why you've held your silence, is it?"

Ander sighed. "I'm not that transparent, am I? What makes you think I'm hiding something?"

"Don't try to bluff me, Ander. There's no need, and it wouldn't work. I'll respect your silence, if that's what you want. But it seemed you wanted to talk."

Ander closed his eyes and rubbed his temples, feeling miserable. "This is so complicated. And I'm still not sure I should tell you. Thane could be hurt." He opened his eyes and looked at Sorel, pleading. "You've felt his pain, Sorel. The way he aches when he thinks of Lucian."

Surprise flickered across Sorel's face. "What do you mean? You remind him of Lucian, he's commented on it before. How could that be a secret?"

Ander shivered, fearing to break his oath. How would Thane feel, discovering a part of Lucian still lived? Would the knowledge rekindle his grief, as Lucian feared?

Sorel held him in a gentle embrace. "Tell me," he said softly. "Trust me to care for Thane as much as you do."

"I'll have to break an oath," Ander whispered. "An oath intended for his protection."

"The decision is yours. But remember, we love him too."

Ander took another deep breath, then looked Sorel in the eye. "Tonight Thane is in the zamindar's hands. Everything has changed." He took a step back, drawing Sorel further into the shadows. "You said there are mysteries in the kei. Things that might help us reach Thane. Sorel, nobody has ever been closer to Thane than Lucian."

"So? Lucian's been dead for ten years."

"Yes, but Lucian and Thane explored the kei together. Loved each other in the kei. Part of Lucian still lingers there."

For once, Sorel was speechless.

"It's true, Sorel! Lucian appeared to me at the Lyceum. He asked me to love Thane, give him release from grief. He's contacted me since then, too. He wants to help, but he's weak."

Belief slowly registered on Sorel's face. "You're not imagining this, I can see that. Maybe it explains why Thane bonded so strongly with you. Did Lucian help forge the bond?"

"I don't think so. Lucian wants to conceal himself. He fears Thane will try to seek him out, refuse to accept his death. The quest would be doomed to failure and heartbreak, but he's sure Thane would try."

"I understand," Sorel said softly. "Even in death, Lucian is trying to protect his beloved."

Ander nodded. "Experiencing the grief all over again would be too much. You know how intensely he feels, Sorel."

Sorel grasped one of Ander's hands. "I do. But Ander, something else has changed. Thane has *you*, now. There's joy to balance his grief."

"I hope you're right. Do you think Lucian's shade can help us reach him?"

Sorel's shadowed features took on a thoughtful look, and he took a long time to answer. "What's left of Lucian exists on a level of the kei we hadn't known about. A spell that keeps us from reaching Thane might not affect a ghost."

"But can we even reach Lucian? Do you know how to do it?"

"I won't try to deceive you, Ander. I don't know. But knowing that we can even *try* is a breakthrough."

A flicker of hope began to kindle. "We should try as soon as we can. He's in grave danger."

"I agree. Let's go inside. I want to hear Nicolai's thoughts on how to work the magic. We'll have to devise a plan for summoning Lucian. And we're working with limited resources, too. We only brought the most basic elixirs with us."

"We *have* to succeed," Ander insisted as they left the alley.

"We'll do our best," Sorel assured him. "Thane's in trouble, yes, but don't underestimate him. You know how strong he is, how determined—"

Ander lurched forward, gasping in surprise, stumbling against Sorel. He bent over and retched. Tearing pain, like slashing claws, ripped at his gut. Moaning miserably, he sank to his knees.

Sorel knelt beside him and steadied him. "What happened?"

Nodding weakly, Ander wiped his mouth on his sleeve. A choked laugh shook him, somewhere between hysteria and relief. "At least we know he's still alive. Our bond just burst open. They've begun the torture."

A NDER LEANED heavily on Sorel as they went inside. Each step brought a wave of disorientation. His muscles jerked spasmodically, reacting to the torments of unseen implements. By the time he staggered into their room, he was ready to gag.

"Ander!" Leif sprang across the room as Ander toppled onto the bed. "What happened?"

Ander tried to answer, but only a moan escaped.

"They've put Thane to torture," Sorel said. "Some of it's coming through their bond. We have to act quickly."

"How?" Nicolai asked, leaning over Ander and brushing hair from his sweaty brow. "We don't even know where he is. And Ander can't help us find him, if all he gets through their bond is pain."

"There may be another way. A way you'd never guess, Nicolai."

The northerner turned to Sorel, an eyebrow raised.

"Lucian. Part of him still lives in the kei." Nicolai's expression shifted to shock.

"Who's Lucian?" Leif demanded.

"Lucian was Thane's first love," Sorel said. "He died ten years ago, under torture. But his shade survives in the kei. He concealed himself to protect Thane from grief."

"How can a ghost help us?" Leif asked.

"He's been in the kei for ten years. He's *part* of the kei. If there's any way to use the kei to find Thane, Lucian has the best chance of finding it."

Ander groaned and pushed himself upright. "But Lucian has only appeared to *me*. I'm too sick to use the art, and that's the only way to go looking for him."

"An obstacle," Sorel said. "But not insurmountable. You're not really sick, you're only feeling Thane's suffering. If we block out the pain, you could enter the kei."

"Imperial sorcerers might notice if we use the art to help him enter the kei," Nicolai said.

Sorel spread his cape on the floor. He unbuttoned one of the pockets and removed his case of elixirs. "There's risk, I agree. But a gamble is all we have left." He opened the case and started choosing among vials of colored liquid.

"But I feel terrible," Ander moaned. "I couldn't even get hard, feeling like this."

"Trust me," Sorel replied. "I know a mixture that should do the trick. Rest with Leif until we're ready. If the potion has the effect I'm seeking, you'll need your strength."

"I think I see," Nicolai said, crouching beside Sorel. "Even with an arrow in his flank, a rutting stag thinks only of mating. I scarcely believed it, the first time I saw it."

Ander barely heard the advice. Curling into a ball, he squeezed his arms around his torso and shivered. His body rebelled against unseen torments. Leif stretched out next to him. "They know what they're doing," he said softly, cradling Ander in his arms. "It won't be much longer."

Ander buried his face in Leif's hair. "I can't tell what they're doing to him," he whispered. "Only that he's in agony."

"Try to think about something else," Leif said. "Remember when we went swimming last summer, and somebody stole our clothes while we were napping on the rocks? How we had to go home wearing nothing but loincloths made from rags?"

Ander groaned. "This is supposed to cheer me up? We were the talk of the market for a month."

"Well, I found out Mina did it. She couldn't resist teasing me about it. So I waited until she and Tannis went to the harvest festival, and—"

Ander's body jerked. His breath hissed through clenched teeth.

"How much longer?" Leif asked, glancing at the mages. Both youths had stripped and were putting away their elixirs.

Sorel turned and held up a vial of dark brown fluid, then knelt beside the bed. "Drink this, Ander. It should be strong enough to drive pain away. But it will cloud your mind, too. Try to concentrate on entering the kei and finding Lucian. You'll be drained after the elixir does its work, so you'll only have one chance."

Ander nodded weakly, shivering involuntarily. "I'll try to remember." He took the vial and put it to his lips. A sere odor, somewhere between sage and sunbaked rock, made his nose wrinkle. He shuddered, then drank the murky liquid in a single gulp. He nearly gagged as the thick, pungent liquid slid down his throat. "What's in that?" he demanded as soon as his tongue functioned again.

Sorel started to answer, but a sound like rushing winds filled Ander's ears. His heart raced. Suddenly the answer to his question didn't seem important. The clean scent of Leif's hair, and the solid feel of his friend's body, were much more interesting. He shifted, tightening his grip on Leif.

Nicolai put a hand on his shoulder. "Ander? Are you listening?"

The words barely registered on Ander's consciousness. His gaze had fixed on Leif's masculine features, the intriguing tilt of his eyes. His friend's tawny skin, the sweet musk of his body, were more arousing than ever. Blood pounded in his cock. He twisted some more and pushed Leif onto his back, holding him by the shoulders and straddling his slender waist. His breath came fast and hard.

Strong hands pulled him away from Leif. He rolled onto his side, blinking. Nicolai stood beside the bed in naked glory. Ander's mouth went dry as he gazed at the northerner's athletic form. Nicolai's years as an acrobat had sculpted his body into sleekly muscled perfection: powerful without being bulky, perfectly proportioned, moving with panther grace. Memories of their lovemaking, and the exquisite pleasure the young athlete imparted, pushed everything else from Ander's thoughts.

"Let's get rid of your clothes," Nicolai said. "I hear your flesh calling out for caresses." Grabbing the garment by its sides, he pulled Ander's shirt over his head and tossed it to the floor while Sorel pulled off boots. Tousled black hair fell in front of Ander's eyes, giving him a wild look.

An inch of Ander's cock extended beyond the waistband of his pants, pressing against his flat stomach. Nicolai brushed the slippery glans with his fingertips, then unfastened the pants. Ander's cock trembled beneath his fingers. "You're as eager as a virgin," Nicolai said, his fingers sliding along the warm flesh of Ander's thigh as he eased the pants down. "You're already slick with desire. Are you ready to begin?"

Ander grabbed Nicolai by the forearm and pulled him down. They tumbled together on the bed while Leif stripped. Ander rolled on top of the northerner and held him with surprising strength, pinning him to the bed.

"Let me fuck you," Ander panted, his cock pressing against Nicolai's hard belly. "I'll go slow, the way you like it." The quivering tension in his body belied the promise.

Nicolai grinned and shook his head. "Later, minx. You'll have to wait."

"I *can't* wait!" Ander ground his cock against Nicolai. "I'm ready to cum *now!*"

Nicolai shifted, throwing Ander off balance and flipping him over. Their bodies strained against each other, like wrestlers seeking a hold. Ander struggled fiercely, flushed and aroused, but it didn't take Nicolai long to pin him. He held Ander in a bear hug, his arms circling the youth's chest just beneath the armpits. Ander's buttocks rested on the edge of the bed and his long legs sprawled between Nicolai's straddling thighs. He panted, straining against the acrobat's strong grip. Nicolai's erection pressed thick and heavy against his belly.

Nicolai chuckled, his muscles bulging as he pressed Ander into the bed. "It's too bad Skorri and Erik aren't here. They love wrestling, especially if you oil them first. They're like horny eels. A lot like you, really."

Ander squirmed, his nostrils flaring. "Let me fuck you, Nicolai! Please!"

"I'm glad to see you're feeling better," Nicolai said. He turned his head and beckoned to Sorel. "I'll hold him still for you. Be careful, he's close." He swung around until he stretched on the bed at Ander's right side, maintaining his hug and squeezing their chests together. His thick blond hair fell forward and caressed Ander's flushed face.

Sorel knelt on the bed at Ander's left side and caressed the deeply carved ridges of muscle sheathing the youth's abdomen. Slick patches of precum, both Ander's and Nicolai's, gave his fingers ample lubrication. "A challenge, making him last when he's so inflamed. I like a challenge." He leaned closer, until his lips barely grazed the quivering penis. Ander's heels pushed against the floor and lifted his pelvis, his cock spearing the air, seeking contact with warm flesh. His scrotum was pulled up tight against the base of his cock and the muscles in his legs formed taut curves.

"Help Nicolai hold him," Sorel told Leif. "He can't restrain himself."

Leif quickly positioned himself between Ander's legs and pressed down on his thighs.

Sorel lowered his head again. His lips slid around the head of Ander's penis and lifted it upright. Ander writhed, moaning loudly, but Nicolai and Leif held him fast. A gush of precum pulsed onto Sorel's tongue.

Once Ander was firmly under the control of the other youths, Sorel's lips began a slow slide down the upward-curved shaft. He moved carefully, heeding Ander's urgent moans.

"*Ahhh*," Ander gasped. "Suck me, Sorel!"

Lips barely touching the rigid penis, using his tongue to hold the shaft in position, Sorel complied with the request and devoted his full attention to pleasuring Ander. His skill as a lover was legendary.

Leif watched with undisguised admiration as the handsome youth sucked Ander's cock. The shaft glistened with slippery spit every time Sorel released it from his clenching throat to lick gently at the sensitive glans. Clear fluid oozed out, and Sorel used the tip of his tongue to spread it around the underside of the glans before slowly encasing the shaft in his throat again. His ministrations were effortless and delicate, despite the size and extreme rigidity of Ander's cock.

Ander shouted incoherently, his whole body straining. Nicolai tightened his grip and pressed their lips together to silence him. Ander responded passionately, wrapping his arms around Nicolai's broad shoulders and plunging his tongue into the blond's mouth. Sorel kept his leisurely rhythm up and down Ander's cock.

Ander's bucking, pushing with strong legs against the floor, made it nearly impossible to keep him motionless. Leif quickly saw the solution to the problem. "Let me lift his legs up so he can't get purchase on the floor," he suggested. "And Sorel . . . do you think I could fuck him while you're sucking?"

Sorel released Ander's cock and looked up. "The more pleasure, the better. Just go slow. You can see how helpless he is. It's up to us to make him last."

"Don't worry. I know his signs. I know when he's going to cum before *he* does."

Ander turned his head, breaking his kiss with Nicolai. "Do it, Leif! Fuck me!"

Leif fetched a vial of oil from their supplies while Nicolai corralled Ander into another kiss. In moments he returned with the lubricant. He applied generous portions to his erect cock and to Ander's ass, then stood between Ander's legs. He put his hands under his friend's knees and lifted the legs up. At last they had him completely immobilized.

Ander felt the head of Leif's cock touch his ass at the same moment Sorel resumed sucking. He shuddered and hugged Nicolai fervently as the wet heat of Sorel's mouth reclaimed his penis.

"Easy," Leif said as Ander's ass clenched. "Let me in. I'll stroke the place where it feels best. Do you hear me?"

Ander couldn't answer, couldn't even nod. Nicolai held him captive in a sweaty embrace, his tongue forcing entry in a deep kiss. But just hearing his friend's voice and feeling his familiar presence was enough to trigger a reaction. His body knew Leif and welcomed him eagerly. The ring of muscle relaxed and the first two inches of Leif's cock slid in.

Ander nearly came when Leif's slippery flesh entered him. His body stiffened and his well-oiled ass squeezed the smooth shaft of Leif's cock like a tight glove. A trembling shudder ran through his body.

Nicolai felt the shiver and broke their kiss. "Did you know that Sorel once kept Skorri hard for five hours before letting him cum? It's still a record at the Lyceum."

The distraction was just enough to divert Ander from a climax. He blinked, still in a daze of lust, slowly digesting the information. "I can't wait five hours!" he croaked.

Nicolai grinned. "You'll cum when we're ready, and not before. But I think you're ready for more of Leif's cock now." He rubbed noses with Ander, keeping him off balance.

Taking the cue, Leif pressed forward while Ander was still bemused by Nicolai's diversions. His cock slid in without resistance until his pubic hairs pressed against firm buttocks. After a few moments he pulled partway out and held Ander's feet high, while arching his back and moving his pelvis in small circles. His cockhead slid repeatedly over the sensitive spot that drove Ander wild.

Ander soared in a whirlwind of lust and pleasure. He tried to crane his neck to see Sorel and Leif, wanting to watch them create the amazing sensations that filled him, but Nicolai's powerful embrace held him immobile. His head fell back to the bed and he looked at Nicolai with dazed lust.

"You're more beautiful than ever when you're being fucked," Nicolai said. "You glow. I could cum just from watching you."

Releasing his grip on the acrobat's broad shoulders, Ander reached between Nicolai's legs. The northerner still knelt on the bed with his knees spread wide like a wrestler. Ander wrapped his fingers around Nicolai's straining phallus, smearing precum over the glans.

Leif began sliding his cock in and out with slow glides. Sorel coordinated his sucking, bringing his lips to the base of Ander's cock as Leif pulled out. They moved in perfect unison, attuned through keen awareness of Ander's body.

Ander panted, inflamed by Nicolai's sweaty scent and muscular embrace. The sensation of helpless captivity made Leif's slow fucking feel deeper than ever. His tight body quivered in response to the pleasure being lavished on it; he felt like an appendage of the other youths, like a cock being lovingly stroked by its proud owner.

Sorel let Ander's cock slip free. It slapped against the boy's ridged abdomen and glistened with spit, its head straining past Ander's navel. Sorel licked the shaft's underside while Leif increased the tempo of his strokes.

Ander growled and surged against Nicolai's weight, delirious. The acrobat's thick cock throbbed in his right hand; his palm and wrist were coated with slippery fluids. Nicolai fucked into the grasping hand, caught up in Ander's frenzy. His heart beat powerfully against Ander's chest.

Leif pushed his cock all the way into Ander's slippery ass and swivelled his hips. "You're the best fuck in the world," he said. "The most beautiful boy, and the horniest." He resumed his slow thrusts, deep and inexorable. "Your cock's so hard! It trembles when Sorel licks it. How does it feel, Ander?"

Ander's tongue was thick, his mind barely rational. He couldn't respond to the question. Leif's slow fucking made him feel like he floated in surging tide. Waves of pleasure swept through him. His vision blurred, everything tinged with golden light. Nicolai's thick blond hair fell in shimmering glory around his face like a curtain of sunlight. The handsome northerner gazed into his eyes. "Remember the kei," he whispered. "Remember Lucian."

Then Sorel's lips slipped back over Ander's cock and caressed the cockhead with the tip of his tongue.

Ander's ass clenched at Leif's probing penis. His toes curled and his head pressed back into the bed. Sensation tore through him like lightning. His muscles convulsed and the first jet of his ejaculation spewed into Sorel's suckling mouth. He howled, totally captivated by the three strong youths making love to him.

Leif slid his cock in to the hilt and geysered a fountain of semen. The hot fluid pulsed again and again against Ander's sensitive flesh. At the same moment Nicolai flooded Ander's hand with a slippery flood of cum.

In a searing instant of overwhelming awareness, Ander felt the minds of his three friends. His mouth watered at the sweet taste of his own cum, and he felt the hot blast of Sorel's orgasm as their minds touched and pleasure surged through Sorel's body. The burst of Sorel's anima pushed him over the boundary between ordinary reality, into a realm beyond.

His cock still shooting streamers of milky semen into Sorel's mouth, Ander's mind soared free of his body's bonds. For a moment he looked down from above and glimpsed four young males tangled together, convulsed in wrenching orgasms. Then a geyser of shared sensation propelled him into ethereal light.

He floated, naked and nearly unconscious, on a warm tide of golden light. His body buzzed with energy, but a distant murmur kept him anchored. The whisper took on Nicolai's voice. Then he remembered. *Lucian.*

The air around him filled with motes as his awareness focused. They sparkled brightly in thousands of colors, and began to swirl as he formed an image of Lucian in his mind.

As Thane had taught him, he let the shape of his thoughts guide his movement through the kei. The mage believed that thoughts and the kei were part of the same thing, somehow tied. Ander didn't understand, but the techniques worked nonetheless. The sense of direction and movement grew stronger. The motes of light coalesced into billowing clouds. Like a hawk, he gathered speed and plummeted through the clouds toward his target.

He emerged in the sky above a sunny hillside. Wildflowers followed a meandering stream between boulders. On one of the largest rocks, a mottled gray slab shot through with quartz veins, lay a nude youth.

Ander blinked, then found himself standing beside the slab. The sleeping boy was Lucian. His long black hair glistened in the sun, and his slanted eyes remained closed. Seeing Thane's first love in slumber, Ander could appreciate his virile beauty. His eyes and tawny skin were reminiscent of Leif, but far more strongly shaped by eastern ancestors. Ander shook him by the shoulder. The flesh was warm, and Lucian's smooth chest rose and fell with slow breaths, but he didn't wake.

Ander shook again, more forcefully. Again there was no response. He was at a loss. Every other time he had encountered Lucian, it had been the shade's doing. He had no idea how to rouse a shade.

He climbed onto the stone and knelt next to the sleeping youth, grasping him by both shoulders. "Can you hear me? It's Ander." He shook Lucian by the shoulders again, then moved his hands beneath the boy's head. "Wake up, please! We need your help. Thane needs you!"

Lucian's eyelids fluttered, and he took a shuddering breath. He grimaced, then opened his eyes with agonizing slowness. Only when he focused on Ander did he seem to become aware of his surroundings.

"Lucian! What happened? What's wrong?" Ander slipped an arm around the youth's back and lifted him up. Lucian slumped against him. His breath came in shallow gasps. Ander hugged him tightly, fear filling his heart. At last Lucian lifted his head and took a deeper breath. He put an arm around Ander's shoulders and sat straighter.

"The zamindar's sorcerers are draining the kei," Lucian said. "I don't know how. They understand the kei a different way than we do. Like a victim to be ravaged."

Ander brushed hair from Lucian's face. "We need your help.

Nobody knows the kei as well as you. We need to find Thane."

The mention of Thane's name sent a tremor through Lucian's body. "Find him? He's not with you?"

How much more can he endure? Ander put both arms around the shade, amazed at his warmth and solidity. Meeting a ghost in the kei was totally unlike meeting one in the physical world. "I'm sorry," he whispered. "I wish I could spare you from this. But Thane was captured by the zamindar. He's been put to torture. You . . . you know better than I what that means."

Lucian pressed his face against Ander's shoulder and his body quaked. Hot tears wet Ander's skin. He shared the boy's grief, but couldn't avoid what had to be done.

A shuddering breath soon signaled the shade's recovery. He knuckled tears from his eyes with a determined swipe. It was easy to see why Thane had loved him so intensely.

"I'm sure I can find him," Lucian said softly. "He's the fire that keeps what's left of me warm." He nodded, eyes half shut as if his mind was already searching. "Yes, I'll find him."

"Thank the gods! But we need even more, Lucian. We need to free him from a spell that overpowered him."

Lucian's confident expression dissolved. "The zamindar's *sorcerers* have him?"

"Yes, though it hasn't been long." Ander grimaced with remembered pain. "My bond with him is mostly blocked by a spell, but I could still feel some of what they were doing to him."

"If the sorcerers have him, we've lost." Lucian's voice was a whisper. "So much struggle. All for ashes and blood."

"No! We can find a way to help him!"

Lucian shook his head, bitter defeat bringing new tears to his eyes. "You don't understand. The kei is being poisoned, me along with it. I lack the strength to overcome any spells."

Ander paused, remembering the time he had helped Nicolai defeat a cantrip guarding a doorway in Fochelis. The energy required for the effort had left the northerner weak and drenched with sweat, and Nicolai was an athlete in peak condition.

"Perhaps we don't have to overcome the spell," Ander urged. "We might find a way to slip through without undoing the wards."

"I tell you, I don't have the power to defeat a spell. Or even to subvert it."

"I'll give you whatever anima I have," Ander said. "Take it all, if you must. But we *can't* leave Thane to die on a torturer's hooks!"

Lucian regarded Ander with sad calm. "I was right about you, at least. You love him as much as I. But it can't be done. I have

176

no body to hold your anima. I'm little more than a remnant of the real Lucian's anima, fragments left over . . ." Lucian's voice trailed off. A thoughtful furrow creased his brow and he gazed into the distance.

Ander held his breath, not wanting to interrupt whatever thought had interrupted the ghost's denials. Finally Lucian took a deep breath and met his gaze. "You can't share your anima with me. But I could give *you* whatever I have left. It might be enough to let you see the kei as I see it. Perhaps you could find Thane, and have the strength to break through to him."

"But . . . what would happen to you?"

Lucian looked down, his noble features enigmatic. "Nothing would be left, at least not in the kei. My anima would be yours, mingled with your spirit. Perhaps I could even touch Thane again, through your hand." His voice ached with yearning.

Ander touched Lucian's cheek, brushing away a tear. It was clear the boy wanted no delay. "What should I do?"

Lucian slid off the rock. His lithe body glowed in the sun like bronze, his long black hair glistened. He somberly extended a hand. "We'll share anima as if we were working a spell. But I have no body to sustain, and will hold nothing back."

Ander stood and took Lucian in his arms. The youth's body felt warm as real flesh, hard yet supple. Its masculine curves slid against him, irresistibly erotic and demanding. They kissed tenderly, their spirits uniting in a single desire.

Their breath came fast as they hugged each other tightly. Lucian's skin tingled beneath Ander's hands. They pushed against each other insistently, like lovers, and their hearts began to beat as one. A wave of strangeness passed through Ander, disorienting. He gasped and broke their kiss. Both their bodies shimmered with traceries of silvery light.

Lucian met his gaze and smiled gently. "Now I'm yours. Together, we might succeed. We *must* succeed!" He closed his eyes briefly. When he opened them again his smile was gone, replaced with desperate hope. "Give Thane my love." He pressed his face against Ander's shoulder. A final squeeze, accompanied by a whiff of fragrance like rare spices carried on a sea breeze, and he vanished in a pulse of golden light.

Ander staggered, momentarily unbalanced by the loss of Lucian's strong embrace. He sat on the stone slab and took a deep breath. He felt stronger than before. The lush vegetation covering the hillside seemed more vibrant, and he sensed an elusive connection between everything—the rock, the earth and plants, the sun overhead, his own being. Even Lucian, the indomitable spirit that refused to leave his lover, was still part of the matrix. *Everything is connected, if you just know where to look.* Marvel filled him. "I won't fail you," he murmured. A whisper of affirmation brushed his mind, a resolve carrying the flavor of Lucian.

He lay on the warm rock, facing the sun and spreading his arms like wings. Closing his eyes, he felt for the linkages submerged in a deeper level of reality. Sunlight warmed his fair skin, and a gentle breeze caressed him. He trembled as he caught flashes of towering mountains the wind had touched, vast distances where the light had traveled. The beauty, intricacy and mystery of the kei nearly overwhelmed him. Then a point of white light flickered into his mind's eye. He focused on it, anchoring himself. The light seemed alive, purposeful. It expanded to the size of an orange, then began to drift away.

Instinctively, Ander tried to follow. Awareness of his body faded. Incomprehensible sounds filled his ears: speech in unknown patterns, growls of animals that formed nearly human words, music seemingly formed from the sound of dry leaves skittering in the street. Visions of comets and bizarre landscapes streamed past his eyes. Subtle pressures buffeted him, and the sense of speed increased. But the white light still glowed before him. His body left behind, he soared after the sphere of light.

As he dove after the light he began to notice a foul odor, like rancid blood in an abattoir. It grew stronger as the sky around him darkened. Suddenly he burst from the maelstrom of images into clear night sky. The walls of Pella spread before him and the reek of blood choked the air like a battlefield after a massacre. The source of the stench was immediately clear. Near the center of the city, on a hill containing the oldest buildings, stood the massive Ziggurat of Baalik. The first three levels, receding tiers of limestone blocks darkened by moss and age, looked as they always had. But the fourth tier, crowned by Baalik's shrine, radiated an angry ocher light.

As he neared the vast pile of stones Ander began to feel a burning in his bones, a faint echo of the pain he had felt in the alley while talking to Sorel. He stopped, seeming to hover in the still air above the temple. The small white light that had guided him flickered and disappeared.

He had expected the light to lead him into the zamindar's encampment, but there was no mistaking the powerful magical energies radiating from the ancient ziggurat. He moved closer, tensing against expected agony, but found that he was now able to bend the kei in a way that deflected the pain. His new perceptions vibrated to the thrum of power coming from Baalik's shrine.

Ander reached out with his mind, cautiously exploring the web of energy. A spell of fearsome complexity tied the strands together. His excitement mounted as he worked deeper into the spell. Deep within it, nearly buried beneath suffocating bonds, he felt a desperate struggle taking place. *Thane! This is the spell that binds him!*

Eagerly, he bent his will to the first knot. Multicolored strands of power slowly parted. Exhilaration surged as the knot fell apart. He felt Thane's pain more sharply, but the increased closeness only spurred him on. A sense of supremacy filled him as he grasped the subtle connections revealed in the kei. The way through the spell lay before him.

The second part of the spell fell even more quickly than the first. He plunged ahead, racing toward Thane's release with nearly blinding anticipation. Curtains of energy surrounded him like sheets of rain. Another magical ward surged with force.

He extended his mind toward the knot, feeling for the points where the bonds were anchored. He was about to touch the knot when he noticed a tiny black thread looping around the intersection of two larger cords of force. It formed a circle, complete in itself, anchored in nothing except the knot that contained it.

An inner voice screamed. Ander froze. His excitement cooled as he remembered the power of the zamindar's sorcerers. He examined the new ward closely, and realization dawned. *A cantrip! Release the spell, the thread redirects the force. But to where?* Delicately, using all the perception Lucian's anima had brought him, he focused on the trap. Its workings fell open before his mind. Shock sickened him.

The trap was perfect in its simplicity. Releasing the magical bonds would also break the trigger thread. And the bonds were attuned to the trigger, so that removing the trigger would be detected. In either case, the force of the bonds would instantly be diverted in a new direction: into Thane.

Reeling with disappointment and frustration, Ander pulled away. His concentration shattered in a thousand fragments. In the space of a single heartbeat he found himself back in his physical body. Searing pleasure instantly pushed all thoughts from his mind. Nicolai's powerful embrace held him pinned to the bed. Leif still stood between his widespread legs, his cock still thrusting deep, pulsing strongly as it spewed cum. The head of Ander's cock rested on Sorel's tongue, and was spitting semen onto the slippery flesh.

Ander's body convulsed, overcome with pleasure, but his friends held him tight and milked every possible drop of sensation from his flesh. His muscles contracted once more in a helpless spasm, then he collapsed in exhaustion.

Leif pulled out, his cock glistening with cum and oil, then Nicolai pulled Ander fully onto the bed and cradled him.

Ander gasped for breath, his senses still swirling. He pushed hair from his eyes, forgetting the copious ejaculation Nicolai had released in his hand, smearing the blond's cum across his face. Sorel and Leif joined them on the bed, creating a tangle of sweaty limbs.

As his breathing slowed, Ander began to remember. His journey in the kei had been outside time, had the feel of a dream, but as it came back he realized that the elixir had done its job. Memory of his failure returned in a rush. He shuddered, his breath suddenly harsh.

"You've been away, haven't you?" Sorel asked. He put a hand on Ander's cheek, gently wiping away some of Nicolai's cum. "Were you able to contact Lucian?"

Ander took a shaky breath, then nodded. "Yes. And he showed me where Thane is. But . . . but I couldn't free him from the spell! I failed!"

Sorel turned Ander's head to the side and gazed into his eyes. "While he lives, there's hope. But the elixir is potent, you'll soon pay the price for using it. Tell us what you learned."

Ander tried to respond, convey the urgency he felt, but the elixir, the sex and his efforts in the kei had left him too drained. His eyes closed and unconsciousness claimed him.

INSISTENT VOICES drew Ander back from blackness. He tried to ignore them, but strong arms lifted him upright. A pungent mint odor made him snort. He opened his eyes, feeling groggy and disoriented.

"Drink this," Nicolai said. He held a vial containing pale blue liquid to Ander's lips and tilted it up. The liquid numbed his tongue and throat, but Ander's head cleared. "It counteracts the first elixir you drank," Nicolai explained. "But you'll still be weak. You've exerted yourself more than you know."

Sorel sat beside him and offered a cup of water. "Can you tell us what happened?"

Ander took a small sip, which seemed to help. "It's strange," he said. "No time at all passed, did it, while I was gone? But it felt like I was away a long time."

"Time is different in the kei. Don't worry. Just tell us what you learned."

Sorel's insistence reminded him of the urgency of their task. Struggling against fatigue, he forced himself upright.

"They're holding Thane at the Ziggurat of Baalik. I tried to dissolve the spell they're using to bind him, but couldn't do it. It's constructed so that releasing the bonds would kill him."

Sorel looked startled. "You attempted such a feat? Reckless, Ander! You're not experienced with the kei."

"No, I'm not," Ander whispered. "I had help. Lucian . . . he gave me his anima. It gave me the power to see far more deeply into the kei than I could before. And it seems to shield me from Thane's pain as well."

"He gave you *all* his anima?" Sorel asked.

"Yes," Ander confirmed. "Lucian's gone now. I'm sorry."

"But he helped you find Thane," Leif said, rubbing the back of Ander's neck. "It's not your fault you couldn't free him."

Nicolai nodded. "If we can't attack the spell directly, we'll have to attack the sorcerers who weave it. Could you tell if the temple was heavily guarded?"

Ander tried to remember what he had seen. Four sets of towering walls, sloping inward to terraces at each level, the shrine at the summit surrounded by pillars. Torches had burned at the corner of each terrace, but the ceremonial ramp inclining from street to shrine on the ziggurat's west side had been dark. The large iron doors at the structure's base were lost in darkness, but if there had been soldiers their armor should have caught the torchlight.

"I don't remember seeing guards," Ander said. "The spell they're using is strong. Maybe they're relying on magic."

"Interesting," Sorel said. "Maybe the imperial sorcerers understand something of Thane's powers, and want to keep the information to themselves." His eyes narrowed. "I've heard there's tension between the sorcerers and the military. Each is jealous of the other's influence. The zamindar plays them off against each other."

"How does that help us?" Ander asked, fighting drowsiness. His eyelids kept sagging, and he felt as if he were made of lead.

Sorel slid off the bed and crossed the room in two quick strides. He picked up his pants and put them on. "Like Nicolai said, we'll have to physically remove Thane from the source of the spell that's binding him. It would be impossible if they held him in the zamindar's camp. But I think the sorcerers are trying to hide Thane from the military. Maybe we can draw the sorcerers away from the ziggurat. Then we can rescue Thane, without having to get past the zamindar's guard!"

"Where are you going?" Ander asked. He tried to swing out of bed, but the effort made him dizzy. He fell back with a woof.

"To retrieve those crystals Nicolai and Thane hid at the garrison commander's house." He finished buttoning his pants and reached for his shirt. "If anything can attract the attention of the zamindar's sorcerers, it's those crystals."

Nicolai slid off the bed and joined Sorel by the pile of clothing. "A job for two, surely. I know exactly where the crystals are hidden."

Sorel's grin showed no surprise. "Just like old times. Did you ever tell Ander about our cat burglar days?"

Nicolai looked pained. "We merely liberated property from people who had taken it unjustly. That's entirely different."

"If you say so," Sorel replied. He gave Nicolai a slap on the back, then handed him his pants. "We've got to be quick. Thane's strong, but we know how persuasive the torturers can be."

"How can I help?" Leif asked.

"For now, take care of Ander," Sorel said. "He'll be defenseless until the elixir wears off. He shouldn't be alone. His protection from Thane's pain might only be temporary."

Leif nodded, then sat on the bed next to Ander. "I hope you know what you're doing. That house is well guarded."

Sorel shrugged, undaunted. "Then we won't let the guards see us." He finished dressing, making sure his throwing knives and other weapons were easily accessible. Soon both were ready. They fastened their cloaks, then unlocked the door. Sorel paused before opening it, giving Ander a thoughtful look.

"Rest well, Ander. Your strength will be tested again before the night is out." When they were gone Leif bolted the door and rejoined Ander on the bed.

Ander nestled against his friend. Despite his anxieties, sleep took him quickly.

It seemed as if mere seconds had passed when he heard softly spoken words. He opened his eyes. The fire in the hearth had burned down to glowing embers. Nicolai and Sorel were removing their cloaks while Leif lit a candle. The room filled with flickering light. Nicolai's shirt was cut near his left shoulder, and blood stained the leather down to his elbow.

Ander jerked upright. "Nicolai! What happened?"

The northerner looked chagrined. "A mere scratch. A guard came from the house while I was loosening rocks in the wall." He made a face. "Thane missed his calling, I think. He should have been a mason. That damned wall will outlast all the rest of Pella. It took nearly—"

"The guard, Nicolai."

"Well, he was armed and I wasn't. But Sorel was lurking in the shadows, and wasted no time." He pulled a face. "It always makes me nervous when he throws a knife at someone I'm wrestling. But I'm not complaining."

"Prudent, as always," Sorel said as he reached into one of his cloak's pockets. He pulled out a silver box the size of a deck of cards and showed it to Ander.

Leif peered at the box, then touched it carefully. "This is what the sorcerers have been seeking? It's so small."

"Appearances are often deceiving," Sorel said. "The crystals can gather anima, save it until there's enough to restore the zamindar's own life force. He'll stop at nothing to regain them."

Ander swung his feet out of bed, surprised at how refreshed he felt. "So we'll use them to tempt the zamindar's sorcerers away from the ziggurat? That's the plan?"

"They'll fly out of the temple like bats from a hollow tree," Nicolai predicted. He turned to Ander. "How do you feel? Better?"

"Much," Ander confirmed, stretching.

Sorel handed the silver box to Leif. "You'd be the best person to scatter crystals in the city. You know your way around. And you're not ready to deal with what we're likely to encounter tonight."

"Blood magic," Leif said, frowning as he accepted the box. "Are you sure *you* can survive it?"

Ander started dressing. "Aside from Thane, Sorel and Nicolai are the best mages at the Lyceum. Nobody has a better chance of success. And there's no time to try anything else."

Leif nodded, then put the box down and collected his clothes.

"Make sure the crystals are hard to find," Ander said. "Drop one in a well, perhaps. Or feed one to a wild dog, if you find a piece of food. *That* should keep the zamindar's sorcerers busy. Just don't touch them any longer than you have to. They can hurt you."

"I'll lead them a good chase," Leif promised.

They finished dressing and left the inn. The street was deserted, and fog hung thick in the air. Ander pulled his cloak tight around his body. Dawn was only two hours away.

"Luck," Leif whispered, touching Ander's cheek in a fleeting gesture. Then he turned and vanished into the mist. Ander, Sorel and Nicolai went the other way, toward the Ziggurat of Baalik.

Moving stealthily, they worked their way into the city's heart. Once they saw the fog brighten with the yellow glow of a torch. They took shelter in an alley, waiting breathlessly, but the patrol passed by. When they reached the ziggurat they concealed themselves behind the statue of a long-forgotten temple patron. The damp air smelled of moss. As they had hoped, there was no sign of guards.

"Hard to judge the time when the moon's shrouded," Sorel whispered. "But Leif should be near the market by now."

"The sooner the better," Ander answered. He wiped a sleeve across his forehead, his hand shaking slightly. "I'm starting to feel Thane's pain again. Perhaps because he's so near."

Sorel nodded, his gaze never leaving the massive iron doors at the ziggurat's base. "I feel some of it too, though my bond with Thane isn't as deep as yours. At least we know we've come to the right—"

Nicolai grabbed Sorel's shoulder. "Quiet! I heard a lock opening!" They sank deeper into the shadows. Moments later an iron door swung open with a loud creak.

Two men hurried out. Both wore ordinary clothes, but carried orbs like the zamindar's sorcerers had been using to search Pella. They moved frantically, one nearly dropping his orb as he fastened his cloak against the chill. As soon as the gate was locked they hurried down the street toward the market.

Ander leaned close to Sorel. "How many do you think there are?"

"The innkeeper said six have been seen in the streets. We'll give Leif time to scatter a few more crystals, and wait until they stop coming out. At least we know the bait works."

Suddenly Ander's side ached as if he had just run a marathon, and his right foot felt as if a red-hot coal lay in the bottom of his boot. He suffered in silence, wondering what agonies Thane endured.

Ten minutes after the first pair, two more men hurried from the ziggurat carrying metal orbs. These were noticeably older than the first searchers. The new pair scurried east, toward the brothel district.

Fifteen minutes later another sorcerer emerged. This one was nearing old age, and appeared to belong to a different class. His head was shaved and a ring of arcane symbols was tattooed around its crown. His girth suggested years of self-indulgence. Menace seemed to exude from him like a cloud of foul gas. He started for the brothel district but turned right at the first street, his eyes never leaving the glowing metal orb cradled in his hands.

The sorcerer's passing hit Ander like a kick in the stomach. He crouched behind the statue, arms wrapped around his body, trying not to vomit. They waited in silence, time dragging painfully while Ander slowly recovered from the sorcerer's influence.

Ten minutes passed, then fifteen. Ander's anxiety mounted steadily. He couldn't feel anything through his bond, a sensation even more troubling than pain. "Hasn't it been long enough?" he whispered to Sorel. "It's been half an hour since the first sorcerers left. What if they find the crystal quickly? They might come back while we're still waiting."

"He's right," Nicolai said. "We don't know how well Leif managed to hide the stones. Our odds aren't likely to improve if we wait."

Sorel scowled at the fog-enshrouded ziggurat, slowly weaving a black throwing knife between the fingers of his right hand. After a few moments he slipped the knife into a sheath strapped beneath his left sleeve. "I'll test the lock," he said softly. "Stay back until I've got it open." He slipped out from behind the statue and started across the street.

Ander started to rise from his crouch, but Nicolai put an arm on his shoulder and pushed him back down. "He knows what he's doing. He's best suited for this job. Trust him."

Nicolai was right about Sorel's skill at picking locks, but Ander was sick of feeling helpless. He shrugged off Nicolai's hand. "Maybe I can help. The kei is more open to me, now. I might be able to see dangers that Sorel misses."

Nicolai looked doubtful, but didn't argue. "Then I might as well go too." They sprinted across the street.

Sorel glanced away from the lock as they approached, looking mildly annoyed but not surprised. "As I feared, there's a cantrip. It doesn't feel like a locking spell or a trap, though. Just a warning spell."

Ander extended a hand toward the doors. He closed his eyes and opened his mind to new perceptions. Unlike the wards binding Thane, the one on the door was simple. He held his breath and pushed with his thoughts. Faint tingling warmed his fingertips. Then, without protest, the cantrip's links bent around on themselves and left the lock outside the spell's protective circle.

Ander opened his eyes and nodded to Sorel. "I've taken care of the spell. Can you open the lock?"

Sorel raised an eyebrow, then reached toward the lock to confirm Ander's success for himself. After a few seconds the skepticism left his expression. "Very good," he said softly. "I think you'll surpass all of us, save Thane." He removed a small tool kit from a pocket and selected a pick. The lock, ancient and large, quickly yielded to his expertise. He stood up and swung the heavy door open.

The stench of rotting flesh made Ander gag. Inside the ziggurat, a single torch guttered at the far end of a tall gallery. Corpses littered the floor, their mutilation apparent even in the feeble light. Arms and heads were strewn around carelessly, bodies were torn open as if wolves had fed on them. Ander's stomach churned as they crept into the charnel house.

"Steady," Nicolai said. "Thane still lives. Remember that, ignore the rest."

Gulping, Ander nodded and followed Sorel into the chamber. The floor was sticky with blood. Shock turned to disgust, then rage, as they passed pile after pile of victims. When they reached the far end of the gallery two staircases confronted them. One led down into blackness, and an even more terrible stench. The other ascended into the heart of the ziggurat.

"You're sure he's in the shrine?" Sorel asked, pausing at the base of the staircase.

"Yes." Ander felt no doubt. "We go up."

"I'll go first," Nicolai said. He drew a dagger from its sheath and started up the stairs. Ander went next, then Sorel took the torch from its bracket and followed.

The staircase worked its way upward through the ziggurat's

core. The zamindar's sorcerers had done their butchering above and dragged the remains down to the gallery. Stone walls were smeared with blood and worse, and confinement made the air thick. Narrow passages stretched into darkness at each landing. The air at the landings was stale as a dusty crypt, but at least it offered a brief respite from the reek of death.

Sweat soaked the back of Ander's shirt and stung his eyes. They were leaving the sixth landing when an ominous rasping sound, like a saw cutting bone, brought him to an abrupt halt. "Wait, Nicolai! Did you hear it?"

The northerner nodded, his body poised with knife at the ready. "We're near the shrine. The air's getting fresher. Stay close—"

A guttural cry tore the air, hoarse and anguished, but unmistakably Thane's voice. Ander's hackles rose and his bond with Thane pulsed with fire. He sprang past Nicolai and bounded up the steps.

He burst into the shrine crowning the ziggurat. Cool air blew through tall windows, and oil lamps burned at each corner. The shrine was ornate, but Ander didn't even notice the intricate mosaics and painted reliefs covering the walls.

Two thick timbers, fixed into square holes in the floor, stood upright near the back of the room. Thane sagged between them. He was shackled at wrists and ankles, and stripped to the waist. Blood ran from his nose and mouth, and his gaze swept over Ander with dazed disbelief. Livid welts streaked his torso. The shackles had bitten into his flesh during his struggles, covering his arms and feet with rivulets of blood.

Two imperial sorcerers stood beside Thane. They turned when Ander barged into the room, Nicolai and Sorel on his heels. One sorcerer looked as ancient as the ziggurat itself, tall and desiccated. A gray beard concealed most of his skeletal face. His clawlike right hand held a jeweled dagger whose blade sparked with green flashes of light. A younger sorcerer holding a barbed scourge stood to Thane's right.

Wrath burned red in the elderly sorcerer's eyes and stung Ander like a swarm of hornets. Nicolai had no such distractions. He leapt forward and crashed into the younger sorcerer. They tumbled against the back wall. Nicolai rolled to his feet while maintaining his grip on the man's robe. With a powerful heave he lifted the sorcerer off the floor and spun him around. The man flailed as he whipped through the air, but his journey was short. His head hit a stone windowsill with a thud. Nicolai turned to the remaining sorcerer.

"Get back, or he dies!" The bearded sorcerer put the tip of his dagger to Thane's chest just above the heart and pushed hard enough to break the skin.

Thane jerked at his shackles. "Kill him!" His voice was hoarse and ragged. His eyes had regained their reason, but held profound fear. "Kill him *now*, you won't get another chance!"

The old sorcerer grinned like a malevolent skeleton and pushed the knife deeper into Thane's flesh. Green light sparkled and danced across Thane's broad chest, and he screamed.

"The blade is ensorceled. If you kill me, the knife will take his life even without my hand's help. You've lost, fools!"

Nicolai halted his advance, though he stayed in a perfectly balanced crouch.

"*Kill him now!*" Thane wailed. "He's Najja, you can't—"

The sorcerer jerked the dagger upward, bringing its point beneath Thane's chin and forcing his head back. Thane bent back painfully, every muscle taut, as he strained to avoid the knife's point. A mirthless grin curled Najja's lips.

"At last, everything comes together. I'll soon have the crystals and your secrets as well. Even the zamindar will bow to my will!" His grin grew to a sneer. "And to think I had a band of stupid boys to thank for delaying my plans. Incredible! But now you'll pay dearly for your interference."

Keeping the knife at Thane's throat, he reached with his other hand for a glass amulet hanging on a gold chain around his neck. Thick black liquid filled the small container.

Thane couldn't speak, but his guttural moan was eloquent. His warning wasn't lost on his friends.

Ander's heart pounded. He had seen such an amulet before. Smashing it would sound a magical alarm, foreclosing any escape. Numb with shock, he realized their lives were forfeit.

Out of the corner of his eye he saw Sorel reaching surreptitiously for the throwing knife concealed beneath his left sleeve. He glanced to the other side and saw Nicolai coiling to spring. Perhaps their deaths would not be wasted. *Maybe I can distract him enough for Nicolai or Sorel to get through.* He lifted a foot to spring forward, but before it reached the ground the sorcerer's eyes flashed red as rubies.

Ander fell backward, feeling as if a horse had kicked him. He struggled to sit up. His body was like lead. Even drawing breath was a desperate struggle. Nicolai and Sorel had shared the blow; they sprawled on the floor like discarded toys. Najja's eyes burned like hot coals.

Ander felt a grip tightening around his chest, squeezing the air

188

from his lungs. His vision began to dim. He groaned, struggling to resist Najja's spell. The air between him and the sorcerer seemed to thicken. At first he thought he was losing the battle. Then the air began to shimmer and take form. At first indistinct, then more and more solid. Ander blinked, and suddenly Lucian stood between him and Najja.

The sorcerer gaped. His dagger dropped from loose fingers and clattered to the floor at Thane's feet. "No! What are you, demon? Be gone!" Najja redoubled his efforts, focusing the power of his attack on Lucian. The shade's presence only grew stronger, as if feeding on the energy coming from the sorcerer's attack.

Thane hung between the timbers, thunderstruck. "Lucian?" He choked on the word. He jerked at his shackles, oblivious to the metal cutting into his skin. "*Lucian!*" Tears and blood mingled on his stricken face.

Lucian's form became as solid as real flesh, and the forces employed in the magical battle became visible as well. Shimmering waves of power radiated from Najja like ripples on the surface of an invisible lake. They splashed off Lucian and bathed the shrine's walls in rainbows of flashing light. The ghost's eyes were fixed on Thane, and his expression was serene.

Najja snarled, his face twisting with fury. Lightning flashed and hurt Ander's eyes. But at the same time, he felt some of the staggering weight leave his body. He managed to get onto his hands and knees and started to crawl forward.

Waves of power lashed his back as he crawled into the middle of the conflagration. Energy howled in his ears and disoriented him. The battle between Lucian and Najja heaved like a leviathan all around him, stretching and straining the fabric of the world itself. Somewhere in the whirlwind came Thane's wrenching cries, frenzied entreaties to both Lucian and Ander.

Ander's mind reeled, but he kept his eyes focused on the patterned marble floor and moved forward inch by inch. After what seemed an eternity of excruciatingly slow progress, the sorcerer's jeweled dagger lay before him.

He felt his body would fly apart at any moment, but he grasped the dagger. Cold metal filled his palm. He nearly collapsed with exhaustion. Then he lifted his gaze from the floor. Thane was only a foot from him. Mindlessly seeking contact with his beloved, he reached out and touched Thane's leg.

Their bond sprang open. Torrents of confusion and pain surged through him. But Najja hadn't broken Thane. Along with the pain came a jolt of desperate strength.

Ander gripped the dagger more tightly and staggered to his feet. His vision blurred and his body swayed. Moving as if in a trance, he lifted the dagger to the height of his chest, then fell against Najja. The dagger tugged at his hand as if alive. Its blade plunged into Najja's heart.

A howling shriek, unearthly and terrifying, split the air. At the same moment Lucian's form flared incandescent as the sun. Then silence.

Ander swayed, numb with fatigue, his eyes closed and watering. Then he remembered Thane and opened his eyes. Thane hung from his shackles, his powerful body limp and motionless. A withered corpse in sorcerer's robes lay at his feet with a dagger protruding from its chest.

Momentary panic dissolved into relief. His bond with Thane was open again. Their hearts felt one another, responded to the contact. Thane's eyes opened and he lifted his head.

"Ander . . . Ander, I don't understand . . ."

Ander smiled wearily, reached out to touch Thane's cheek. Blood and grime streaked the mage's face, making his young visage look older. "Later. We're not safe yet. The sorcerer's minions could return soon."

Thane licked his cracked lips. His eyes were haunted. Ander felt questions pouring through their bond, but knew that the answers would have to wait.

Nicolai had recovered from Najja's onslaught almost as quickly as Ander. He immediately began to search the sorcerer's body for keys. He found them in a pouch attached to Najja's belt and quickly unlocked Thane's shackles. The battered youth fell into Ander's arms.

Taking turns supporting Thane's weight, they made their way through the ancient passages and the gallery filled with the remains of Najja's victims. The cold air in the street smelled as sweet as life itself.

Returning to the inn was painfully slow, and Nicolai had to carry Thane the last third of the distance. Dawn tinged the horizon as they carried the mage up to their room. Leif had returned just minutes before and watched them anxiously, but held his questions. They laid Thane on the bed and covered him with thick quilts while Leif fetched a goblet of water.

Ander held the goblet to Thane's lips and made him drink it slowly. Even without the knowledge imparted through their bond, Thane's shaking hands would have told him all he needed to know about his lover's exhaustion. But he also knew the mage wouldn't rest, *couldn't* rest, until his question was answered.

Ander handed the goblet to Leif, then combed his fingers through Thane's short hair. "No, you weren't dreaming," he said softly. "You saw Lucian. A part of him that didn't die with his body."

Tears welled in Thane's eyes, but his gaze never left Ander's. "Why? Why didn't I know? Why didn't he come to me?" Anguished grief poured through their bond.

Ander took one of Thane's hands and squeezed it. "He was just an echo of Lucian's spirit. It was impossible to restore what you had shared, and he didn't want you to go mad trying." Ander felt hot tears on his own cheeks. "He still loved you, even in death. Too much to cause you more grief. I sought his help when you were captured, and he gave me all that remained of his anima. But now even that's gone. Defeating the sorcerer took all that was left of him."

Tears streamed down Thane's face, but his eyes showed understanding. "He's saved us again," Thane said, his voice thick. "Najja hadn't shared the secret of using the kei to gain immortality. Not even with the lesser sorcerers. He was planning to betray the zamindar and keep the power for himself. The zamindar is denied his prize."

"*You* defeated him, too," Ander replied. He bent down and pressed his cheek against Thane's. He remembered Lucian's final wish, that he might touch Thane again through Ander's hand, and his heart ached. *Fate was never kind to Lucian. But he saved Thane. Perhaps he'll rest peacefully after all.* He lay on the bed beside Thane and held him in a tender embrace. "Rest, jirí. And tomorrow we'll remember Lucian."

BOOKS FROM LEYLAND PUBLICATIONS / G.S PRESS